Torchbearer

RIFTSINGER PRESS
PERTH, AUSTRALIA

Paperback Edition 2022
ISBN: Paperback: 978-0-6488113-2-9;
ePUB: 978-0-6488113-0-5;
Mobi: 978-0-6488113-1-2

Torchbearer

STEVEN THIELE

RIFTSINGER PRESS

THE WASTES

TALON REACH

EASTERN PLAINS

IMBRA

STORMFIELD MARSH

LERANION

ESTREA RIVER

FALLKIRK

KINAR RIVER

MT. SANCTI

THE THORNWOOD

PRIAN

STALLOR

THE SEVERED PEAKS

BIRALAM

AMALDAS

N
W   E
S

MAP OF
EKRA

CASALIS

VALMOR

RENEGADE
HAVEN

Chapter 1

Sanctuaries do not guarantee safety.

Eli idly brushed the wooden curve of his bow, eyes fixed intently ahead. Deep amongst the towering pine trees, the gentle morning mist twisted in the cool breeze. He fought the shiver and resisted the temptation to draw his hood further over his head. Not when a doe was lowering its head to drink, across the stream just twenty metres away. He grasped the string and drew back, the yew creaking, until his fingers brushed the light stubble across his chin.

The leaves rustled again, and he sighed, relaxing the string. A second creature glided out, barely half the height of its mother. Dammit. The wind whispered through the woods, carrying the scent of pine as the rising sun crested the wooded hill. Blowing his scent right towards the magnificent animals. Hooves thudded away, and he rolled his eyes and slumped back against the trunk. Rough bark clung to his fingertips as he traced its ancient surface. All the while, he mumbled monotonous greetings to Nestham—ritualistic rather than fervent, drilled in over the years.

He moved as gracefully as the animals he hunted, soft footsteps over brilliant leaves, brushing through the trees until that pine scent covered his clothes. His pants soaked in the frigid stream that glittered in golden rays, covered by wisps of fog. Without hesitation, he plunged his face into the water until he threw his head back, blinking rapidly, gasping with the chill. But the chill spread to his heart, controlling his body until his fingers numbed in the water. No. Not again. The wind shifted, rustling the black fletches in his quiver. Eli coughed, bile shooting up the back of his throat as an acrid stench seared his mouth and nose.

1

He straightened, the hood falling from his head, light flitting across a sharp face framed by short dark hair. His heart began pounding again as he grabbed his bow and fled the stream, angling his body through the dense forest. The birds, once so vibrant, fell silent. His feet rustled through the leaf-litter, and he ducked under an outstretched branch, his movement an elegant dance, until he emerged from the pocket and stopped on the banks of the river glistening in the morning sun, gazing at the solitary peak reaching into the sky.

He didn't hear the hiss of the arrow as it cleaved the air. A piercing scream tore from his lips as it slammed into his shoulder, tearing sinew and bone. Eli collapsed to the ground, his tanned skin pressed into the dirt that smudged his clothes and face, blood mingling with mud. He scrabbled for the arrowhead protruding through his chest, but more muscle tore and he reached new heights of agony. Boots, soggy from crossing the river, appearing in his line of view. A bulky figure, crouching next to him. A voice, rasping in his ear.

"Do you serve the Jinnam filth?"

Eli shook his head; colour leached from his skin. Fear entwined with pain as the figure snapped the arrow and pulled it through, rolling the hunter, ignoring his agonised cries as he pocketed the bloody arrowhead. The voice swore as a faint light glimmered around Eli's wrist. A knife, coated in blood, rested on the injured man's throat. "Goodbye, heretic." He slashed the blade across Eli's neck. Hot blood spurted from the wound until Eli let out a soft gasp and lay still. Verdant grass stained with red, pooling out from the slain hunter. The figure coughed once and strode away, indifferent to the boy behind.

* * *

Orange rays flickered in the west, gleaming through a thick haze. Eli groaned and stirred, pushing through the blood on the

2

ground to rise, his face coated in filth. A small, ornate wooden pendant lay on the ground in front of him, its simple clasp still attached to a snapped cord. He reached for it, running his fingers over the engraving, remembering. ES. He stashed it in his pocket.

He grunted as he stood on trembling knees and traced with shaking fingers the wound at his throat. Nothing more than a mere scratch, the blood barely bubbling. A blue light dimmed as the hole in his chest gradually healed. He should be dead. What in the Five Hells was going on? He leaned on his knees and retched pitifully, hot bile surging up through his throat. The faint cheers echoed in his mind, but he brushed them aside. A stench filled his nose—that nauseating, sickly-sweet smell. His hands tensed up, sweat already covering his palms, and his breathing fluttered.

A low groan sounded behind him, and he whirled, head aching with the blood loss, and gasped. A man drifted in the river, clad in a sodden brown robe. His right hand worked feverishly to keep him afloat, while the left—a severed stump, thick with scars—clutched a leather-wrapped package. His eyes half-closed in exhaustion and his remaining hand fell limp, his thickset body spinning gently in the ebbing river.

"Alsair!" Eli yelled and dropped onto the soft grass, reaching down the drop and grasping hold of his friend's coarse robe. Eli grunted as he hauled Alsair up the rocks, finally depositing him on the grass and sighing with relief. The sun dropped over the horizon as he met Alsair's jade eyes, rimmed with red.

"Eli," the monk whispered. "Thank Nestham!"

Alsair's gasps for air formed a counterpoint to the bubbling of the river behind them. His right hand, creased with age, twitched almost as if there was something missing, something he should be holding. He let the package under his

3

other arm drop to the forest floor as he groaned, rubbing his left stump, the scarred flesh now hidden beneath ancient cloth. Eli sat back down, his face washed clean, his blood now swirling amongst the pristine river water.

"How's the arm?" Eli asked, nodding at the missing limb.

"The cold isn't helping," Alsair grunted.

Eli finally mustered the courage to ask what loomed in his mind. "What in the Five Hells happened?"

Alsair gazed at the dirt. "Eternal Guardsmen attacked the Mount. I couldn't get any monks out."

"No. No." Eli whipped his head back and forth. It couldn't be true.

Alsair shook his head sombrely, and Eli's stomach dropped to the dirt. The earth trembled and wind punched through him like a fist as a roar rushed through the trees, cracking and tearing wood. Eli's reddened eyes lifted to the horizon as orange stained the sky—but the sun was long gone. He stood up to discover the source of the strange light, and almost vomited from the dizziness that coursed through him.

"Careful," Alsair muttered. Eli ignored him, forcing himself to stay on his feet and stare at the Mount, at the smoke trailing into the sky.

"What in the Hells is that," Eli breathed. The mountain that had been his home, once proud and majestic, now spewed flame. As he watched, the disfigured remains of Mount Sancti exploded outward, debris crashing onto the sprawling plain.

Alsair's face paled even further. He dropped to his knees to murmur a prayer, all the while stroking the medallion at his neck. A wooden carving of a dove, the symbol of the Jinnam monks.

Former symbol.

Alsair was now the only Jinnam left.

4

Eli needed to leave, but he couldn't. The sight transfixed him like a mouse in a snow leopard's maw. He fell to his knees. What had been a pristine plain was now scorched earth, littered with rock and the blood of his friends. The mountain had crumbled. A vermilion mass of soldiers gradually left the plain, leaving faint cheers and whistles in their wake. Keening resonated behind Eli and he turned, finding Alsair kneeling, mumbling the liturgy, beseeching Nestham to take the Jinnam monks and shelter them in Paradise.

"We can't stay here," Eli whispered.

"I know. I have a place in mind." The afterglow of the sun faded over the trees as they staggered like drunks along a faint track.

* * *

Eli couldn't raise his gaze, couldn't think, couldn't do anything but place one foot in front of the other, blindly following Alsair's hulking figure bent beneath sorrow. Not even the stars were out now—they were covered by thick roiling smoke, as if Nestham had turned his face away.

He stumbled on a root and fell to the ground in silence, only pausing to dust himself off and keep limping. Alsair turned back to him briefly but never spoke.

The tangled undergrowth stopped and opened into a little clearing, overshadowed with looming silhouettes, the shape of small huts. Eli squinted but couldn't make out anything else in the pitch black. How Alsair had managed to guide them, he had no idea.

Alsair led him to the largest shadow and pushed on the dim outline of a door. As it creaked open, Eli coughed at the mustiness that filled his lungs. Alsair pointed down the hall as he lit a candle, the flame sputtering into existence, flickering. Eli glimpsed downcast green eyes just before he followed the pointing finger, bumping into coarse wood until he reached a bedroom. His bow clattered to the ground and his quiver fell off his shoulder before he dropped onto the bed in silence.

The terrors came that night, the screams of an old woman, the cry of a girl reaching back across the years, a shattered dove and a strange, flickering light. But every time it came back to the same sight. A mountain, with fire spewing from stone, a wail of death surging across the flame.

* * *

Eli awoke to golden rays through stained windows, the sunlight catching on the floating dust. He surveyed his surroundings in silence, catching his reflection in an ancient mirror leaning amongst the cobwebs. A shiver ran through him at his hollow reflection. His silver eyes, eyes that had earned him strange glances from many, were today dull, drained.

He swung his feet onto the floor, pausing as they scraped patterns in the dust, next to a freshly set out tunic and pants. Eli glanced at the blankets surrounding him and choked, horror stealing through him. The faded blankets were now marred with his bloodstains, the same for his clothes. He changed quickly, his breath catching every time he glimpsed another blotch of blood.

He moved to the door with the athletic grace drilled into him through years of movement and combat training. Training that would never leave him. He sheathed his knife at his belt, and followed the corridor outside the bedroom into a simply furnished living room. A crackling fire had already been lit, casting light on the elder man fumbling for breakfast. His movements were slow, stiff, sapped of energy. Eli drew breath to comment, but the man turned and Eli blinked at the dark rings under his haunted eyes, the scratches on his skin.

He knew.

"I thought he'd do a better job," the monk finally said. Eli frowned at him. "A friend of mine should have cleaned this place while I was in the Mount. But at least he kept food here." He jerked his head to Eli. "Wash trough is out the back." The boy sighed and shuffled off to wash himself.

He returned shivering, his hair dripping wet, but even that carried no feeling. Alsair deposited eggs on the table, cradling the bread under his stump. A cheerful whistle signalled the coffee's readiness, and he poured steaming dark liquid into tankards from the shelves.

Despite the heaviness on them both threatening to dull his senses, Eli couldn't shake the feeling crawling up the back of his neck. "Are we safe here?" His question cut through thick tension.

Alsair nodded slowly. The monk hesitated for a moment. "How ... how are you feeling?"

"I don't know," Eli said as he shook his head. "There's just one thing I feel, and it's rage." A fire burned within him, stoked hotter and hotter through grief and pain.

"Bad idea," Alsair shook his head.

Bad idea to let it out. "How can you be so calm?" Eli burst out, chunks of egg spraying from his lips. Alsair sighed. "I'm a man of peace now. My soldiering days are over."

"A man of peace," Eli snorted, a bitter mirth rising within him. "Of course. That's why you were so keen to train me, to beat me every day in that rabbit warren you called a monastery." The knife clattered onto the table, but Alsair ignored the ringing note—and the bad manners.

"That was for you, not for me," Alsair replied with a raised brow. "You wouldn't have stayed for two breaths if I hadn't."

He was probably right, but Eli didn't want to stop there. "Fine. Then are you going to stay silent?"

Alsair's face was serene. "I will remain peaceful. The Jinnam wouldn't have wanted you to get involved. But if you want to exercise, there's an armoury out the back."

Eli stomped off and crashed open the door, his eyes immediately alighting on the small hut beyond the back porch. His nose caught whiffs of that substance again and he coughed, tears pooling in his eyes. He pushed open the door and let sunlight spill around the room, flickering on gleaming weapons. A man of peace indeed. A vast variety of weapons hung on racks lining the walls, some crumbling and rusted, others freshly polished. The deep ring of a sabre's blade as he tapped it was reassuring, though he frowned at the flaky brown coating it left on his skin.

He pushed his way through these weapons to the back wall, but grunted as his toe banged into wood. Eli glanced down to see a small wooden chest, barely big enough to hold a loaf of bread. He tried the handle, but a lock sealed it, ancient and flaking away. He studied it, brow narrowing in concentration. The shape rang familiar, yet he couldn't place it.

He briefly considered Alsair's desire for secrecy but gave up, grabbed a knife from the rack and jammed it into the bolt. Screeching metal and jarring wood. He swore as the dagger fractured and splinters cut jagged lines into his hands.

A faint blue gleam flickered through the room, but he ignored it as his fingers closed around the leather hilt of an axe and lifted it, his arms strengthened from years of training with Alsair. He slammed it down, a perfect cut on the lock, and it shattered, thudding to the ground.

Inside lay a small, tattered wrapping of cloth. He reached in and pulled it open. Two small shapes made of a strange grey metal. He brushed one gently and his hair stood on end. Waves of energy coursed through his body and he let out a yell. An icy blue light pulsed through the room. But it wasn't coming from outside. It was coming from *him*. It wreathed his right hand—light, endless, eternal light. He'd seen that once before.

When he died.

"What are you doing?" Alsair roared from behind him and he jerked his hand away. The light faded as Alsair stormed past him and threw the lid shut, turning on the boy. "This is not your business," he hissed. Something in Eli wanted to stand back and roar, but he winced and nodded. Alsair reached into the racks and tossed a pair of short swords to Eli. "Get outside."

Eli paced outside, hands making idle cuts with the swords, swaying from side to side. He scanned the countryside on instinct, a habit learned in his days as a hunter. Because even if you were hunting, you were always someone else's prey. A gurgling brook wound its way through the paddock, plummeting over a cliff on the far side and forming a small waterfall.

Alsair finally shouldered the door aside and stared at him, new shadows in his eyes, tanned skin creased beneath grey hair. In his only hand he held a broadsword with no struggle, hefting it with the grace and strength of a born warrior. He gave no warning and smashed the sword right onto Eli's blade. Eli parried with his right hand, but the sword just kept coming, bludgeoned his guard and pointed directly at his chest.

"Dead."

He knocked the blade out of the way and swung again.

Alsair stepped to the left, tripped him and rested the sword on his neck. "Dead."

He kept pushing. Sweat poured off him as he relentlessly circled the old man, never making a mark on him. Alsair moved with breathtaking speed, always anticipating his movements. Unsurprising, since he was his trainer.

Eli finally stopped circling. "Do you miss them?" he blurted.

9

Alsair blinked at him. "Of course I do, but they're with Nestham now."

"Doesn't the Order serve Nestham? And their soldiers slaughtered the Jinnam. Your people. Our people!" Alsair had no reply, merely swung his sword with a ferocity that caught Eli off guard. Alsair at last held up his stump.

"We're done here. Inside."

Chapter 2

The sun's rays glittered through a smoky haze as Jayne Farer straightened from her place by the charred remains of firewood, snuffed out hours ago. She brushed the dirt off her knees and grabbed the sword resting near the fire pit. The leather hilt was worn and stained, bearing the signs of an active year. Her eyes—ocean-blue above dark circles—probed the forest surrounding her valley and the cliffs that hemmed them in. Jayne breathed a quiet sigh and glanced down the mountain path, at the young man fitted in dark armour marching up it. A smile tugged at her lips as he let out an exaggerated yawn, running a hand through tousled black hair, mussed from sleep.

She nodded at him, once. "Luca."

"Ghost." He smirked.

Jayne glared at him. "You know how much I hate that name."

"But you don't have another one," he crooned.

Her glare was pure steel. "Do you really want to be chopping wood for the rest of the day?"

Luca straightened and saluted. "No, Jayne. Is there something you require?"

"Yes, there is." A smirk began to creep across his face again and she rolled her eyes. "Oh, for Nestham's sake, has Anar left yet?"

Luca nodded abruptly. "He and Ginlun left moments ago. Where are they going?"

"On a scouting trip around the valley. The Order has been too quiet since we got this last group out of Imbra, and I don't like not knowing about it."

"Yes, you really miss Imbra's whispers," Luca grinned.

She ignored his comment, instead placing a hand on his shoulder. He straightened, hand dropping unconsciously to his sword.

"I need you to find another way out of this valley. We've never looked, but if the soldiers find us, we're trapped. Only an idiot would lead us into that situation."

Luca frowned. "Jayne, we would trust you with our lives."

Jayne pursed her lips. That was a trust she wouldn't take lightly.

He spun with his hand gripping the worn hilt of his sword and strolled off. After two steps he turned around and stared at her.

"You weren't rostered for watch last night," he said. She didn't answer, and he sighed and turned away, slim shoulders shrugging as he strode.

Jayne tightened her dark gloves over tanned skin, then clasped her hands behind her back. The quiet valley began to stir as men and women emerged at the valley's base, from the well-hidden tents set around the crumbling ruins of the chapel. Why anyone had thought there would be faithful out here, she had no idea. She grabbed the polished metal from its box by her side and flicked it back and forth, flashing the light across to the sentry on the opposite ridge two hundred paces away. His returning flicker dazzled her eyes, and she tossed the metal back into its box. She picked her way carefully down the steep slope, avoiding rocks and snags looming amongst the grass. Tripping now might cost her a serious injury.

As she did, she caught the smells of the camp, wood smoke dissipating now they had cooked the food. Never leave the fire going in the day: the first rule of hiding from superior forces. There was no telling who was around these parts. One figure flicked a smile at her as they filed into the chapel. Jayne reached back instinctively with her right hand, tapped the sword strapped over her armour, and followed.

She stopped at the stairs of the chapel, gazing at crumbling stone only held intact by curling vine. The door hadn't lasted the first opening, and remained on the grass as it had for months. The rotting wood was a sharp reminder of how long they had stayed here. She mounted the mossy stairs and entered.

She was the last person to do so, and as one the group turned to her. Scholars from Imbra and some outlying towns, one travelling merchant claiming to have seen the Wildborn, and three women who'd declared a demon had possessed the Archbishop of the Eternal Order. They all waited on the ancient pews, surrounded by familiar faces—the warriors and soldiers who had gathered in her name.

The scholars hadn't told her their story, but she could easily pick them—they huddled together, several scribbling on parchment that seemed to have appeared from nowhere. The merchant's shoulders tensed, though he remained sprawled on pews next to the outspoken women. His eye twitched as she narrowed her focus on them. Two of the women held her gaze: one blonde and young, the other matronly and clutching a baby to her chest.

"Everyone sleep well?" She smiled. The crowd let out a nervous chuckle. "I know you're a little concerned about the recent shift. To those new among us, we welcome you into our little band, until we can get you somewhere safe."

"Where would that be?" the mother piped up. The air tightened around her and the scholars ceased their murmuring.

Jayne raised her hands to placate her. *Smile, ease the tension,* she told herself. "We're still working out the best place to send you. In the meantime, if you want something to do, some of my team will offer training and exercise." The

13

merchant pursed his lips, and one scholar, a young man with flaming-red hair, looked up at last and smiled handsomely. Several dark-clad men and women lining the walls nodded. "In the meantime, please report to Tamryn if you wish to assist the camp." She gestured to the greying man to her right, her chief cook and taskmaster. "And don't worry, you're completely safe here."

The refugees muttered amongst themselves again, but they seemed reassured. The trainers within her band stepped forward to meet those willing to fight. Among them, the red-haired young man and the blonde woman seemed the most energetic.

A few minutes later, Jayne listened to the clang of steel-on-steel as some of her warriors faced off with the refugees outside the chapel. The red-headed man moved uncertainly, as Lillin instructed him in basic use of the staff. Jayne's most confident warrior took it slowly, calling time in the sharp barks she'd become known for. Grey-streaked dark hair hung to her collar, shifting as she showed a basic chain of swings, and he followed, albeit even slower.

Eventually, Lillin called a break, and he stopped dead, chest heaving as he grounded his staff on the floor.

Jayne paced up to him. "What's your name, man?" The redhead glanced at her with a jerkiness that surprised her, his blue eyes like ice, ice that melted in his smile. Despite herself, heat crept up the back of her neck.

"Trayse, ma'am."

"Drop the ma'am, Trayse. I'm Jayne." She glanced at Lillin.

"Go grab some food, Trayse," she said, eyes still fixed on her trainer. "You've earned it." She grabbed the staff from his hand as he headed off.

"He's a fighter, that one," Lillin said, barely out of breath. Jayne twirled the staff idly and circled to her right, waiting for Lillin's gentle strike. It was a training technique Lillin had used before, maintaining a conversation whilst still parrying every stroke, increasing the speed each time.

"I'm not quite convinced," Jayne replied, riposting and barely blocking Lillin's counter. However, Lillin had always been an excellent trainer. She'd improved Jayne's skill with the staff even after several years of training. "But there's no harm in training him in some self-defence before he leaves. How good do you reckon you can get him in two days?"

The older woman's eyes gleamed with the challenge. Lillin was no-nonsense, and saw talent regardless of position. It was why Jayne had recruited her six months ago. "I can get him to be better than you, that's for sure. He's a quick learner." Jayne grinned at the greying woman. Lillin chewed her lip before whipping her staff towards Jayne. "Truth be told, he may not want to leave."

Jayne sighed, even as she blocked. Most of the refugees they helped were eager to accept the lessons and leave, but some had tried to stay with their group despite the danger. Protecting refugees from persecution and the Order's secret war was no easy task. Few had succeeded. She wanted no liabilities in their line of work. Particularly when said liability was an untrained warrior who could get them killed. "I'll help you with the trainees tomorrow," she said. "I just wanted to see how you were holding up. This group is the third we've had in two weeks, and I know some are friends of yours."

Lillin grounded her staff and held up a hand. "I know. You don't miss much. Truth is, I'm wondering if we're doing enough." Jayne motioned for her to go on. "Look, you've assembled a powerful band, and they're all loyal to you. Luca, Anar, Tamryn, and the others would die for you." She took one look at Jayne's expression and amended, "Though I hope that isn't necessary. But we could take the fight to the Order and put a stop to this."

Jayne lowered her staff and breathed deeply. "I thought of that too, but the Order has hundreds of soldiers," she said.

"Doesn't the King have more?"

Jayne arched her brows once. "I won't set the King against the Order. That would rip Leranion apart."

Lillin's expression was like a thundercloud, and her staff twitched in her hand. "You're still loyal to them, aren't you? You told me what happened in Imbra. They cast you out and left you to die. If Luca hadn't found you in the wilds, you'd be dead."

"If Luca hadn't found me in the wilds, we'd all be dead," Jayne said, ignoring Lillin's point. She couldn't still be loyal to the Leranion nobility after how they had turned on her. But somehow, she was. "I'll put it to a vote tomorrow night, when Anar and Ginlun get back," Jayne said, and saw Lillin's agreement.

She turned as rapid footsteps thudded behind her. Luca skidded to a halt, beaming in every line of his reddened face. "I found it," he burst out.

* * *

Luca led her down the southern end of the valley to the rock wall that enclosed them. No climbing would be possible here, even with a rope, but he pressed his side to the featureless surface.

"I don't see anything," Jayne commented.

He grinned at her. "That's because there's nothing here."

"Excuse me?"

16

He chuckled and pointed off to the side, before unbuckling his sword and pressing it to his chest. Behind an outcropping, Jayne could faintly make out a small gap, covered in shadow. He pressed his way into it, light and nimble. Jayne hesitated once, biting her lip, then unstrapped her blade and stepped in after him.

The walls seemed to press in on her, as if they were merely waiting for the right moment to collapse, to bring the mighty valley down on her. The air tightened in her throat, thick and hard to breathe. Luca glanced back at her.

"You okay?" he mouthed. She nodded and pressed on, focusing on keeping one foot in front of the other. The passageway twisted and turned as narrowing stone grazing painfully on her back. It scraped on armour and skin, and she took one more step, but then refused to budge. Panic rose in her throat, and she flailed her arms, until a slim hand grabbed onto her own and yanked her through.

She coughed deep and wretchedly, shielding her hands from golden light. Jayne forgot all about the pain and fear as she stared out at the landscape. It had transformed, from the verdant greens of her valley to barren plains, rocky and harsh, stretching out before her. A faint acrid stench made her nose twitch in discomfort.

"Strange," she whispered. "It wasn't like this a few days ago." The sun passed behind a cloud and the scene darkened in warning. The moment passed and sunlight gleamed over the horizon once more, but she glimpsed something ahead of her. "What's that?" she pointed. A thin trail of smoke now faded into the distance. She pulled out the map she always kept on her, and frowned. "Isn't that where Mount Sancti is?"

Luca leaned over her to check the map, glanced around them, and then nodded. "Then where's the mountain?" he asked nobody.

17

A chill fell over Jayne and she jerked her thumb back at the passageway. "We need to get back," she said. "But first, let's hide this passageway. I do *not* like the idea of soldiers sneaking through the back and ambushing us."

"Always paranoid," Luca joked.

"Why are you surprised?" she shrugged.

They made quick work of disguising the passageway. Some foliage still clung stubbornly to the rocky ridge, and they simply dragged it to cover the entrance. Jayne frowned as she studied it from the inside. "We should put a sentry here."

Luca nodded his assent, ever the loyal Second. "I'll add it to the rotations."

They squeezed back through the passageway and blinked as the light dimmed. Evening already. Tamryn was lighting the fires he would use to cook their meals—some meat her hunters had brought in. She noticed them cleaning their equipment and smiled. Immediately, Luca charged off to help Tamryn, barely throwing a goodbye over his shoulder. She chuckled as the young man reverted to his boyish self, shedding the young warrior for the irrepressible helping spirit.

* * *

They gathered around the campfire and passed out some cheap wine. It wasn't much, but it was enough to make the refugees comfortable. They also doled out blankets, but kept the spare clothes. They were becoming much harder to get a hold of, unfortunately. Tension rippled through the air, so much so that a chill ran down her spine. She glanced around for the source. There was nothing, but everyone was still on alert.

"Is everyone accounted for?" she asked Tamryn.

The cook nodded. "All refugees happy and healthy. Two have volunteered to help with the passageway duty."

18

Jayne took a swig of the wine and immediately regretted it. The thin taste was something she wouldn't be able to get out of her mouth for a while. She finally raised her brows at the cook, who smiled at her discomfort. "Not bad," she coughed.

Once they had served the food, the combined mass of humanity separated, as members of Jayne's group began to shuffle over to her. At last, they formed the command circle. "How are the rest of the refugees looking? Any other promising recruits?" she asked. Nina, one of her hunters, gestured at the blonde woman next to the young mother.

"That one there, Rinna," Nina said. "By the time I got back from the hunt, she was making good progress with a bow thanks to Mick." She nudged her younger brother.

Jayne pursed her lips. "Do you reckon she'd want to join us?" she asked, but Nina shrugged.

"I doubt it, she'll probably want to stick with the other heretics, but we can train her, anyway."

"Don't call them that," Jayne sighed.

Nina shrugged. "That's what the Order calls them. Straight to the First Circle if they get caught."

The chirruping of crickets swelled to a cacophony as darkness set in. "I'm thinking we send this group to the Plains," Jayne said. "There aren't any safe places in Leranion anymore, the Order's influence is too strong." She chewed her lip. "Stallor should be safe enough. The Duke has most of the land secure south of the Thornwood. The scholars will do well there anyway, they always want researchers in the Archives."

"How are we going to get fifteen people across to the Plains?" Mick asked. "We've barely taken anyone east of Mount Sancti."

The name struck Jayne, and she glanced at Luca meaningfully. He nodded. She gathered herself. "Mount Sancti is gone."

The band sucked in a collective breath. Silence fell across the campfire and belatedly she realised the refugees were listening as well.

"How?"

"I don't know. We'll see if Anar has anything else to report."

"When will he return with the others?"

"I expect him and the other two to return by sundown tomorrow. With luck, they'll have more information for us besides what we already have." But as she gazed around the circle, the mood seemed to darken even more than the surrounding night.

She didn't want them to get any worse, so she nudged Tamryn and the old cook nodded meaningfully. "You got any good stories, Tamryn?" she asked.

A twinkle glimmered in his eye as his gaze swept around the group. "Have I ever told you all about the tale of Temero, the wicked demon?" He grinned.

A shiver went through Jayne. Not this one. Anything but this one. But she refused to speak lest she show her fear.

"Oh, not this one," Mick grumbled. "It's a load of rubbish."

Tamryn cleared his throat. "When the world was young, Nestham ruled undisputed as Lord of All, surrounded by his angels of light. Yet one among the armies of angels sought to dethrone him, and came to Ekra, seeking power amongst men."

Her heart quickened, and a bead of sweat began to trail down her neck.

"He took men and animals, and twisted them, warped them, and left only the shells. Every time he placed a bracelet of his own making on them, he filled them with his spirit. They became demons. They became his legions." Nervous looks flicked around the fire. "His force was unstoppable, and darkness covered these lands."

"And how did it end?" Luca breathed.

Tamryn smiled beatifically. "He was killed by the kings and queens of the realm. By Nestham's Chosen."

"Of course," Mick butted in, "it's nothing more than a folk story."

Tamryn glared at him. "Is it?"

Every time, the story of Temero made Jayne pause. She could never explain why. Perhaps because Tamryn was closer to the truth than she could ever tell.

Chapter 3

Dinner was meagre, and the conversation even more so. Footsteps thumped on the wooden step outside and Eli froze. Alsair glanced at him, deep-set eyes assessing their position. The monk flicked a finger and their chairs glided back in pure silence. Eli drew his belt knife and dropped into a fighting stance away from Alsair. The hilt of the knife quickly moistened in Eli's hand. He wished to Nestham he had his sword, but it was most likely under piles of rock at the remnants of the Mount. His heart thrummed in his body, his breathing steadying. He nodded at Alsair, and the door rattled as someone pounded on it.

Alsair took one step towards the door, his foot sliding across the dusty floorboards, and nodded at Eli. The door rattled again. Alsair threw it open fluidly, reached and grabbed. He dragged an elderly man through and slammed the door shut. The newcomer let out a piercing screech, but behind him, Alsair rolled his eyes and leaned against the wall, shaking his head, while Eli sheathed his knife.

"The last time I saw you, Ginlun, I think I threw something," Alsair sighed.

The greying man clutched a bent back, but a faint hint of mischief gleamed in his eyes. Even though Ginlun was old, it was clear a brittle strength remained in his bones, even though they would probably crumble to dust within a year. He stood with a warrior's confidence, despite his frailty.

"Good to see you, Alsair," Ginlun said, his smile somewhat forced.

"It isn't good days for anyone anymore," Alsair replied, but surprised Eli by bowing. Ginlun didn't copy the gesture.

"You really have fallen," Alsair said as he straightened with a groan.

Ginlun shrugged. "I made my choice, same as you did. I merely wanted to know if you survived."

"How did you find us?" Eli asked, his eyes narrowing. If anyone else had followed Ginlun, they'd have a fight on their hands.

"Nobody knows you're here, don't worry." Ginlun waved a hand dismissively, flipping a coin in it as he did so.

"I'd worry less if you told us how you knew."

"He knows me well," Alsair assured him. "Ginlun was a companion in my soldiering days. We joined the Jinnam together, yet someone"—he added with a pointed glance—"couldn't really take the solitude."

Eli fought back a smile. He knew the feeling. But Ginlun scowled at Alsair, a heavy scar over his cheek adding emphasis to his anger.

"That wasn't exactly how it went down, was it?" Eli murmured.

Ginlun blinked once and perked up, sensing an ally. "No. I decided not to follow Nestham after what I'd seen. And despite what Alsair thinks, the Order isn't proving me wrong at this point."

"I'd have to agree with you there," Eli admitted.

Alsair crossed his arms and glared at Ginlun. "What do you want?"

Ginlun raised his hands in supplication. "I'm sharing information you'd want to hear. But first, who's this?" A wrinkled hand pointed at Eli.

"My apprentice, Eli Serae." An unspoken message flickered between the elder men.

The man's eyes flashed, and for a brief instant, he glared at both of them, but he quickly replaced it with a genial smile.

"You trained him?" he asked. Alsair nodded and Eli smirked. "I'd love to see him fight."

Eli straightened and glanced at his mentor. Alsair's nod was discreet, but Eli understood. Despite the burden of grief and guilt on his shoulders, using his skills was a secret delight.

"Perhaps another day," Alsair said, taking another step forward. Eli instinctively pivoted away from him, forming a wider range of combat, space for superior numbers to take their places. His head reasserted control from his body. Ginlun's brows raised and when his eyes met Alsair's, only resentment gleamed there.

At last, he sighed. "Fine. The Archbishop is working on a new secret project in Imbra. Apparently, there's some chemical involved."

"Why is that my concern?" Alsair rebuffed him.

Ginlun held up spotted hands in supplication, though when tremors shook them, he shoved them in his pockets. "Look, I'm just taking this to everyone who will listen. I've been working with a new group near here and I think you'd be proud of them."

"I told you. I want no part of this. I left that life a long time ago. You'd have a better chance of finding the Nameless Heir."

Anger marred Ginlun's kind face, yet something else gleamed in his eye. "So, what? You'll just sit on your backside and do nothing?"

Alsair drew himself up to his full height. "We're done here. Get out. Go back to your group."

Eli frowned. This was not the Alsair he knew.

Ginlun sighed and pushed the door open, but stopped on the threshold, holding the coin again. "You know, I think your apprentice might disagree with you."

The door thudded shut and soon his footsteps vanished into the night. An eerie calm settled over the cabin, but Eli couldn't look Alsair in the eye.

"I'm not hungry anymore," he said and went to bed. Even as he lay on the mattress, his thoughts whirled. A chemical, Ginlun had said. Could that have destroyed the Mount? Eventually, he fell into an exhausted slumber.

* * *

Thunder rumbled in the distance as Eli rose from the bed, and made it with fresh sheets. He grabbed his bow and a sword from Alsair's armoury, ignoring the small wooden chest, and stopped in the flattened training area outside the cottage, breath misting in the morning air as he scanned the tree line. Satisfied, he moved into the rituals he had long perfected after years of hard training, fast and deadly as ever. Sweat poured off him despite the chilly air, until at last he set the sword down on the ground and reached for the grey sky, stretching his muscles. He swept his eyes across the tree line once. Paused. His hair stood up on the back of his neck and a small tingle ran through his hand as he slowly scanned back.

Glowing silver eyes, wide and observant, stared back at him. His breathing fell silent and his skin rippled with goosebumps as two gazes of silver collided. Those were not the eyes of an animal. He gripped his bow and nocked an arrow. Forget knowing what it was; he wanted it gone. The bow's spine creaked as he drew, barely aiming between those luminous eyes. The string dug into his calloused fingers. Just as he was about to release, the eyes closed and vanished. They reappeared closer. He swung his bow to account for it and fired.

The arrow hissed as it spiralled to its target, but the bush merely rustled as an arrow slammed into it. The eyes reappeared. He fired again. And again. Those damned eyes shifted all around the field, and he fired constantly until his quiver ran dry. Finally, the eyes vanished, yet their burning gaze remained as a brand on his heart.

"Did you at least hit anything?" He whirled, hand reaching automatically to his quiver, grasping at empty air. His panicked gaze homed in on Alsair and he fought to relax. The man's green eyes stared right through him. "What in Nestham's name were you aiming at?" Alsair asked casually. Eli debated what to say as the silence stretched longer.

"Just target practice," Eli finally said.

Alsair's mouth thinned, but he shrugged regardless. "Well, by all means, retrieve your arrows. Breakfast is ready."

Eli waited until the old man went back inside before unsheathing his knife and cautiously marching over the grass, hunter's feet on chilled ground. At least the winters were milder in southern Leranion. Up near Imbra it would be much worse.

There was no sign of the eyes, yet as he studied his arrows, each had flecks of a metal on them, shinier than war arrows had any right to be, and gleaming with a faintly blue aura. He left one in his hand, twisting it in the air as he headed back inside, and he nearly tripped up the stairs to the cabin. Once breakfast had concluded, Eli suggested they talk about Ginlun's visit.

The monk leaned back in his chair and shrugged. "There's nothing to talk about," Alsair said.

Disbelief washed over Eli at the swift dismissal. "Nothing?" Eli retorted. "You want to sit here and not help anyone?"

Alsair's eyes flashed. "I will do a lot more by finishing your training."

"I've trained for almost ten years! I think I'm ready. But even if I was, you wouldn't let me go out there anyway, would

26

you? Because you"—he jabbed a finger at his mentor—"don't think I'm ready."

"The Order has an enormous army. It doesn't matter how skilled you are; they will destroy you. And what are you going to do anyway? Just kill the Archbishop? Whatever is going on, this strange purge—it's more than just religion. This is out of character for the Order!"

Good! But that wasn't helpful to anyone. "Well, I'm sure the history books are a great help on the subject," Eli said. He slammed his hands on the table, and Alsair barely blinked. "People died two days ago and we don't know why! All we know is that they destroyed the mountain and slaughtered all the Jinnam." He pushed himself away from the table and stood up. "I'm doing something about it. With or without you."

Alsair's eyes turned mournful. "Don't do this. Please."

Eli was undeterred. "I'm going to Imbra, and I'll find out what the Archbishop's working on. And I'm getting justice for the monks," he said. And perhaps he'd find out what that light was. Within minutes, he was armed with a sword from the armoury, a knife and his bow. In a pack were water and food. It was decidedly heavy on his back.

He crossed the threshold, already torn. Alsair had sheltered him for so long. But his anger wouldn't let him rest until he poured salt into Alsair's gaping wound. "It seems one of us has to." Belatedly, he wondered if he was convincing Alsair or himself.

He slammed the door shut, leaving the monk alone.

Eli hesitated on the step. The expanse of the forest loomed over him as the birds fell silent, the clouds hiding the sun from view. He cast a mournful glance back at the cabin, at the smoke that crawled out of the chimney. He shook his head and glanced up at the sun, trying to work out the direction. He settled for north and set off. From what he remembered, it was at least a few days to Imbra. He'd hunt on the way there and grab food from the nearby towns. All while avoiding any lingering Order soldiers.

How had it gone so wrong?

There was nothing for it but to keep marching. A flash lit up the sky and rain plummeted from the heavens. He was soaked in seconds.

Chapter 4

As the sun reached its peak over the valley, the group gathered around the charred remains of the fire pit.

Jayne couldn't hear exactly what Mick said, but it was hilarious and laughter spilled from her entire team. Many of the refugees were relaxing in the noonday warmth, though the younger ones were keeping Lillin active with a variety of sparring sessions. Finally, she studied Trayse. He moved sluggishly, though better than yesterday. He at least worked through the combinations with more coherence. Jayne pushed herself off the ground and strode over to the sparring ring. Once she reached the heap of staves, worn through constant use by the exiles they had trained, Lillin winked at her and nodded. Jayne grinned back and grabbed a staff from the pile, idly twirled it as she approached the red-haired man. She waited a breath, two. When he showed no sign of letting up, she coughed once.

Trayse jerked his head to her like a frightened rabbit, and she retreated half a step, continuing to smile. At last, a casual smirk replaced the startled look in his eyes. She ignored the flush that threatened to creep up the back of her neck and focused her gaze, blocking out everything but him.

"Let's see what you can do." She dropped into a fighting stance and waited for his unsure nod. She began slowly, an overhand strike easy to block. Trayse hesitated once, yet raised his staff and caught the motion. She smiled reassuringly and swung again. The refugee blocked again, this time adding his own riposte. Jayne countered easily, but her appreciation of him grew.

Time to switch it up a little. She spun the staff in her hands once, twice, until it was a bewildering blur of force. Just to see how he'd react. She lashed out with a barrage of blows, aimed at various parts of his body.

His piercing blue eyes, once clouded by fear, snapped into focus and his own weapon flicked out, countering every single one. She kept at it, increasing the tempo until smooth wood tapped her on her thigh and her heart stopped.

"I see my work here is done," she coughed, before flicking a surprised smile to him and arranging her staff back in the bundle. Lillin's grey brows rose in an appraisal as she left.

Minutes later, Trayse reached the campfire. A swagger was in his steps, at odds with the unsure man she'd seen only just before. Jayne flicked her eyes around the group, caught Tamryn's steady gaze. She nodded once, instant agreement with him. The communication they'd developed as a unit for months. Suddenly, Trayse was standing in front of her. She craned her neck up to look at him, wishing she could have stood up, put herself level with him. But it was too late now.

"Jayne, I was wondering about something," he began. "What happens when we leave?"

Her heart picked up, but she fought to maintain a professional standard. "We'll take you to a safe place and let you live your new lives," she said. His mouth twitched, and she caught herself staring at it. Would he remain with them?

He scuffed the grass. "What if I didn't want to settle down?"

She shrugged, though her mind screamed otherwise. "You're free to go wherever you wish. We won't stop you."

"Could I stay with your team? I can fight and help," he said, almost breathlessly.

Despite her plan to ask him, the question caught her completely off guard. "Uh—of course." She smiled, knowing her group was watching every move she made. "We're always happy to have some new recruits."

His smile became shyer, as if he lost ten years of age in an instant. "Thank you." He sauntered back to the scholars.

She glanced round at her team. Only smiles lit their faces. "Well, I guess that settles the matter," she said. Jayne sat back down over the map beside Tamryn, but her eyes kept darting to the handsome man smiling at her.

* * *

The sun had completely fallen by the time Anar returned, Ginlun in tow. Their faces lightened as they approached the fire, yet its dim light showed the bags beneath their eyes, their dragging steps along the ground.

"Have some food," Tamryn offered, ladling out the rich soup. They sighed gratefully and sank to the ground, accepting the proffered bowls.

"Anything to report, Anar?" Jayne said.

The man sighed again as he took a sip of the soup and prepared himself. "Mount Sancti's gone," he stated. He looked at the unsurprised faces. "But I see you already knew that."

"Jayne found out when they found another exit from the valley," Tamryn said.

Anar pursed his lips. "Do you know who did it?" he asked Jayne.

"I suspect the Order, but we don't know how." She shrugged. At her words, Ginlun raised a brow. When she glanced at him, he hastily rearranged his features into a frown.

"Did you find out any other information?" she pressed.

Anar shook his head. "We just saw one figure heading off to the mountain, but we didn't get close enough to make him out. Ginlun headed in a wider range, and I went directly to the mountain." He hesitated, his eyes gazing into the distance.

"What did you see?" she asked. He shook himself alert and fixed wide eyes on her. She tensed for the blow.

"There were bodies littered across the plain, all Jinnam monks. I saw some tracks leading away from the battle, so maybe someone survived."

"We should help them," Luca said.

Jayne shook her head. "We can't risk the refugees. We swore to protect them; we can't just charge across the plain for anyone who's in trouble."

Luca's head snapped to her and she tensed.

"Is it not our duty to protect the innocent?" he said.

"Our duty? Our duty is to the people in this camp," Jayne cautioned him.

"It's our responsibility to find out why the Order is suddenly purging the other faiths," Luca hissed. "Now they aren't content to do it secretly, they're making a statement. If the Jinnam are gone, it leaves only the Musadim and the Eternal Order."

Jayne repressed a frustrated sigh. Luca had always been the one to see others in need and feel compelled to help them. He would have made a great healer had he not shown exceptional skill in tracking and combat, making him a born candidate for the Royal Scouts. Even then, he hadn't stayed long before being recruited by Jayne.

"What do you say, Jayne?" Anar said.

It fell to her, as always. Just once, she wished the burden wouldn't rest on her shoulders, but it never failed to do so. There was nothing she could do to avoid it. "We're staying here. Just for a few days."

"I say we make a break for it," Mick butted in.

Jayne's throat dried, but she fought to maintain a steady tone. Something rose inside her, like a slumbering beast opening an eye, but she relentlessly clamped it down and adjusted her gloves. Anar caught the gesture and his eyes widened.

"There are probably hundreds of Eternal Guardsmen out there," she said. "Our only chance is to stay safe in the valley until they pass."

Luca was standing now, face flushed with passion, hands on hips. "If we don't leave now, they'll find us and kill us!" he shouted. Anar groaned and dropped his head in his hands. The yell rang out over the camp and immediately the other fire fell silent. Her glare could have melted a stone wall, and Luca promptly dropped to the ground. She flashed a reassuring smile at the refugees, but turned back to Luca.

"Your responsibility is to this team," he breathed. He brushed a hand through his dark hair.

"That's right," she said evenly. "And I'm fulfilling it." Her voice quietened. "I'm not abandoning this team, but you still need to listen to me." Jayne glanced over at the other fire, noted the toll of worry and fear on the faces of the refugees. Trayse raised a brow as Rinna leaned on his shoulder, her eyes closing slowly. Quiet conversations bloomed once more. "Enough," she said to her group. "We remain here for two more days. The Order soldiers should move on by then. If anyone has any issues, you know where to find me. Mick and Nina, you're on watch tonight." Their grumbles were short, but they nodded as one.

"I want everyone to rest now," she said with a glance at all of them. "Get some sleep if you can, or talk to the refugees if you can't. We're a unit, and I won't allow any division here. If you have something to work out, take it up with me." Some faces showed frustration, but nobody disagreed. Thunder cracked overhead and rain began to splash on the ground. "Everyone inside the chapel," she commanded, and the refugees scurried in. Jayne waited until they were all inside, save for Mick and Nina, who had drawn the short straw. Jayne grabbed the cloth they had used to seal the entrance and threw it over the doorway, gratefully accepting Luca's help. As one, they turned to the frightened escapees.

"There's a group of Order soldiers roaming the plains," she said, "but we are completely safe here. Everyone, get some sleep."

The stones of the ancient building shook in the storm, but the refugees stayed still, kept talking. Her team lit some candles, spread the furs out on the floor. Fortunately, they'd amassed a good stock in the last few months. Everyone spread out between the pews in pairs or groups. The young mother held her baby tightly as intermittent rain replaced the rolling thunder. Jayne grabbed a place in the corner, leaned against the wall. Despite the calm smile she kept on her face, her heart continued to pound. She wondered if she'd made the right choice. Eventually, her eyelids fluttered and her head dropped onto her chest, spiralling into darkness.

Just before she did, a tall, red-headed figure left the chapel, hand tightly gripping the woman's next to him.

* * *

She jerked awake as lightning flashed overhead, gleaming between the gaps of crumbling stone. Eyes strained to see in the pitch black, yet her skin prickled with unease. Finally, pure darkness became dim shapes, and she reached for her staff, brushing the smooth wood with a calloused palm. The dim outline of the pews guided her as she picked her way over the outstretched bodies on the floor.

A soft voice startled her as eyes opened sleepily beneath her foot.

"Where are you going?" Luca whispered.

She shrugged. "Just outside. I need to check something."

"In the pouring rain? The hells you're not." A hand clamped on her lower leg and she quickly forced down the temptation to whack it with her staff.

"That's enough, Luca." The hand disappeared into the darkness.

"Fine. Then I'm coming with you."

She didn't show the relief she felt at his promise as her staff brushed aside the cloth. She stopped at the entrance as the lightning threw the valley into stark relief, and the rain kept pouring. A flicker of orange, quickly extinguished, caught her attention.

"Did you see that?"

Luca stopped behind her. "What?"

She kept staring at the spot, but nothing changed. "Never mind." A cry echoed across the valley, silenced swiftly by the thunder. So swiftly she wasn't sure it was even real. An invisible hand on her shoulder pushed her forward into the pouring rain. She was instantly soaked, the heavy coat drenched in water, her hair plastering to the back of her neck, the chill running down her back. Her grip on the staff slipped as the world plunged back into darkness.

The next flash of lightning revealed the tree line, and they pushed their way through the heavy curtain of water, boots sinking into the muddy grass. Luca stumbled, and she reached a hand behind her, hauling him back up. As they neared the forest, the trees grew denser, as if they were physically pushing her back. But that crawling sensation returned, as if a hand rested on her shoulder, about to push. She stepped forward again and yelped as she stumbled over something soft, yielding. She stretched her hand out to save herself, landing hard against the ground, mud pressing into her face.

The lightning flickered again, and she stared into Rinna's cold, unseeing eyes. With a mass of blood around her neck.

Her blood ran cold, and she pressed her hand to her mouth, stopping a silenced scream. Thunder rumbled, but that damned lightning flickered again, and she raised her eyes to the tree above. One letter carved into the ancient wood above Rinna.

T.

Trayse. She choked on the gasp that rose from her shredded soul. Her training reasserted itself and she scanned the area, water running into tear-pricked eyes. Thank Nestham, the murderer had fled. She bowed her head and whispered a prayer to Nestham to keep Rinna close, to protect the woman's soul, even as the coppery tang of blood filled her nose. She reached out a trembling, sodden hand and closed the girl's eyes. After a year of running and fighting, she'd lost one.

Luca's bitter curse cut through the roaring thunder and he fell to his knees beside her. His expression said it all. Rage and grief warred across his face, settling on a wrath not easily woken. A killing fury. The last time she'd seen it, he'd slain several pillagers roaming from the Plains border.

Jayne placed a bloody hand on his shoulder. "We have to warn the others and get them out tonight," she said, forcing herself to tear away from the dead woman. Luca nodded, and they began to run. But they stopped dead at the tree line, her muscles caving in as a new light filled the valley. Not lightning. It was like a flare of the sun, brilliant flaming light that fell to the ground, emitting a fierce light, enough to illuminate men in blood-red jerkins, bearing naked steel.

Dizziness swept through Jayne and they ducked down, knees pressing into mud. Shouts filled the clearing as dark shapes rushed the chapel and dragged out staggering figures.

Illuminated in the glow of the lights, Tamryn's stooped form stumbled amongst the soldiers and she swore viciously.

"What can we do?" Luca asked.

"We need to assess the situation first," she replied, though every bone in her body was *aching* to go to them, to fight for them as they had done for her countless times.

"We need to get them out of there!" he hissed, but she slapped a hand over his mouth. One hand on his chin, she drew his eyes to her focused, red-rimmed gaze now dried of tears, narrowed in a concentration she'd practised over a year of fighting and running.

"You will do *nothing* until I say. Is that clear?"

He swallowed. "Yes, sir."

A barked command rang out from across the clearing and she flinched as she recognised that honeyed voice, once so charming and now utterly twisted. "Kill them." No. No!

The men moved methodically, skewering the refugees. Yells of pain, fear, and grief vanished in the storm. Jayne tried to move, but she couldn't. Her legs refused to obey her. She buckled into silence whilst Luca seethed beside her. The soldiers reached her team, the men and women who had followed her. Beside her, through the pouring rain, she sensed the leaves shift and turned to find her friend rising.

"Don't you dare," she hissed, but Luca had apparently decided enough was enough. He let out a piercing scream, raw and raging, and charged at them, waving his sword like a madman. She let out a choked sob. There was nothing she could do without getting herself killed.

Hope rose in her heart as Luca flickered in and out of the pouring rain, a man on a death run. Given over to his rage, he was wrath made form. Trayse glanced at him once, then lifted one finger. An arrow lodged itself in Luca's heart and he collapsed to the ground. A strangled cry cracked out of Jayne as her nails tore into mud.

She could only watch as Trayse sliced the throats of her team. Ginlun and Tamryn went quietly, a faint smile on their faces, determined not to show fear. Anar held a glare with Trayse the whole time. Mick roared and shook off a soldier, launching himself at Trayse. His muscled form seemed to slow in the air as Trayse whirled and unsheathed a wicked sword. Mick's head dropped to the ground before his body.

Nina's screams became shrieks, and she followed suit. Trayse hesitated as he reached Lillin. The elder woman merely grinned fiendishly at him. Jayne's breath caught. Maybe he'd spare her. Her vision narrowed to Lillin's mouth. She'd always been good at reading people's lips.

"She'll kill you," Lillin said.

Trayse's grin was darker. "She can try." He waved for the soldiers to end her. He spun and marched off into the chapel.

Jayne collapsed into the mud. All hope, all rage, Trayse had snuffed it out, as if a dark shadow had reached up and clutched her heart. She began to shudder uncontrollably as devastation took over. They'd never had a chance to defend themselves. There was no chance anymore. The mission had failed. The rain kept pouring. But though that was constant, the world had changed, emptied just a little more.

Footsteps crunched in front of her and she held her breath, casting a fearful glance up at a broad-shouldered figure. Trayse. He smiled, that winning grin now sardonic in the lightning.

"Hello, Jayne." She tried to raise her staff but her arms were numb, refusing to obey any command. She could control nothing. All semblance of that had died tonight along with her team.

A strong hand grasped her under the arm and hauled her out of the foliage. She lashed out with her fist, but Trayse easily intercepted it and put her arm in a vicious lock. Her staff he left in the tree line, marching her back to the army of Order soldiers and throwing her down. She fell with a cry, landed on a corpse. Ginlun. Her trusted adviser. The one who'd listened to a girl standing over the bodies of three Eternal Guardsmen and dreamt of a better world.

She had failed him.

She had failed them all.

"Monster," she spat. "These were good people. They gave you a home." Trayse's smile didn't falter. If anything, it became even more twisted.

"I had my mission, just as you had yours." He turned to the men assembled around her. She took one look at the expression on their faces and recoiled at the mix of bloodlust and animal-like intentions. They were foul creatures. "We leave for Imbra in the morning. Take her inside. Don't touch her. She's for the Chosen." One man hauled her up and marched her into the chapel. The lack of any sleeping bodies, the empty pews, it tore the hole in her heart even wider. How often had the team assembled here, laughing, joking, getting ready to make a difference?

The furthest corner was the least open to the elements, and that was where he dropped her on the stones behind the altar. She skittered back to the wall and drew her knees up at the stare he gave her. Her sodden hair fell around her like a curtain. She was grateful for that at least. It hid her weakness.

Her shame.

Her cowardice.

The storm stopped, and the clouds parted, illuminating the bodies in crystalline moonlight. And it struck her how Nestham only turned his face towards the scene of injustice once the deed was done. Into the blackness Jayne swore that the moment she had the chance to avenge her team, to avenge Luca, and destroy Trayse, she would take it. There would be no hiding from her wrath. The men who had caused this would wish they were dead. That was a fool's hope, yet she clung to it all the same. Her eyes were used to the dark by now, and she made out shapes and individuals. Her gaze homed in on Trayse, on the glint of silver he rolled deftly across his hand. He flicked it up in the air and watched it fall back into his palm.

"What was your price?" she whispered.

Trayse glanced away from her. "You don't know what you're talking about."

"No, I want to know. What made you work for the Order?"

"The Eternal Order's coffers run deeper than the King's, little girl. The peasants tremble in fear in the face of holy wrath. I'm merely Nestham's will made flesh."

"You're nothing to Nestham," she said. "When judgement comes, I will tear you limb from limb like the monster you are."

"Monster? Am I a monster, Jayne?" The voice grew hideous, slithered across her skin, as he reached for her. Instinctively she shied away, and he grinned. He enjoyed the power, the control over others. She forced herself to stay put, to straighten her spine and glare back at him.

"You're a monster in who you are and what you stand for."

"Perhaps I am," he shrugged. "But at least I'm not heading straight to the torture chamber in Imbra's dungeons." She couldn't hide the shiver that raced through her and knew he had won. He knew it too.

"Why don't you just kill me?" she breathed.

He reached over and caressed her cheek gently, drawing a quiet shudder from her. "You're too beautiful to just throw away."

She fought the urge to recoil, instead glaring at him. "But Rinna wasn't?"

"I wish it didn't have to be that way. She was stupid and made a mistake. I didn't want to kill her ... but it would have happened nonetheless. Your cause is nothing to the Order. The scholars and the monks wouldn't have survived for long. Besides, I imagine they'll want information out of you."

"Did the Order destroy Mount Sancti?" she asked.

He smiled. "So you know about that?"

"*Did they?*" she hissed.

Trayse shrugged, handsome features now utterly vile. "The monks were worthless. They deserved to perish."

"They were more human than you are," she whispered.

"It doesn't matter," he smirked. "When the dust settles, the Chosen will claim it was Nestham's will that destroyed the Mount." *Chosen?*

She repressed a shudder. "You're twisted."

"Go to sleep. You've got a long journey tomorrow," he taunted. She fought the tremble that threatened to undo her. The steel in her spine had long crumpled.

That night, the wolves howled and the crunches and squeals pierced Jayne's ears, as much as she pressed her hands over them, trying to block them out. And so there was no honourable burial for any of her friends. No memorial. Not even an unmarked grave.

Once the baying stopped, she hesitantly lowered her hands, still shaking from the screams. The moon slowly rolled past as silent tears tracked paths down her face through the dirt and the blood.

Chapter 5

He could make it to Imbra, couldn't he? Eli crouched under the pine boughs, pressed against the bark. It was a few weeks away from spring. Here in the heart of Ekra, snow fell only in midwinter. Steady, miserable rain was all they got for the rest. His hood was sodden, as was the small flap of cloak he drew across to protect the vulnerable flights on his arrows. His bow he held in his cloak, trying to shield it from the rain.

If this was meant to be an adventure, then it was a pretty pathetic one. Good. He deserved this.

Wings flapped somewhere near and he tensed, but then the rain on his head ceased. He glanced up. A single wing was outstretched overhead, shielding him from the rain. The feathers were a vibrant brown, speckled with white. Intelligent eyes stared down at him, their ancient wisdom shrinking him until he was nothing but a small morsel for this incredible bird. The world fell still for a long moment, as if there was nothing but the two of them, and for the first time since Mount Sancti, warmth stole through his heart.

The rain stopped, that constant sound fading to nothing. Eli blinked as the hawk flapped its wings and vanished into the forest. The comforting presence fell from him, and a shadow lay across his soul. Dark whispers slipped in to fill the gap.

He hauled himself up, grunting as he wiggled his toes in sodden socks, and pressed on. His limbs were heavy, and he couldn't raise his eyes from the sodden ground, where the water had formed pools that he kept squelching in. There was only his damp feet.

At last, the forest ended, and the clouds pulled back, revealing hundreds of stars glittering over the sky. Eli blinked. It had gotten so late and he hadn't even noticed. The moon shone brightly in a crescent. Wind Moon would soon be upon them. Eli flicked his eyes ahead, a reflex reaction. He noted Nestham's Shield—five brilliant stars, the one at the base gleaming brightest of all.

He refused to let himself enjoy the splendour. Not anymore would the stars bring him joy. He only needed Nestham's Shield because the base pointed north, all the way to Imbra. The open plains stretched before him. And beyond ... the towering peaks of the north of his continent. Nestled among them, the Citadel in the hills. His capital. If only they could do something about the Order's purge. Give him answers, help, anything. He stumbled, fatigue pressing in on him.

"I guess this could be a good place to make camp," he said. He blinked as he realised he was talking to himself. "I should really stop doing that," he muttered, and shook his head. He grunted as he lay down on the damp grass, setting his quiver aside, but keeping the dagger close to hand. The blanket of stars was an alien sight as at last he tumbled into the blackness.

Strange sights came for him that night. Eli opened his eyes to find the plains bathed in sunshine. He stood clothed in shining armour, a fine sword at his waist. Behind him, a roaring army, clad in blue and white. And in front ... a horde of beasts, uncountable and unrecognisable. Twisted and misshapen, they were darkness given flesh. He shivered as they charged towards him. As one, the army stilled and looked at him. Eli went to pull the sword from his scabbard, but it refused to budge. He tugged again, panic fuelling his reactions. But it still wouldn't budge. A scream shattered the air, and a beast pounced on him, crunching its jaws down on his neck.

Eli shot up straight, panting. Sweat covered his brow as he tried to control his breathing, calm the racing heart pounding within him.

One who bears Nestham's Mark shall be a sacrifice.

The words echoed around him, nothing more than a whisper in the night by some unseen being. He grasped in vain to catch them, learn their meaning. But the voice never spoke again. He lay back down on the grass and gazed up at the stars as they wheeled overhead, but he could have sworn he felt the ghost of a hand brush his shoulder as he did so.

The sun rose again, and he blearily followed suit, wiping his eyes to clear them. He trudged over the plains, pushing through the grass. By midday, the sun beat down mercilessly on him. His tongue grew dry, and he began to move listlessly, gasping at nothing. He dropped his pack to the ground, reached inside for a waterskin. A jangle of metal alerted him and he pulled out a heavy leather bag. He opened it and his eyes widened. Gold and silver coins. He didn't remember putting them there. He left that in the pack and pulled out the waterskin, squeezed it hopefully.

A trickle of water rolled its way down his hand, tracking through the dirt. He shifted the bag and cursed. A gaping hole had torn inside the waterskin, leaving it completely ruined. His eyes began to cloud as he tried to sit down. Instead, he collapsed to the ground. Anything could take him at this point. His tongue swelled and dried inside his mouth. But when he opened his eyes, a curved leaf filled with water lay in front of him.

A hawk flapped away from him, its eyes flashing violet.

Chapter 6

Morning dawned bright over the little valley, though the storm was still on the horizon as Trayse dragged Jayne by the chains on her wrists. Her knees locked at the pure malice writhing in his icy gaze. Trayse snapped his fingers, and a shadow loomed behind her. She whirled, arms seeking a target, but he yanked on the chains. Her teeth sank into her lip as she stumbled forward, manacles cutting into her wrists. Blood bloomed in her mouth and metal bit into her neck. She couldn't draw breath to scream. The cold steel was a vice around her throat.

Trayse leaned closer. "The Chosen says we're not to harm you," he warned, "but if you even *try* to escape, you're fair game." His smile grew wider. Jayne glared at him, but he seemed to enjoy the defiance. His men did too. They split up around her, one leading her by the chains attached to the collar, the others watching her at all times, as if they could expect a significant threat from the Ghost.

But they wouldn't need to do so. The Ghost was broken.

* * *

The heady aroma of coffee hit her first, swirling out of the mountains on an icy breeze, making her suck in a breath, closing her eyes, stopping her stirring heart after days of travel. Trayse braced his hands on his hips, shifting his bright red jerkin, the uniform of an Eternal Guardsman. He sighed contentedly. "Not far till home, now, huh, boys?"

It felt like a betrayal, somehow, to enjoy the same scents as him. Her smile plummeted to the damp ground, but a harsh hand gloved in sweat gripped her chin and raised it to the

45

skyline. Her breath caught as she surveyed the rolling hills, the pillars of smoke towering from behind them.

She was heedless of the men and women clad in homespun cloth who took one look at swaggering Order soldiers and stepped off the path to avoid them. They at least were safe from the Order. Jayne craned her neck and glimpsed burning gold, tucking that small glow in her heart to endure what would surely be a nightmare, one from which there was no waking. Trayse pushed her on.

At last, they reached the foothills and began the winding climb. The well-travelled path had seen better days, but it was major trade route. People covered the road, even loading wagons on the paths cut into the hillside. Imbra lay nestled between the hills they were climbing and towering mountains beyond. Despite the occasional drops to the side, the soldiers had no compunction about pushing others out of the way. Some cast looks at her in kindness, others in condemnation. None dared challenge the Guardsmen.

As they ventured along the hillside path, the wind picked up and drifting snow glided from the heavens, gathering in her hair. She ignored its icy touch, but soon she was shivering— horrible, racking shivers as the cold pierced her rough shirt and pants meant for the warmer south. The soldiers fared no better, but Trayse seemed immune to the cold. That cursed smile was still on his face, a melange of charm and sadism. Wind hurled through the chasm, stirring the frenzied snow. The travellers sped up, banding together to huddle through the storm. Jayne hunched down, seeking shelter in the lee of her guard, dropping her eyes to her feet, to the chain with the loose link.

Blinding whiteness blotted out the rest of the path. The only things visible were the flickers of golden light—the Eternal Torches—guiding their way.

"We need to find shelter," one soldier said.

"The next shelter is beyond the first watchtower. We press on until then," Trayse replied. The path up to Imbra could be dangerous in this weather, and shelters on the route dotted the hillside, allowing weary travellers to wait out winter storms like this one.

A larger flare of light signalled the first of the watch posts. Ancient fortifications, created in the days of the war against the demons. An age long past, a time when golden warriors battled against pure darkness. The wall still held strong. Some miracle of craftsmanship kept it standing. Black rock polished almost like glass by the snowy wind. Above it, the swirling golden power of an Eternal Flame. A beacon lighting the path towards Imbra.

"Halt!" The challenge swirled on the gale. Trayse didn't bother, instead leading her forward. An arrow whistled out of the blizzard and skittered on the icy rock. At last he paid heed to the guards. "State your business," the same voice said.

"Lieutenant Trayse of the Eternal Guard," he announced. "Passing to Imbra."

A beat of hesitation. "Never heard of him," the sentry roared.

Trayse pressed forward into the lee of the watchtower, his men following. "Let us pass or there will be consequences."

By now the sentry was visible, clad in ordinary Leranion uniforms of blue and white. Soldiers of the Kingdom.

"Sterking Ordermen," another sentry muttered under his breath.

Trayse drew his sword like a striking snake until it rested on the chin of the first sentry. Razor-sharp steel glittered at his throat. "Let us pass. Now."

The sentry gulped. "Understood, Lieutenant."

Trayse turned and clutched Jayne's jaw. "Not a word," he breathed into her ear. She wanted to scream, to cry out, to cause a scene. But he was gripping her so tightly she'd have bruises tomorrow, and Trayse wouldn't hesitate to cut her down.

They shuffled past under the watchful gaze of the sentries. "Wait!" the guard yelled and Trayse turned back with a frigid smile on his face. "Yes?"

"Who's that with you?" The sentry stepped out of the watchtower and made his way into their little group. He pointed right at Jayne. Her heart pounded, and she began to twitch in Trayse's grasp.

"Oh, her? She's nobody," Trayse replied. Jayne frantically shook her head, blinking endlessly at him. The sentry didn't seem to notice.

He certainly didn't notice the words she was trying to whisper.

Help me.

"Carry on." And those words were a punch to the gut.

He retreated into the watchtower, into the warmth and security. Trayse yanked on Jayne's shackles until she complied, and they trudged through the snow again. The icy ground betrayed Jayne, and she fell to the ground, biting her lip at the scream. The manacles had worn tracks on her skin, now red and bleeding. At last, her strength had left her. After walking across the land with no hope, her legs had given up on the slopes of the northern mountains.

A hand grabbed her hair and hauled her to meet Trayse's gaze. "You can walk," he smirked, "or I can drag you." She tried to get up but stumbled again. He gripped her around the arm and hauled her along the path. Ice scraped her legs until bloody welts smeared tanned skin.

At last, she glimpsed two flaring flames on the path and breathed a quiet sigh. Trayse rapped on the carved door set into the mountainside, and it swung open. The roar of fireplaces and the chatter of wayfarers were deafening, but despite the flames, there was no smoke in the air. These halls had stood for centuries, and ingenious shafts filtered out the excess smoke. Trayse took a step in and tugged once on Jayne's chain. She winced and followed him in, sucking in a breath at the size of the hall. It kept going back, teeming with people around the tables by the bar, on rugs on the floor, and scattered around the many fireplaces. They laughed and joked, idly waiting until the storm passed.

One by one they fell silent, until hundreds of eyes blinked at them. Jayne again tried to communicate, to send a signal. Surely one of them would help her. None would meet her gaze as Trayse cuffed her on the head and began to push through the masses, swaggering as his weapons swayed.

Trayse pointed at the corner of the hall, and the soldiers bullied a path through the throng and claimed a spot near the fire. Families shuffled away, glaring at the soldiers when they weren't looking. Jayne glanced at two young girls who looked at her with a mixture of fear and guilt. Their father shifted slightly to block them from the soldiers' view, but they kept staring, peering at her with wide eyes and pale skin.

Jayne slumped to the floor, her chains pressing into her skin, until she found a relatively comfortable position. The soldiers were even more vigilant now. A spark kindled in her heart. Maybe now. She'd been working on these chains for days. One slip of the metal would be all it would take. The older man, Vin, had been puffing all the way up the mountainside. Even now, he was dozing, spittle dripping over his second chin. She prepared to twist the metal, ever so slightly. Hot breath curled in her ear.

"Try to escape, and everyone here dies," Trayse sighed, soft as a lover. Her skin paled, and she fought the urge to vomit. The Guardsman merely bared his teeth at her, and she fought back the tears brimming in her eyes.

He saw anyway, and smiled at her, brushed a finger over her cheek. Hate and grief raged in her eyes, but he held her gaze until she dropped her eyes to the floor, keeping her breathing silent. The talking had resumed, albeit tense, and people directed furtive glances her way almost constantly, so much that the skin on the back of her neck pricked every time.

A scrape of wood on stone caught Jayne off guard and she jerked her head towards the sound. It was only the young girl, and the steaming bowl of soup pushed her way was a welcome surprise. She glanced back. Trayse was closing his eyes against the stone wall, but the man had senses like a snow leopard. Any move she made would wake him. His reflexes had been surprising even back in the camp. Before he slaughtered her team.

She blinked back tears at the memory, at the pain that sliced her heart in two. The girl was still standing there, watching her. She never moved, merely cautiously studied her like one would study a caged animal. Jayne supposed that was an accurate depiction of her, right now.

She took the soup and smiled at the girl in thanks. The girl's green eyes crinkled, and she skipped back to her family.

Just before she settled in, she glimpsed a handsome face across the hall. Silver eyes flicked over her chains and the surrounding Guardsmen. She could have sworn his face twisted in anger before he looked away.

Chapter 7

The wind stirred into a frenzy as he arrived at the shelter, following the trail of people stumbling up the path. The ancient doors opened and he pushed his way through the crowd, heart thrumming in his chest, hand on his sword. He jostled until he found a spot on the wall and reclined against it, with nothing but his weapons. His stomach growled, but he had emptied his pack a day before. The only thing remaining was the gold on his belt. A serving girl brought over a bowl of steaming stew and he accepted gratefully, offering her a brief smile and a coin.

Her pretty smile faded fast as she glimpsed his eyes, and she stepped back hurriedly, turning away. He sighed. Always the same. He quickly glanced over, pretending to be interested in the conversation next to him, as an elderly man recounted his journey to a matronly woman holding an infant. Satisfied, he reclined his head against the stone wall and his eyes fluttered shut.

The door swung open again, and the wind howled, causing the flames to sputter. The clink of chains echoed as the conversation in the hall died away to nothing. A man strutted in, garbed in a red jerkin and a dark cloak. He swaggered to the bar, and yanked on something in his hand. A gleaming chain, leading to a collar attached to a lithe young woman, bloody and bruised, shackled and hobbled. Escorted by armed soldiers. Order soldiers.

Eli's nails gouged the palms of his hands, and the elder glanced at him, as if sensing the angry energy rolling off him. Eli ignored him and kept staring, taking in every detail of the scene. The conversation started again as the men shoved their way to a prime spot by one of the many fireplaces. They forced the young woman to sit in the centre, surrounded by the

Guardsmen. Even if she could free herself, she would have no way out. What did she do to deserve the Order's capture?

The hackles stood on the back of his neck as the leader loomed over the girl, his handsome face twisted into a sneer. She pursed her lips and made a brave face of it, but it was clear she was faltering. Eli's fingers tapped the side of his leg, inching toward his sword, but as his eyes scanned the room, they alighted on the serving girl. She blinked at him twice, then shook her head. He sighed and slumped against the wall. She was right. Starting something here in this crowded hall wouldn't help anyone. So, he watched and waited until the hall gradually fell into silence, and he drifted off.

He blearily awoke the next morning, his shoulder shuffling as someone shook it. A pretty face with dark brown eyes loomed over him.

"Time to go," the girl said. He blearily shook his head and glanced around. The hall was nearly empty. He must have slept like the dead not to have heard them leave.

"Have you seen those soldiers before?" he asked, but she merely shook her head. He hauled himself to his feet and stumbled to the door, pressing a hand against the wall.

"A word of advice?" she called behind him. "Don't get involved. You'll only make things worse."

He glanced at the open door, at the shining blue sky beyond, and shook his head. It seemed he couldn't help anyone these days. Boots trudged through the tracks the others had left behind, but even though the sky was bright, a shadow had fallen across his heart. Hours later, as he crested a rise, it lay before him. The twisting Kinar River descended from the north, the main course skirting the southern border of the city. The shining city walls were ringed with golden light, and on the mountain beyond lay the Citadel, a mighty fortress in its own right. Imbra, the beating heart of Leranion. Finally. He steeled himself and paced through the snow towards the city.

* * *

Morning sun glinted off the snowy peaks as Eli shuffled towards the gate, and thumped across the bridge over the Kinar River, which flowed down from the northern mountains and skirted Imbra. This time of year, floes of crystalline ice drifted on fresh mountain water. The steel gate yawned ahead, like the maw of a sleeping beast.

Metal glinted as the sentry on the battlements shifted his weight on his spear and gazed intently at him, his blue and white cloak keeping him much warmer than the others on the bridge. Eli hunched further down, but he still couldn't shake that gnawing feeling, the prickling on the back of his neck, that something was amiss. As he shambled into a seething crowd of despondent humanity, the shadow of the gate fell across him and a shiver ran through him. A man bumped his shoulder, trying to push further into Imbra, and Eli kicked him, then shuffled away whilst the stranger looked around for his assailant.

As Eli emerged on the other side, he glanced back at the gate. Hanging from either side was a blue and silver banner, emblazoned with a snarling snow leopard. The symbol of Leranion for as long as anyone could remember. Back when kings were brave enough to find one of their own.

The main road into the city diverged, one leading to the Citadel high above, but the press of the crowd forced Eli onto the path of the town. The snow-capped buildings seemed to stand proud despite the prevailing winds. Imbra still hadn't fallen, even throughout the struggles over the centuries, the wars that had scarred Ekra. Some of the stone shuddered under the weight of snow and leaned precariously over the street. Eli quivered as a strong wind flickered through the twisting alleys, and pressed his face deeper into his cloak.

Raised voices echoed up ahead and he tensed. A rich, rolling tone rang above all the clamour.

"Nestham is watching you," the red-clad crier yelled. "He has appointed us to bring you to His unknowable self! Do not anger Him, or you will face His wrath!" A shudder ran through the crowd as the Order crier stepped down. Eli swore under his breath. No anger, no resentment. Just a city held in the Order's grip.

A little bridge appeared ahead, marking a stark divide between two parts of the city. At least where Eli was now, the buildings still stood, somewhat. Across the bridge, they were mere shanties, crumbling under the snow's inexorable force. He marched up to the bridge and thumped over it through the snow. Cracking ice loitered by the edge of the stream, parts of it breaking and drifting onwards. He halted as he reached the other side, surveying the crumbling buildings. Not a soul entered or exited, as if the entire city held its breath. Eli hesitated, eyes probing with that relentless hunter's gaze. He pushed in between two buildings and paused. Something within him sensed he'd found what was watching him.

A push from behind sent him stumbling against the wall, hand dropping to his sword. He whipped around in time to see a dark head disappear around the corner. He patted his belt, checking sword and dagger, and groaned. His money bag had vanished.

He sprinted after the thief. His feet pounded on cobblestones as he pushed his way through narrow alleys. The quarter had suddenly come to life and eyes were peeking out of askew doors. One banged open as Eli ran forward and he spun to the side, narrowly avoiding the unspeakable liquids tossed in his path. His eyes watered but he kept running, just hoping for a sign.

The alley opened onto the stream before him, and he froze. Nothing but moored boats, surrounded by ice. The stone walls of the river were in disrepair, but as they went deeper into the slums, wooden walls replaced them, and eventually nothing held back the river.

A flash of black darted into an alley across the river. There! But there was no bridge, nothing to let him cross.

Light flared and power began to surge through him. His senses sharpened. The world became crystal clear, the smells infinitely more pungent. He glanced behind him to the alley and shuffled back before taking a deep breath. Then he was at the edge of the river, moving faster than a human had a right to. But he didn't stop at the edge. He gathered the strength in his legs and leaped.

Wind ruffled his hair as he flew through the air, the world slowing down, pausing—he landed on the far side and rolled to stop his momentum, before jumping up and sidestepping wandering onlookers. Mentally, he cursed himself. What the hells was he thinking? So many people had just seen something inhuman.

There was nothing for it now other than to keep running.

But the strange light didn't stop shining from his hand.

So he bolted through the streets. He dodged a woman lying on a mat, her eyes covered with black cloth. He sidestepped a man hobbling with the help of a cane.

Finally, he glimpsed the hair darting into a building. The door slammed, and he heaved his shoulder against it and drew his dagger.

He surveyed his surroundings quickly. A darkened room, with no furnishings, covered in cobwebs and dust from disuse, with no other entry or exit. And a young boy glaring defiantly at him from the corner. He slammed the door shut and stalked towards him, every inch the trained and lethal warrior.

"I think you have something that belongs to me," he murmured. He thought he could detect a flicker of fear in his eyes, but the boy shook his head vehemently.

"You're off your head," he coughed.

Eli raised a brow. "My money?"

"Look, I was just walkin' home, okay?" the boy said in a thick accent, raising thin, shaking hands to ward him off.

"From where?" Eli glared.

"Uh, the tavern, my mam works there."

Anger rose in Eli. "Just stop. Stop lying to me." He studied the boy. Oh. "You're not a boy, are you?" he breathed.

Ire flashed across the child's face. "What the hells, gruntah? You can't just walk in here and say that!"

"Try me," he said evenly. The boy twitched, and he coughed. "You're not going to be able to pull that off for much longer," Eli continued. "How old are you?" The question hung in the air, and he was content to let it stay there.

"Thirteen," the boy hissed.

"I doubt that."

"Eleven." Eleven.

Eli's heart cracked. "Why?" he didn't need to say more.

The girl's mouth twitched, as she debated what to say. "Streets are tough," she finally murmured. "It's easier to be a thirteen-year-old boy than to be an eleven-year-old girl. You wouldn't understand."

"Oh, believe me," Eli replied. "I would. So how about I make you a deal? You give me my money back, I put down my sword, and we go get some dinner from the tavern. My treat."

He could see the fear in her eyes, the walls strengthened by years of mistrust and betrayal.

"I give you my word that no harm will come to you." A promise, one he intended to honour.

"Useless. Swear it on your mother's grave."

"Fine." A little smile threatened to twitch his mouth, but the situation didn't warrant a smile.

The little dagger she was holding in her dirt-covered hand wobbled slightly. Eli crouched down, as if he was dealing with a frightened animal, and gently lifted the dagger out of her grasp. As he went to sheath his own, he glimpsed his right hand.

Not just ice-blue light, but a star, glimmering at the base of his hand, just above the wrist. As he stared it down, it faded away completely.

* * *

The shouts and bustle of the tavern were deafening as Eli and the girl—Amora, he'd learned her name was—devoured their meals purchased with the little gold Eli had left. He'd had time to observe her in the way Alsair had trained him. Though he didn't believe her to be a threat, she was still worth watching. He noticed how her dark eyes were never on her food, instead flickering around them, searching for targets—or threats.

A man roared with laughter and bumped into the table, causing Amora to jump. Her eyes glittered for an instant, betraying the fear within.

"Excuse us, friend," Eli said. The man muttered something under his breath and staggered away. Eli furrowed his brow and glanced at the girl, but she was already glaring back at him.

"What?" she asked.

"Are you okay?"

"I'm fine," she snapped. He winced and placed his elbows on the table.

"Where are you from?"

"Been in the slums my whole life," Amora said. "I don't want to talk about it."

"Sorry. You just ..." He hesitated.

"Look different?" she said. It was true. Though Imbra was a successful capital, few other than Leranion-born settled there, with such a cold climate. With her night-dark hair and eyes, she could have been from the Eastern Plains, not the heart of Leranion. He shrugged helplessly. "Can't help it," she glared, but a glimmer came into her eye and he tensed. "What are you doing here?"

"What if I live here?" He shrugged again.

Amora smirked. "Please," she said. "Locals don't walk into the slums on purpose."

"I don't want to talk about it," he said, mirroring her response exactly. She grinned quickly, but cynicism edged it until it lost its mirth. The tavern roared with laughter at something beyond them, but she just kept staring. Her narrowed eyes bored into him, setting a little shudder through him. That one so young could appear so wise ...

"Then how d'you come by these weapons?" she pressed. "You know, you're not allowed to wear a sword in the city unless you're one of the grunts." She flashed an easy grin. "Course, doesn't matter in the slums."

He covered the sword hilt with his cloak. "You ask a lot of questions."

"You're not dressed warmly enough, either," she wagged a finger. "Imbra's damn cold in the winter."

Another shiver racked his body, almost on reflex. "Don't I know it."

She grinned. "That's it. You were shuddering all along the alley. Made taking your gold dead easy."

"Please don't remind me of that." He smiled in return. The girl's quick wit made it impossible not to. They lapsed into silence for a while.

"Do you have a place to stay?" she asked suddenly.

Eli pursed his lips and hefted his bag. "Any good inns around here?"

Amora stood up so fast he jumped. He followed her out of the tavern down the next street. They stopped on the threshold of an inn, and Eli blinked rapidly, the flickering torches dancing sparks in his eyes. Men in rough cloth paused and glanced at him, sizing him up, weighing the risk. Amora ducked behind him. Strange, the girl. So brave one minute, then utterly vulnerable the next. She'd need to control that if she wanted to stand strong. He increased his swagger, playing a new role, his weapons marking him as someone not to be crossed.

Eli flicked over a gold piece to the innkeeper, a greying woman who nodded with a surly expression and pointed upstairs. He tapped Amora's shoulder and headed in that direction.

A young woman, one of the staff by the looks of it, forced a smile but retreated a step. Eli paused. Was that how he really looked? She led them up and pointed at the room, but she still trembled as he walked past.

She took a deep breath and rushed out, "There's a washroom down the end of the hall. You and your brother are welcome here." Her refusal to meet his gaze belied the words. Not how he'd expected that to go, but good enough.

He opened the door and ushered Amora inside, watching as childlike joy took over and she bounced on the bed, while he sagged and dropped the bravado.

"Do—do you feel safe here?" Eli asked hesitantly.

Amora let out a strange laugh. "I never feel safe anywhere."

He frowned at that. "Look, I understand if you don't want to be around me."

She shrugged, her bony shoulders visible through the rough cloth, the picture of irreverence born and raised in hopelessness. "I'll stick with you for now. On one condition—tell me why you're really here. Why Imbra?"

"I'm looking for answers."

"Ah, mukk. Thought you were a gruntah. You one of those head-in-the-clouds scholars? You know, people who think they know everything just because they can read and write?"

"You can't read?" he burst out before clamping his lips shut.

She shrugged again. It seemed to be a common trait of hers. "Don't need to. Just need to pick and steal and survive."

"That's no way to live," he said, anger coursing through him. "Why hasn't anyone done anything about it?"

"Oh, they tried," she grinned. "But the slums are their own world."

"What's a gruntah?" he asked.

"You."

He rolled his eyes. "Try again."

"People who grunt all the time. Ordermen, City Guard—gruntahs."

"I'm not one of them. Have you heard anything about what the Order has done?" he asked, but her blank, ash-smudged face was answer enough.

"They destroyed an entire mountain," he said heavily.

Her lack of concern couldn't have been more obvious. "Why should I care? Nobody has ever done anything for us. The urchins. We've just tried our best to survive."

60

"Well, I guess you don't have a reason to care," he sighed.

He left the room and paced down the dimly lit corridor. His boots squeaked as the floorboards, uneven and unkempt, groaned under his weight. His thoughts began to churn, and he slumped against the wall. He'd come here for answers, and he'd become stuck with a street urchin he needed to take care of. He shook that thought off. There was no place in his mission for a young girl, but, dammit, he couldn't turn her loose. Not after meeting her. The Jinnam had taught him that much.

He marched back to his room, sighing at his lack of options. The door creaked open, and he leaned in, prepared to say something. He stopped and stared at Amora. The girl lay under the covers, eyes closed and breathing evenly. Any residual thoughts of turning her loose now vanished completely from his head. He trod silently to the other bed and dropped onto it, leaning forward and putting his face in his hands.

"Gruntah?" a soft voice whispered. He jerked up, hand dropping to his dagger. A soft gasp pierced the air and Amora darted to the corner, pressed into the wall. She was completely frozen, eyes never leaving his. He wondered how long she'd been learning to act like that.

"I'm sorry," he whispered. Like a camouflaged insect, she hesitantly uncurled herself from the wall, as if she could remain there forever if needed. "When did you get into the slums?" he breathed.

She sighed. "Born there. Never knew my father. Mother died when I was two. Been with the urchins ever since. Millan looks after us," she said.

"I'm trying to find out what the Order is up to. Will you help me?" he asked. He was prepared to offer gold—the poor girl surely needed it—but she nodded, her entire body shaking with the motion.

Chapter 8

The clink of her chains through the snow-covered city streets was enough to draw the attention of wanderers and merchants alike. Jayne's gaze remained firmly on the ground as she swayed with her last reserves of energy. Vaguely, she registered an old man on the side of the street with a shovel and a bucket, scraping the snow from the path with the energy of a much younger man. Even he stopped and stared. The collar chafed at her neck, the last remnants of flesh now scraped raw, her wounds aching and festering. She listed to the side, but a heavy-handed guard grabbed her shoulder, forcing her to walk straight.

She nearly stumbled into the guard, halted in her path. Ice pooled in her veins as ethereal music floated on the chilly air. Soaring melodies and thundering crescendos—it was a gift to Nestham. At least, if they meant it.

Rich marble pillars soared into the sky. The Order's Cathedral, the bastion of their presence in Imbra. It also housed the elite of the Eternal Guard. The rest of them were housed in other cathedrals scattered throughout the city. Supposedly to keep the peace, yet that was also the role of the City Guard.

Trayse handed her chain to one of his men and sauntered forward, rummaging underneath his cloak for a sealed scroll, which he tossed to the sentry, a skinny, bearded man garbed in red and black. His spear gleamed in the morning sun as he pursed his lips and surveyed Jayne.

"Are you sure this is the Ghost?" he asked. The sentry next to him started awake, his bleary eyes blinking rapidly.

"Eh? The Ghost?" He yawned.

The bearded one grunted. "Trayse thinks he's caught the Ghost." The sleeper straightened, and Jayne could feel his eyes trace her body, though she glared firmly at the ground.

"This slip of a girl? She's not much to look at, is she?" the other chuckled. "Not sure Trayse is right in the head."

"That's Lieutenant Trayse," her captor insisted, but she heard the tremor of anger in his voice. A small flicker of humour crept over her, but she couldn't muster a smile. "I'm taking her to the Chosen," Trayse said firmly, ignoring the chuckles of the guards. Any mild amusement she felt at Trayse's humbling fell away and she tried to swallow, but her mouth refused, too parched.

The sentry grunted and let them pass.

"Try not to spill blood on the carpet," Trayse hissed at her as they marched her inside. She avoided looking at the grand paintings on the walls, the gilded art. A king's treasure lay here, all for the glory of Nestham.

Trayse marched her straight down the grand hall, past rows and rows of carved pews, worn and smooth from decades of service. Not unlike her chapel back in the valley; the thought sent a lance of grief into her heart. A silent choir stared from the pews as Trayse made straight for the door at the back of the hall, behind the speaker's lectern. It opened silently, and he stepped through, pausing at an ancient desk dominating the room. A young woman waited there, pretty, red-headed. Her pale eyes widened as Trayse smiled at her, and a small tremor passed through her. Jayne's arms tensed, but when the woman glanced at her, she dropped her eyes.

"I'm here to see his Excellency." Oh, mukk.

The assistant swallowed. "His Excellency isn't taking visitors at present," she stammered. Trayse glared at her and stepped closer to the desk, placing his palms delicately on the table.

"This, he'll want to see." The woman shuddered but nodded, granting Jayne a horrified smile. Trayse turned back to her and a thundercloud of fury crossed his face. She held up her

63

chained hands, pulling on them till blood dripped from the wounds. Forming a spectacular stain on the rich carpet. She'd had to clench her teeth to stop herself from screaming, but it was worth it.

He hissed at her and yanked on Jayne's collar, so hard and so suddenly she let out a cry despite herself, as he crashed through the door. Two men were inside, hunched over something Jayne couldn't make out.

An elderly man laughed and her insides churned even faster. "And your piece falls," rich tones purred, as a guttural voice swore. "That makes seven hundred gold pieces."

Archbishop Finon looked up from the luxurious hellin's board and his eyes narrowed on Trayse. "I hope you have good news, Lieutenant."

Trayse grinned. "Indeed, Excellency." He clicked his tongue and hauled Jayne forward, heaving on her chain until she swayed in front of him. A heavy hand forced her to her knees.

"Get out," Finon growled. His opponent and Trayse's guards left the room. "The Ghost, whom I dispatched you to hunt down, you believe is this girl?"

"Yes, your Excellency."

A sharp bark of a laugh rang through the room and she forced herself not to wince. "Let me see."

Spindly fingers wrapped around Jayne's chin, forced her to meet snake-like eyes under greying brows. Those eyes widened, and he swore viciously. Despite herself, she wanted to grin like a fiend at the poisonous old man.

"Who else has seen this girl?" he demanded.

Trayse shrugged. "Only the people who saw her on the way. We put the rest of her team down." Jayne's teeth were so tightly clenched she feared they would break.

Finon's graceful gestures became frantic. "Put her in isolation here at the Cathedral. Let *no one* see her or your head is on the chopping block next."

* * *

The door slammed shut on the cell as Jayne slumped against the stone wall. Nothing but a straw pile and a bucket, their dim outlines barely visible. She shuffled over to the straw, sighing as she fell into the pile. Hours of nothing but the wretched ceiling.

Until she slept.

And dreamed. She stood alone in a grassy valley. The sun beat down on her, wringing sweat from her clothes. The air was still, the grass unmoving. But she was no longer alone. An army of faces stood before her, just floating in the air, wisps of vapour streaming from their heads. They had no bodies, but the voices were as familiar to her as her own.

"You let us die," Luca hissed.

"We trusted you," Tamryn roared.

"And for what?" Lillin screamed. "You led us like sheep for the slaughter!"

Jayne fell to her knees, her shoulders caving in. Just as in the valley, her limbs refused to obey her. The tears flowed freely, cascading down her cheeks, her breath coming in hiccups. There was no saving her, no repentance.

An ear-shattering howl pierced her senses, and she looked up with bleary eyes. Her loved ones gained forms, but nothing like their old bodies. No, they were twisted and misshapen, glistening skin splotched with stains. Their eyes grew unnaturally large, and where they had gleamed with hate, they now paled to a milky-white—sightless and deathly. Teeth became reddened fangs as skin became scales. An army of monsters, bred to kill.

65

Luca led the charge and the army of the dead swarmed her. All that remained were her cries of pain and agony as her loved ones tore her apart. Jayne screamed herself awake, covered in a sheen of sweat.

But in the cold, damp cell, there was nobody to hear her.

Chapter 9

"Are you sure this is the best idea?" Eli asked. He leaned against the alley wall, glancing up and down the quiet passageway.

Amora glanced up at him. "Of course. Nobody else in the poor quarter knows what Fallin knows."

"I don't trust him," he muttered.

Amora grinned at him. "Good. You're learning, gruntah."

Eli shook his head at the cynicism. "And what, I'm just supposed to walk up and ask what the Order is up to?"

"Of course not. You need to buy something first."

"Fine," he shrugged.

"Just—don't act like a stranger," she mumbled.

"How am I supposed to do that?"

"Try not to be an idiot. Off you go," she chirped.

Eli left Amora and strolled around the corner and through the street, angling for the drab shop on the far side. Snow was falling from the awning in drops as it melted under the midday sun. As he pushed through the crowd, he noted how travellers immediately cleared a path for him at the sight of his weapons. More than one glanced at him with curiosity, met his silver eyes. Several faces lit up at the sight of him and his fine weapons, and he kept them in his awareness as he pushed open the faded green door. The hinges squealed, a warning to Fallin just in case soldiers came knocking; he'd have time to prepare.

The shop was almost empty save for a surly man in the corner, idly cleaning a knife with a filthy rag, probably putting more dirt on than he was taking off. Eli took one step towards him but stopped. Amora's voice echoed in his ears, the advice of a street urchin with years of fending for herself. Fallin would never talk to someone who approached him directly. So he scanned the items. Fishing supplies, leather items, assorted jewellery. A small bag with a considerable bulge in it seemed like it would do. He tossed it on the counter. The old man barely looked at him as he pulled an armlet out of the bag.

"Three silvers."

"Four," Eli amended. The price going up—he wanted information.

A light of comprehension flicked into the man's dark eyes. "Four," Fallin agreed. He held his hand out and Eli pulled out four silver coins, placed them on the counter with a soft thud. Fallin waited patiently. Eli covered them with his hand and stared at Fallin's deep brown gaze.

"Word is that the Order is attacking other faiths. What do you know of it?"

Fallin's face almost resembled fear. But a deal was a deal.

"Alright. They first started with fear, forced people out of their homes. Made them exiles. Then they sent soldiers to destroy artefacts and writings. They started with the outlying towns, but have worked their way in. It scares even the Musadim. They've left almost no witnesses, and they're convincing people that it was Nestham's will. They've been executing heretics or taking them to the Cathedral. And word is"—he dropped his voice to a plotting whisper, despite their isolation—"they've caught the Ghost who's been operating in secret to rescue scholars and refugees."

Eli's brows rose. *How do you know this?* he wanted to ask, but he trusted the information.

"And the Archbishop? What do you know of him?"

Fallin glared at him. "That's more than one piece of information, boy." Eli snarled softly and relinquished another piece, which Fallin quickly snatched up. "He goes by the moniker of Chosen, now. Thinks he's the one called to

Nestham's teachings above all others. He's been meeting with some Vindicators. Things are getting shifty there." He stuffed the armlet back in the bag. "Watch out, boy."

Eli frowned. "Thanks."

He grabbed the bag and walked out, meeting Amora's gaze, the girl slouching against the wall, hunched into a surly youth's posture.

"So?" she drawled.

He nodded as he handed over the bag to another vendor for one piece of silver. "Here's not the place to talk about it." A brilliant green glowed within the bag as Amora turned her back on the vendor and followed Eli.

* * *

Eli shut the door on their room as Amora crashed on the bed. "You alright?" he asked.

"I'm fine," she replied, but she didn't meet his gaze. "So, did you learn anything?" She stared at the ceiling.

"Some. The Jinnam in Mount Sancti weren't the only group purged by the Order recently. And they've caught someone called the Ghost who's been rescuing refugees."

"Catching a saviour? The Order has really slumped to a new low."

Eli rolled his eyes. "I guess there's nothing else to do but try the source itself."

That got her attention. "You better not be saying what I think you're saying," she said.

Eli shrugged. "Why not? Nobody outside the Citadel has any idea what's going on."

She glared at him. "You really want to get into the Citadel?"

"You've got a way in?"

"Yes, but it's probably going to get you killed."

A single waterfall lay ahead, icy water plummeting to a moon-kissed river a hundred metres below. The river provided all of Citadel's water. And possibly one weakness. Eli had studied all the fortress walls from their place in what seemed to be an expensive part of town where the bluff was some ten metres above the water. Beneath the sheer cliff on the far side, a dark fissure extended from the water's surface. A yawning tunnel emerged from there, just behind the waterfall. There was just one problem. There was no way to climb up it without first entering the lake.

"I said I had a way, but it's probably got a bunch of guards," Amora pointed out after she showed him.

"This is your way in?"

"Yes. But of course, you don't want to go there, do you?" she said with a wink.

He just stared at the waterfall.

"It might be okay. It's well hidden. The lake would discourage most people." Amora turned a hunched back on him, and when he glanced away from the waterfall, he frowned and tapped her shoulder. "What's wrong?" The question faded away into nothing until she spoke over her shoulder. Her voice lightened, softened.

"I just don't want you to get yourself killed. You're—you're the only person who's shown me kindness."

Eli's heart melted for the girl. "I'm coming back," he reassured her. "Once I find out what the Archbishop is planning, we can leave Imbra forever." He would *never* call him Chosen. Not after the Jinnam's slaughter. She twisted to him so fast he blinked, and threw her arms around him. After a brief hesitation, he returned the gesture.

"Don't you dare get caught," she hissed.

He grinned. "Keep these for me, won't you?" He handed her his sword, bow and arrows. The climb would be enough of a challenge without the extra weight. He kept his knife.

He marched to the edge of the bluff, hesitated. An icy wind swirled from the northern mountains and whipped at his hair. He took deep breaths, preparing for the jump. Once he went in, that would be it. The cold wouldn't allow him the strength to go under again. He would jump, swim under the waterfall, climb the rocks behind it, and enter the tunnel.

He pushed off the cliff. Or tried to. His heart was hammering, but his boots wouldn't move. Fear rooted him to the spot. A brilliant blue light flared on the cliff as a shimmering outline appeared behind the waterfall. Flickering under the water, one detail remained clear. Silver eyes, blazing with passion. A ghost of a hand smacked his shoulder, and he jumped.

He fell for an eternity and yet a split second. He plummeted through the air and hit the water. It was like hitting stone. It knocked all the breath out of his lungs and he clutched his throat, desperate for air. He made frantic motions to rise through the water, but he was too deep.

It was pitch black in the lake, an area that likely never saw light. An unconscious connection clicked in his mind, like a door that opened into a storm. He sank into the strange power and let the star flare. His light pierced the water, illuminating the icy lake. Nothing but stone and water.

Except ... gold glimmered on the cliff wall. A sharp symbol, with three lines forming a triangle. Pointing up. Eli grimaced, pulling himself through the water. The cold setting in, as was the lack of air. He kept swimming for the symbol. His blood pounded in his head and his arms refused to obey him. *No, not now.* But he couldn't move ...

A strong hand grasped his arm and heaved him bodily out of the water. Eli turned and vomited up water on the stones, but when he turned around, there was nobody there.

Only the roar of the waterfall and the lake beyond.

It was impossible to see in the grotto. It seemed nobody had been here for hundreds of years. Eli shuddered to his feet. The cold vanished, replaced by a strange sense of peace. He drew his knife and, though he didn't mean it to happen, his light flickered. Cold blue brilliance illuminated the cave as he dripped his way along the stone. To the left, a gaping tunnel, to the right, a set of stairs. He went right and cautiously ascended the steps, boot steps ringing on rock as he spiralled to his right. Within moments his legs were burning, his energy drained by the freezing swim. Finally, a glimmer of light. Golden light. An Eternal Torch flickered up ahead. After what must have been a hundred steps, he emerged onto the Citadel battlements. The moon glimmered overhead as he stood alone, a figure cloaked in darkness. The Mark dimmed, and he shoved his hand into his pocket.

Steps from behind him. He whipped his head like a snake, tensed to spring, but paused at the bizarre sight awaiting him. A gleaming silver tattoo wound its way around the man's cheek, but there was no expected glimmer from his eyes. The man took another step forward. No, more of a shuffle, his feet scraping on the stone. Bare feet. What in the hells? Another step. He tripped and stumbled forward, bumped into the stone of the battlements. A muffled snore echoed through the night. Eli stared, struck senseless by what lay before him. Because that was surely a Vindicator, a sworn officer of the Crown, sleepwalking in front of him. Fully dressed, fully armed, but fully asleep. The Vindicator turned slowly and took one more step forward on the flagstones, away from Eli.

72

He leaned forward onto the battlements. Too far. His torso fell into thin air and he began to drop like a stone, only a little wheeze emanating from his mouth. Blue light flared as Eli lunged for the man, grabbing onto rough cloth. He collapsed onto the flagstones with a thud and lay there, aching. His fingers strained as he held the Vindicator, but they were slipping. Eli grunted as he shifted his weight behind him and hauled the man up, depositing him on the battlements.

Prone on the stone floor, the Vindicator merely began to snore again. Eli sighed. "I hope whatever you're dreaming, it's worth it."

He strode through the streets of Citadel, looking for all the world like he was a soldier, but never fully advanced into the light. At last, the building he sought appeared up ahead. Graceful lines soared to the heavens, a celebration of Nestham. At least that was what the Order claimed. Though it seemed more self-adulation than anything else.

No priests outside, no wandering Eternal Guardsmen. Just two bored sentries with spears. Evidently, piety did not equal pacifism these days. Eli shuffled forward and hunched his shoulders, looking for all the world like a fervent parishioner desperate for late-night prayers. The steps forward felt like an eternity, as the road lengthened before him. His heart quickened as one of the sentries pounded his spear into the ground.

"Name?"

Eli's mind went blank. *Name?* "Uh—Jynn. Jynn Lanter."

The guard glared at him. "Purpose of visit, Lanter?"

"Prayer, sir."

A bloated silence filled the air. Eli's heart beat even faster. The other guard shifted his stance, ready to aim his spear in a blink. "Very well. Pass, please."

Eli blinked in surprise. The guard gestured over his shoulder. "Go!" He smiled and passed through, to the entrance of the cathedral. It was even grander inside. Sweeping vistas of long-dead saints and priests, angelic beings. But as Eli passed through the hall, ignoring the other worshippers, something snagged his gaze. A large gap between the paintings, as if one was missing.

He found a seat on the wooden pews and closed his eyes, listening for anything. He sat there for over an hour before he gave up. The night had been a failure. A muffled thump echoed from behind him and he spun around. A closed door, gilded and locked. He glanced furtively around him. The hall was empty, the others having departed within the hour. He trod on the polished wood, inhaling the sweet smell of incense. He pressed his ear to the door.

Silence. He tried the door handle. Locked.

But it hadn't closed properly. He pushed his shoulder to the door and nudged it in, wincing at the squeak on rusty hinges. A stark office. Another door beyond. He twisted that handle. Locked. He tried twisting it again, and blue light flashed on the walls. The lock splintered, and the door opened. He stepped into a much grander room, rich furniture and a stack of documents scattered over the desk. Idly he pulled some out and leafed through them.

"Mount Sancti destroyed ... Jinnam eliminated. King still opposed." His eyes widened. He scanned the room. A cabinet with expensive-looking flasks and bottles, a grand sword mounted on the wall, bookshelves lined with ancient texts.

A soft tread on the ground pricked his consciousness.

A thump on his head made him lose it.

Chapter 10

The bluff hadn't changed from when he'd last seen it. A snowy cliff overlooking an icy waterfall, the roar of water echoing in his ears. Alsair stood motionless before the glimmer of gold in the sun, before the walls of the Citadel looming on the far side. Though his legs ached constantly, he didn't fancy the cold creeping even further into his body. He shivered under his cloak, beneath the dark hood shielding his face. Any sane person would have gone home by now, sought the warmth of an inn. They would not be peering endlessly at a waterfall, searching ceaselessly for a boy already contained within the Citadel walls.

But his prey wasn't inside Citadel. No, his prey was behind him. He withdrew his hand from his belt and as he raised it in the air he casually drew his cloak over the sword's hilt. He had been lucky to avoid losing it to a sentry.

"If you're thinking of stealing my purse, Amora, it may turn out differently from your last theft." Absolute silence. "I'd rather you didn't shoot me in the back with that bow, though I don't think you could draw it. Who knows? They may make one for you, one day." Still nothing. "I'm turning around." His foot slid through the snow as he pivoted, slowly turning until he faced the tree line behind him. "Amora, you can trust me."

"How do you know my name, smoother?" a voice floated out of the air. He rolled his eyes and kept his smile from showing through the bristles.

"Lucky guess, I suppose," he replied. He kept watching, waiting. The breeze shifted and the bare branches swayed, but the area remained untouched. And at last, a dark head of hair peeped out from behind a tree. Night-dark eyes fixed intently on

Alsair. "You know where he's gone, don't you," he said, and smiled.

She glared at him. "I'm not telling you anything, priest."

"Firstly, I'm not a priest. I'm a monk."

"Same difference."

Alsair raised his arms in supplication, watching how her eyes narrowed in on his missing hand. "I need to save Eli, and I need your help." At last, Amora's eyes dropped the fierce glare, dropped the entire act. She and Alsair sat down, heedless of the snow that chilled them.

"There's nothing we can do to help him right now," she said.

Chapter 11

A scrape on stone, like an object being dragged, roused Jayne from her drowsy state. She blinked rapidly, leaned forward from the wall, but couldn't find the strength to rise. Not after what had happened. Kept in isolation, kept out of sight of everyone. Kept in the Archbishop's pocket. That didn't surprise her in the slightest.

The scrape again, but longer. Getting louder, getting closer. The guard unlocked the door opposite hers and threw something into the cell, a deep thud echoing from the stone, and for a brief moment she glimpsed its form. Cloaked in darkness, the only part she could make out was the short hair on his head.

The guard never looked her way, merely slammed the door shut and thumped out. She waited a breath, two. It was clear her new neighbour wasn't rousing soon. Jayne leaned back against the wall, bringing her knees to her chest. It was some time before he stirred. A whisper, almost like a prayer, echoed out from the darkness.

"I'm sorry, Alsair."

"Who's Alsair?" she blurted out, despite her attempts to stay silent. But there was no response. Hours passed, or maybe seconds. With no light, it was impossible to keep track of the sun's passage. Deep, even breathing became much louder, as if he was panting, fighting off something in his nightmares.

Finally, he spoke again.

"Hello?" he called, a plaintive plea for help.

"Don't bother trying," she said. "There's no one coming." She blinked away the moisture that filled her eyes.

"What?" His voice carried worry, desperation. "Who's there?"

Jayne debated what to say. "The Ghost," she finally said.

"Ah. I see." He fell silent for a moment. "Does the Ghost have a name?"

She held back a snort. He was persistent, at least. "Jayne."

"I'm Eli. Nice to see you." A pause. "Well, sort of."

Her mouth twitched. How was he doing this? Curiosity nagged at her, stirring her from despair for the first time.

"What happened to you?"

He just let out a deep sigh. "Wandered into the Archbishop's chambers. Got knocked out from the feel of it. Where are we?"

"In the dungeons beneath the Cathedral. I thought this was isolation, but apparently not." She could only guess what had happened to the prisoners before her.

"How did you get here?" Eli asked.

Jayne swallowed. "They took me in a valley a day south of Mount Sancti. My team was"—she choked—"slaughtered." The cells fell silent again.

"I'm sorry to hear that."

But for some reason she couldn't stop, fearful she might just shut herself off, that she'd die without the story told, that their memory would be lost forever.

"We were taking a group of scholars south to the Plains, where the Order doesn't have as much of an influence. They died for something they believed in." She was rambling, she knew. But this had to be shared. She had to relive it, if for no other reason than to remind herself of her failure.

"What were their names?" Eli asked gently.

"Luca." Her Second, the one who had pulled her from the raging river. "Lillin." Her mentor, her trainer, her friend. "Tamryn." Her taskmaster, her rock. "Anar." The calm in the storm. "Mick, Nina." Her hunters, her firebrands. "And

78

Ginlun." Her protector, the one who'd found her standing over the bodies of four Eternal Guardsmen, staff in hand, and asked to join her. She massaged her palm, eased out the sharp pains from her nails clenched tight.

"Ginlun?" Eli echoed.

"You know him?" she asked, surprise stealing through her.

He hesitated. "I met him once, briefly. He said he was doing some work with another group nearby. I assume he meant you." Jayne nodded, but he couldn't see her expression, a face forced into stone. "Don't worry. We'll have our chance to tell our stories at trial," Eli said.

Five Hells, he was optimistic. And impossibly naïve. She laughed cynically. "There's no trial. I don't expect to see the sun again."

"You can't think like that," Eli tried to persuade her. The silence stretched longer.

"Try me," she broke it. But even then, his voice stoked the small flame in her heart, the one thing keeping her from giving in.

The dungeon door opened and a single stranger stalked in. At least, she thought it was one stranger. He carried no flame. Even so, a single flicker of light illuminated his face. Illuminated the curling tattoo over his cheek. Her cry caught in her tightened throat as the Vindicator unlocked Eli's cell. She sensed rather than saw the young man stirring, but the man grabbed Eli by the arm at the same time as he pointed a sword-tip at his chest.

"Come with me."

Chapter 12

With little choice, Eli marched ahead of the guard. To attempt an escape would be pointless, with the razor-sharp sword resting on his spine. Corridors twisted and turned in this rabbit warren of a cathedral. He began to count. Twenty-seven steps, then a left. Thirty-nine steps, then a right. He tried to maintain his focus, but a ringing slap to the back of the head set his head spinning and he stumbled forward. Eventually, they emerged into a darkened room, with only one glowing light, a dim flicker of orange. The Vindicator shoved Eli into a chair and quickly clamped manacles around his wrists. The steel bit into his hands, forcing him to suck in a breath as little rivulets of blood pooled under the metal.

The Vindicator faced him, his surprisingly youthful face gleaming with hate.

"I think you know how this will work," he breathed, but the voice was like a hissing snake, filling every corner of the room. "I ask you questions, and if I don't like the answers, I'll start hurting you." Eli swallowed. "Why were you in the Archbishop's chambers?"

"Looking for something to steal," Eli shrugged, forcing irreverence. It might be his only chance.

Something crept up on him, a twisting pain that exploded in his mind, overwhelming, unending until he could barely stop his scream. At last, it stopped, and the silence crept in.

"Let me ask you again," his assailant whispered. "Why were you in the Archbishop's chambers?" Eli clamped down on his mouth as it started again. "It's pointless to hold this back. You're only hurting yourself."

Sweat drenched Eli's chest, soaking through his shirt, but he fought to keep his lie. "I was just looking around."

The Vindicator sighed. "Well, perhaps you are just a thief. We will tell in time. Regardless, I may have need of your skills." He pushed Eli back on the chair and tugged his shirt over his head to expose his chest. Eli shivered in the cold as his pooling sweat chilled, as his breath misted in the freezing cell.

The man moved over to the small glow in the room, touched it gently and hissed. But in the glow, his hand remained perfectly healthy. The light began to move towards Eli and his heart picked up, hammered so fast he feared it would leap out of his chest. Fresh sweat broke out on his forehead, and his tongue glued to the roof of his mouth. The Vindicator's perfect teeth glimmered in the orange flame as he pressed the brand to Eli's flesh.

At first there was no pain, merely shock. Then searing agony, as if every nerve was immersed in flames, travelling up and down his body. He spiralled deeper and deeper into the pain, his screams rebounding off the stone wall. At last, mercifully, his head slumped onto his chest and he lost consciousness.

* * *

The roiling agony of his singed flesh was enough to wake him. It pierced the fog of blissful unconsciousness and his screams started again. The wound was still smouldering, the stench of charred flesh lingering in the air.

"What in the hells happened?" he vaguely heard Jayne whisper, but he couldn't find the strength to reply. He opened his mouth, but it was too late, and bile rushed up his throat. He gagged and retched until it sprayed on the cobblestones, then shoved himself back against the wall, as far away from it as possible.

He tried to curl up, but gasped as his hand brushed against the wound. An ice blue light flickered in the darkness, and a wave of soothing rushed over him, wrapping him in a calm he hadn't felt in so long. Belatedly he realised it was the strange power lying within him, the same that had healed him from the soldier the day Mount Sancti fell. He swore and clamped his hand on the ground, masking his light. White light flared from his chest and agony engulfed him once more.

At last, he slept. When he stirred, the pain was still there, but muted, as if a monster now slumbered within him, satisfied with every drop of torment it had wrung from him. A single drip of water splashed, somewhere in the dungeons. Once, twice, three times. He groaned as he tried to sit up, and cracked opened his eyes. A mess greeted him, reeking and foul. He noticed his shirt just beside it and gingerly pulled it over his head, wincing as it brushed against his aching wound.

"How long have I been out?" he rasped through a parched throat.

"How should I know?" Jayne replied. "I can't tell time here, remember?" She fell silent, waiting. "A while," she said.

"Was that ... me?" he said, pointing at the vomit. His eyes began to water at the smell and he fought the urge to retch again.

"You really don't remember?"

He clutched a breath once, twice. "Nothing past the Vindicator branding me."

"He—he branded you?" Silence. "That's nothing like Leranion or the Order. What the hells did you do?" she pressed.

"Nothing, I swear!"

The guards came, delivered their meals. Mush, slop, every disgusting item on the menu.

"We're not staying here long," Jayne whispered, after they'd eaten, and her voice was fierce, as if something in her had reignited, far from the broken, bitter girl she was earlier.

He let out a hollow laugh and screamed as it set his skin on fire again. "No. You were right. There's no hope left."

"I kept a spoon from dinner. The guard's a mukking meathead for missing *that*. And there's a loose bar on my cell."

"You're still shackled to the wall," he pointed out.

A muffled clink of metal on stone. "Not anymore."

What are you? he wondered. They kept talking throughout the night, laying out their plan.

Heavy, ponderous steps rumbled through the chamber as one guard came to deliver their food, a tray balanced on each arm. As per routine, he went to Jayne first. He unlocked her cell, stepped inside and set one tray down in front of her, his hand on his knife. But she huddled against the wall, chains draped around her wrists. The picture of brokenness.

The moment the guard turned his back, she moved like a whirlwind, leaping up and at him. His own knife plunged straight through the back of his neck. Blood sprayed over the stones as Jayne placed him down, then rummaged on his belt for the keys.

Eli pressed up against the bars as Jayne fumbled in front of him. The keys rattled as she tried each one, his heart thumping louder with each try. Finally, the door swung open, and she unlocked his chains. He glanced up into her face. Even in the meagre light, he recognised her.

"The girl from the mountain hall," he breathed.

Her eyes widened in recognition. "You ..." She smiled and gestured for him to stand.

He leaped forward, then dropped to the floor, still in pain.

"I'm not sure I'll be much help," he gasped. She knelt beside him, grasped his arm and slung it over her shoulder. He was surprised at the innate strength within her as he stood on trembling legs.

"I won't leave you here," she replied, with a voice like stone.

He grinned despite himself. "Don't you think you're coming on a bit strong?"

She snarled at him, low and fierce. "Not the time."

They paced up the steps, one at a time. And at last, flickering lights gleamed beyond them. Eli reached up and grabbed a torch off the wall. "I may as well be some use," he breathed.

She flicked a smile but glanced around, still on alert. At last, he had a moment to study her. And, Nestham above, she was beautiful. Even covered with dirt and filth, blood coating her face, she was beautiful. Deep blue eyes stared right through him and he realised she had said something.

"Where are all the guards?" she said, arching her brows.

"Don't know, don't care. I just want to get out of here." He shrugged.

"Do you remember the way?" she asked.

He pointed to his right. "If that way was where he interrogated me, I say"—he glanced left, to a set of stairs leading up—"we go that way."

"Any reasoning for that?" she asked.

He looked at the stairs, rolled his gaze back to her. "We're underground." He grinned. "The way out is always up."

"You know I can just drop you on the floor." She glared. "You're not funny."

"I thought I was," he gasped through the pain.

Muffled laughter to their left alerted them. Jayne reacted on instinct, shoving Eli against the wall, pressing her weight to him. He raised a brow, and she glared at him from underneath the blood. The laughter died down, and the thump of guards echoed from around the corner, sending his heartbeat spiralling out of control. Jayne's body wrapped around his as he pressed his hand against the head of the torch, extinguished it—searing pain not unlike the brand on his chest. He hissed under his breath, but Jayne pressed her hand against his mouth.

This was it. He nodded at her, prepared to unleash hell.

Screams and thuds made Jayne lean further into him. Then they peered around the corner and Eli let out a quiet sigh. A single man stood there, a calm smile on his face, a slender, curved weapon held in his single hand. He hadn't even unsheathed the blade. His broadsword remained strapped over his back. All the surrounding soldiers were prone, but no blood covered the ground.

"If you two have quite finished, perhaps we can leave?" Alsair said mildly.

Eli bowed his head, unable to speak.

Alsair glared at him. "I'll deal with you later," he said. Eli scuffed his feet on the ground. "Who's your friend?"

Eli sputtered but couldn't reply, so Jayne introduced herself. Alsair's eyes gleamed once, flicking jade over her. "Take this. You look like you could use it," he said. He handed her the sword. The markings were strange, running up and down the scabbard, but it looked impressive. Jayne's ocean-depth eyes widened and a small smile crept across her face. Alsair continued as if nothing had happened. "We just have one more stop."

With that, he turned and marched off.

Jayne glanced at Eli. Her right hand twitched the sword back and forth, her training evident. "Friend of yours?"

"Hopefully," he sighed.

"Hurry!" Alsair called from the next chamber and they followed him through the twisting warren underneath the cathedral.

Jayne studied him in silence. "What's wrong?"

His breathing sharpened, then fell again. He shook his head. There was no way Alsair could be here, yet here he was. "Nothing. Let's go."

They rounded the corner and Eli stopped dead. A semicircle of golden flame, dancing on water. Dead ahead, a great stone carving, of just one symbol. Sharp, jagged lines. Something nagged at Eli, but he couldn't think through it, as the brand flared and he groaned, sagging against the wall.

"I've never seen that symbol," Jayne whispered.

Alsair stared at Eli and jerked over his shoulder at the flame. "Stick your torch in there," he suggested. What? Eli narrowed his eyes at the monk.

Jayne gasped. "This is the Eternal Flame's wellspring, isn't it?"

Alsair gestured at her. "Exactly. Handy to have a torch that never goes out, right?"

"This is blasphemy on so many levels." She smiled, but it died quickly and she stepped away.

She was right, it was blasphemy. The Eternal Flames were set as beacons. No human was allowed to carry one. Ever. Eli stepped up to the inferno flickering over the water. A gust of wind flickered through the chamber and the fire *roared,* flaring higher. He glanced back at Alsair, but the monk just smiled at him, all the iciness gone.

He thrust the torch into the Flame.

His Mark flared, joined by the brand. But the Flame flared most of all. Eli winced and yanked the torch out, but it remained dark, lifeless. He held his breath, waiting, but as the seconds stretched out, his stomach sank lower and lower. Jayne wouldn't meet his gaze, concentrating on tying back her tangled and blood-matted hair. Alsair kept smiling. And somehow it seemed so important that this light would catch. But for the life of him, Eli didn't know why.

He sighed in disappointment. His breath swirled on the torch, a gentle breeze. A small golden glow flickered in the core, just a faint ember. The torch burst into flame, golden light spilling everywhere. Eli grinned.

"Touch the flame, Eli." He whipped his head around, started to protest, but Alsair just nodded serenely. Jayne's gaze was glued on his own silver eyes. Alarm and concern flickered across her face, those delicate brows arched high. Eli held his hand up to the Torch. Stopped. "It's okay, Eli." Emboldened, he thrust his hand into the flame. No pain, no scorching. The flame was bright. His light was brighter. The spell broke at last and his pulsing light faded away. As he glanced at Jayne, her eyes gleamed but she said nothing.

"We need to get out of here," he said.

"Amora's already waiting outside. We'll leave the same way you came in, Eli. These tunnels link all the way back to the waterfall."

They plunged into the musty tunnels, splashing through the water, covering their noses at the stench. Jayne beside him was wide-eyed at their surroundings. Alsair somehow had a sixth sense for the patrols, and at last they arrived back into the waterfall chamber, where Eli had begun his journey. In there, Eli blinked rapidly at the sight of a little boat bobbing in the lake. Eli turned to Alsair.

"Yes, yes, I procured a boat. Enough talking. Get in," he waved. Eli and Jayne clambered in, sending the boat rocking, the packs and weapons tumbling. Eli sighed with relief as he noted his sword and bow amongst the pile. Jayne half-screamed when Amora popped up from where she had been hiding, but

Eli laughed with delight. The girl tackled him and the boat lurched, sending them stumbling. He bit back a scream as his burn pulled.

"You said you'd come back sooner," she whispered into his shirt.

"Sorry. Looks like it worked out okay, though."

Alsair hopped into the boat and shoved off, sending it rocking gently as they bobbed on the water, utterly silent. Each held their breath as they passed through the heavy curtain of water. Finally, they slid out from underneath the cavern and into the stars. A vast drapery strewn across the sky. They were silent as Alsair paddled the little boat down the Kinar River, one of the few parts without ice. He broke the silence at last. "We can't stay on the river forever, they'll get wind of us soon."

"We can head into the mountains," Jayne replied. Eli raised his brows, and she noticed the motion in the Torch's light. "There's an old rebel hideout I know. We can stay there a while."

Alsair glanced around the little group. No one objected. "North it is."

Chapter 13

"Vindicator Monsun?"

Monsun grunted and his bleary eyes opened, fixing on the man standing over him. He wore a blue Leranion uniform, the snarling snow leopard emblazoned in silver on his chest.

"Sir?" the man said.

"What time is it?" he groaned.

"Mid-morning. The king asked to see you."

Monsun's eyes snapped open, and he bolted upright in the sheets. "Well, we don't want to keep his Majesty waiting." He rolled out of bed, garbed in light, billowy trousers.

"There's something else, sir."

"Yes?" Monsun called over his shoulder as he wiped his muscled torso down in the washbasin.

The messenger hesitated. "Lieutenant Porma says you walked again, two nights ago."

Monsun stopped dead. "What day is it today?"

"Sevenday."

His gaze fixed on the soldier, noted the sandy hair and piercing brown eyes. "I've been out for a day and two nights?"

Silence. The man merely nodded. Monsun sighed and untangled his hair, mussed from sleep. He wove it into an inky braid with years of effortless practice. The pristine blue uniform flashed as he swung it over his shoulders, along with the silver half-cape, then strapped his axe at his belt. He swung his gaze at the other doors around him as he stepped out. Cedwin's was still ajar, his room as messy as ever. The youngest Vindicator should have returned by now. He made a mental note to check on him later, before stomping down the ancient stone stairs, ignoring the ancient steel door at the base. A ring of steel echoed from behind it, accompanied by a feminine yell of

89

delight, and his mouth twitched, heart speeding up. He raised a brow at the messenger, whose eyes had flickered to the door, still closed beside him.

"Lucky Vindicators," the messenger muttered under his breath.

Monsun smiled and stalked out, his silver tattoo gleaming in the morning sun. The soldier hurried to keep up on stumpy legs, whilst Monsun's cape fluttered behind him. He merely nodded at the sentries as they opened the great iron door, ancient and weathered, to the shortcut under the Spires. Crossing between these two Spires via the normal route could often be tedious, particularly with all the courtiers who glanced at his ebony skin and curled their lips in disdain. He stepped through, let himself become accustomed to the dimness. Orange flames illuminated the walkway, but it was never wise to walk straight through this passageway. Two steps to either side would send him plummeting to a grisly death. Why the architects of Imbra's Citadel had seen fit to build over a giant chasm, he would never know.

A blinding pain struck his chest, and he stumbled to the floor, breathing heavily. His vision flashed red for an instant and he gasped, fighting against the scream. A tug, stronger than any man, pulled him backwards. Monsun jerked back and blindly thrashed in the phantom grip, trying to get free. At last, it gave way, and he lurched forward, his lungs heaving. A strange force settled inside him, as if it had shoved his soul out. The messenger rushed to his side, eyes wild and frantic.

"Sir, what happened?"

"I don't know," he gasped, pressing a finger to his neck. He glimpsed the steel bars of the prison cells cut into the wall of the chasm, and the empty gap behind them, before continuing. At last, Monsun burst into King Hadrian's chambers. The first thing he saw, ignoring all the rich decorations, was the familiar bright hair, glowing like a living flame. He dropped a knee to the floor.

"Majesty," he said.

The King turned to him and smiled widely. "Monsun, my friend. Up you get."

He arose and grinned at his ruler. The smile died away as he took in the pasty skin and reddened eyes. "Majesty, are you well?"

Hadrian waved a dismissive hand. "Fine, just fine." Monsun wisely decided not to press anymore, instead enquiring after the Queen. Hadrian's eyes glistened. "She's better, but there are some days where she won't get out of bed." Grief could change a person. The door banged open again and Monsun whirled around, glaring daggers at the intruder. Hadrian remained silent, unmoved.

The man wore vermilion robes, a polished golden staff in his right hand. His neat grey moustache twitched as King and Vindicator stared him down. He refused to remove his headgear, the ridiculous towering hat embossed with Nestham's Shield. Hadrian waited.

Finally, the intruder spoke. "Two prisoners escaped yesterday. Dangerous fugitives. I thought you should know, but my men will ensure they are swiftly brought to justice."

"The prisoners you don't keep in your Cathedral?" Hadrian glared at the man. The silence stretched longer.

"Yes," the greying man hissed. Hadrian waited. "Yes, Majesty."

"Archbishop Finon, you are treading on thin ice. I've already heard rumours of the Order moving armed forces. If I hear anything else, you'll be a lucky man to avoid prison."

"With all due respect, Majesty, I only answer to Nestham," Finon said.

Hadrian's gaze could have melted iron. He tapped his gleaming ring, and in answer, brilliant golden light flared from his hand. A blazing star on his right hand, by the knuckle of his forefinger.

"Finon, *I* only answer to Nestham. Take heed lest you meet him sooner than expected." Finon's face blanched slightly, but his eyes narrowed. Those eyes that belonged to a snake. The Archbishop left without another word. Another insult to the King, leaving without being dismissed.

Monsun exhaled softly as he glanced at Hadrian. "I hear he goes by Chosen, now," he ventured. Hadrian merely nodded and rolled his eyes. Monsun sensed something else was bothering Hadrian, but he saw no reason to press.

"You know the capabilities of my ring," Hadrian began, and Monsun nodded. All the nobility did.

"I know when someone is dishonest. It's why I can trust you wholeheartedly." Hadrian sighed, the scratched crown on his head moving with the reaction. "Much of what Finon says these days is a lie."

"He's a politician," Monsun deadpanned. "No offence sire, but your court is a pack of jackals."

Hadrian huffed a laugh. "Why do you think I keep you Vindicators around? But even so, Finon's news is troubling. I think ..." he began, then trailed into silence. Nodded to himself. "Finon just confirmed everything Hyrin told me. He said Finon had a woman brought into the Cathedral in chains. Yes, I think if we were to recover these fugitives ourselves, and perhaps not let the Order know, we might have something of an advantage over Finon."

Monsun's eyes blazed. "How do you even let him live?" he pressed. Dangerous, questioning the King in his own palace. Yet Hadrian had never denied him, making a warrior from

Biralam the youngest soldier ever to hold the title of Senior Vindicator and take the silver tattoo.

The older man sighed wearily, his grey beard twitching with the motion.

"Truth be told, I don't think I can challenge him anymore. I'm not sure how many on the Council support him. It's almost as if my staff refuse to obey me. I swear my ministers aren't telling me something, but I don't know what." He snapped his mind back to the present and clarity shone from his deep blue eyes.

"I need you to bring back the two fugitives. Maybe we can use whatever they have and get an advantage. Can you do that for me?" Not a question.

Monsun snapped a salute. "Your will, Majesty. They will be back within a week. If they try to escape, they die." His chest pulsed again, and he choked on his breath. Hadrian's face showed concern, but Monsun was already striding from the palace, barking orders. Minutes later, a colossal horse with a coat of midnight thundered out of the Citadel.

Chapter 14

Eli shivered with his back to the cave wall, idly watching the sparks dance in the fire, his legs aching from the hours they'd walked after abandoning the boat. Even a day after the escape, his brand still ached constantly. For now, however, it was the numbness in his left arm that was the problem; a solid weight was squeezing all the blood from it. Amora muttered as she slumbered on his arm. Eli sighed and flicked his gaze to Alsair, but the monk hadn't moved from his position at the mouth of the cave, curled up in his cloak, gazing at the snowy landscape outside. A bitter wind swirled through the cavern, cutting through his jerkin, and he shivered, but Alsair was unruffled, as if mortal elements were beneath him.

On the other side of the grotto, Jayne sat with her knees pulled to her chest, hair drawn back in a severe braid. Her arms, freshly bandaged from Alsair's supplies, rested on her knees. Shame the monk hadn't brought much food. She gazed into the fire, as if entranced by the ever-shifting light. He opened his mouth, then shut it. But it was too late. She glanced at him, those deep blue eyes trapping him like an animal in a snare. He swallowed, mouth suddenly dry.

"Where did you say we were going?" he asked.

Jayne cocked her head, the motion strangely feline. "I didn't." He let the silence ring, waited for her to elaborate. But she stayed silent.

"Care to fill in the details? It seems we're stuck with each other for a while until the Order stops looking for us."

"I guess so." Her expression was not exactly uplifting.

"You don't sound thrilled by that," Eli grinned.

She shrugged, gazing at nothing. "I just think I'm better alone." Strange way to live.

94

"How about this," he said. "We stick together for now and see what happens." She bit her lip, calculations flickering over her face.

"It's a place called Dawn Sanctum," she said at last. "It's an old rebel base up in the mountains, very defensible and hard to reach. We should be safe there at least until the Order stops searching for us."

He stopped and stared at her. Jayne's delicate brows arched high in an almost regal expression.

"If it's so hard to reach, are you sure we can make it up there?" he asked.

"It's easy if you know how." She shrugged. Even then, the strength in her voice fascinated him. He smiled at her, noting the faint blush that rose to her cheeks, pale and drawn from her time spent in shackles.

"Can I see the brand?" she suddenly asked. Eli raised a brow at her bluntness, but that seemed to be her way, discarding pleasantries and small talk.

He realised, in all the excitement, he'd never seen the brand in light. He unbuttoned the jerkin and shakily lifted his shirt. She let out a quiet gasp.

"Does it still hurt?"

He shrugged. "Not as bad as it used to." He clenched his teeth as another wave of pain swept over him, though she didn't seem to notice.

"It—it made a light when you got back to your cell. Two of them, actually." Her eyes fixed on his, and he knew she was correct.

"Does it have any symbol you can make out?" he said, completely ignoring her question.

Acceptance quickly replaced the ire in her eyes. "It has one, but nothing I can recognise."

He glanced down, but could only make out jagged and blistered lines. He swore.

She circled back to her earlier question. "Do you know what that light was?"

He sighed. "Look, I don't know you well enough to talk about that yet."

"Fine. But it looks like that's what made you a target, more than snooping around the Cathedral."

He bit back an urge to retort. "I need to talk to Alsair."

She frowned at him, and immediately he knew what she would ask. "What's the story there?" Something prompted him; he wasn't sure what. But despite his reluctance, he felt the urge to explain.

"I used to live in a place called Laif, a few days south of Imbra. Farming community, not much to talk about, but it was home. We used to trade with the monks, sell them grain and other products, and they swapped for good wine and cheese." A fond smile flickered over his face, replaced by swifter shadow.

"But about ten years ago, some raiders attacked the village, killed my father and burned the place to the ground. My mother got me out, got me to the slopes of Mount Sancti. Begged the monks to take me in. A fever took her, sometime after. But a life of solitude and peace"—he sighed—"wasn't for me. I was a restless and frustrated boy. The monks taught me reading and writing, and the history of the kingdoms. Even so, I wasn't a fan of all the constant meditation, and I would wander around and disturb everyone. Eventually, one of the monks put me in a training ring."

"I thought the Jinnam were men of peace," Jayne interjected.

Eli nodded. "That was what I thought too, but apparently not. Alsair taught me how to shoot and swing a sword. Beat me senseless for years in the ring, with just one arm.

I never won once." He nodded at the hunched figure outside. "Perhaps it was kindness, but he never told me why he did it. Then the Order came. They—they destroyed the entire mountain. I found Alsair floating in the river and we left together."

He gently lowered Amora to the floor. Jayne chewed her lip as he trudged outside, shivering in the chilly air and plopping down next to Alsair, who folded a small book shut. His copy of the *Nesthamara*—the Holy Book of Nestham. He must have retrieved one from the cabin. They scanned the darkened woods, listened to the night sounds.

"Boy, how are you feeling?" Alsair asked.

Eli shrugged. "Better, thanks to you." Indeed, he doubted he would have escaped the Cathedral if not for Alsair.

"And the brand?" the monk pressed.

"How—how do you know about that?"

"You're not as quiet as you think."

Eli flushed. This wasn't a conversation he wished to experience again. "I'm sorry for leaving. You were right, I wasn't ready to take on the Order."

"It's alright," the greying man smiled. "It's what I needed."

"What happened while I was gone?" Eli asked. "How long did you wait?" he continued with a grin.

"Not long. I couldn't let my young protégé get himself killed." He nudged Eli and chuckled. His smile died away after a second. "I think you've earned these now." He produced some familiar tatty cloth and handed it to Eli. The boy placed it on his lap and removed the layers. Inside, the ornate vambraces he'd found in the small wooden chest in Alsair's hut. "Put them on." Eli fumbled with the catch on the vambraces, but strapped them onto his wrists. He gently ran a hand over the metal and his hair stood on end, hackles rising on his neck. He pulled his hand back in shock, to see Alsair studying him, eyebrow cocked.

"Something wrong, boy?"

"They're humming. What in the Five Hells?" A flash of light flickered out as his hand lit brighter than ever before. Purest icy light spilled out into the forest, ruthlessly clamped down as Eli covered it. "What are these?"

"They're made of Nesthamir. I expect it will enhance your powers when you're wearing them."

Eli merely looked at him and asked the question he'd been wondering for days. "Alsair ... what am I?"

The monk paused. "You mean—your magic?" Eli nodded. A faint power stirred in him, as if something besides him was holding its breath. "From what I've read, it looks similar to the ruler's Marks." He smiled. "But don't worry, you're not a long-lost King. But the magic increases your senses, as well as speed, strength. You've already shown you can heal at an impossible rate."

That explained it, but he still couldn't shake the nagging feeling. "Am I a threat?" he asked, his shoulders curled up and fingers twitching.

"Only to those who would do others harm." Alsair's smile was almost fatherly. "But enough for now. Go get some rest." Eli nodded and stumbled back inside the cave, noting Jayne refusing to sleep, her eyes staring blankly into the fire, her hand clutching her sword's hilt. On reflex he traced his finger over the metallic surface at his forearm. Before he fell asleep, he could have sworn he felt a hand brush his shoulder.

* * *

Eli and Alsair faced each other, intensely focused, swords in their hands. Hand, in Alsair's case. The sweat was cooling rapidly on Eli's bare torso. Somehow, he'd thought it was a smart idea to remove his shirt in the morning chill, even exposing his brand to the world. Out of the corner of his eye, he caught a flicker of movement, but Alsair's swing pulled him back into the moment. He moved like a dancer, but as he riposted and came close to Alsair, he proved yet again that years of experience were against him. To face a master and walk away unscathed ... no, he would never have a chance against the old man. Eli was always one step behind his mentor, as if Alsair could see all of Eli's strokes before he made them, an ability earned by years of combat training. Alsair brutally blocked Eli's cut and kicked at his ankle.

A muttered curse rang through the air as the young man tumbled to the ground, rolling back up in a practised motion. Alsair grinned at his young protégé and they separated, trading a battle of swords for a battle of glares, until Eli leaped forward again, impatient as ever. They continued their dance, Eli putting all his strength into it, his breathing becoming more and more laboured.

"Are you holding back?" Alsair said, a mocking grin on his face.

"Thought I'd give you a chance, old man," was Eli's immediate reply, but his panting proved the lie.

They circled each other, blood pounding in ears, boots crunching on snow.

"What say we put stakes on it? Loser has to take the winner's watch tonight." Alsair grinned.

"I can live with that. Be nice to get some sleep."

They took off again, faster than before. Eli's blade was lightning in the morning sun, flickering everywhere at once. Something in his mind shifted, a lock springing open. He didn't know how he did it, but it was enough. That brilliant light flickered, blazing blue. His speed and strength recovered, and a freshness flowed through his nerves. He sprang forward and locked blades with Alsair, drew power to push him back.

A muffled gasp gave away their watcher as Alsair shifted his weight. As Eli pushed, Alsair dropped his sword and *pulled,* grabbing Eli's jerkin and hauling the boy over him, through the air and to the ground with a deep thud. Eli groaned as the breath rushed out of his lungs. He tried to suck in air from where his face lay in the dirt. A dirty, tattered pair of boots lay just in front of his nose. And above them, Jayne's beautiful smile. She stepped over him as if he was something disgusting on the ground, and marched into the little clearing where they had set up, rolling her shoulders.

"Eli, some struggles there, keep your guard up next time," Jayne called over her shoulder. Something like incredulity passed through him and he twisted around, showing the annoyance on his dirt-smudged face.

"Care to step in?" he ground out.

Jayne's smile bared far too much teeth for polite company. "If you can still breathe properly."

Eli groaned as he hauled himself up, shaking out each limb to make sure it could move. He rubbed his left shoulder and swore under his breath.

"Good luck, milady." Surprise flickered in her eyes before she glared at him. Alsair nodded quickly and stepped farther away, observing Jayne as she drew her slender blade from its scabbard. It was a short sword, merely suitable for one hand; single-edged, elegant. It bobbed and weaved lightly, a fine weapon. And, clearly, she knew her way around it. A smile twitched at the corners of her mouth as she flicked the blade, and Eli readied himself, read those ocean-blue eyes. Despite the dark rings beneath them, they practically *glowed,* tracing up and down his torso as she fixed her stance, her left hand out to steady herself. The back of his neck heated immediately.

100

"Ready?" Alsair dropped his hand, and they were off.

Jayne darted at Eli, testing his reactions. He was stronger, but not quicker, his light fading away, along with his extra strength. The thoughts flashed through his mind as she parried, dodged and riposted his attacks. Even though his sword had an extra thirty centimetres of reach, she was still nimble enough to avoid his attacks. She feinted an overhand cut then twisted around to knock his blade aside. Eli's sword cartwheeled across the earth and he tensed, preparing to dodge.

"Keep going," he said. She raised a brow but continued even faster. His Mark burst into light and he caught her blow on his vambrace. Her blade never laid a scratch on it. Instead, a single note rang through the clearing, steel on Nesthamir. She swung and swung and swung, but could not get past him. Her vision narrowed further, and she sped up the tempo until the sound of sword on wrist guard was almost a pulsing chime. Eli stumbled as Jayne lashed out with her foot and chopped down with a vicious stroke as he fell to his knees. Eli crossed his arms overhead and took the blade on the guards.

Light flashed, then darkness engulfed him. Eli opened his eyes blearily, almost retching at the light-headedness coursing through him.

Jayne whipped her head around, scanning the clearing. He grunted, barely a whisper, and somehow she heard it. She whirled and lunged for him, the colour draining from her face. "What happened?"

"I don't know," he gasped. Black spots edged his vision, pushing him back towards unconsciousness. He sucked in a breath, willing them away, inhaling deeply to stay awake. Clenching his teeth to prevent the gasp. "What's wrong?"

She hesitated, but Alsair nodded encouragingly, letting her speak.

Jayne pointed over to the right. "That's where you were when you crossed your arms. You vanished and reappeared here." Eli's brows shot up and he glanced to Alsair for confirmation. He received it in a stoic nod.

"Is this something you've seen before?" Eli asked. A small shake of the head was Alsair's only response. "Well, let's not do that again," he ground out. He tried to stand but stumbled. On instinct, he reached out, but Jayne was already there and grabbed him under the arm, draping it over her shoulders, hitching a breath and closing her eyes. He bumped into her, muttered an apology. He stepped aside and forced his trembling legs to lock in place.

"I'll go check on Amora," she said, before striding away, adjusting her dark gloves. Eli watched her slender figure for a long moment as his breathing evened. Once she was out of sight, he glanced at Alsair.

"Did you know what these things can do?"

A beat of hesitation. Alsair shook his head. "No, I had no idea."

"And do you have any idea who she is?" said Eli.

"None whatsoever," Alsair replied.

Eli sighed in frustration. "You're not very helpful today, are you?"

Alsair grinned. "Can't help what can't be helped."

Eli sucked in a breath. "Well, this seems useful. Let's figure out how I did it."

"Didn't you just say you don't want to do it again?"

"Yes, but I feel better now."

Alsair just rolled his eyes and motioned him to go on. Eli tentatively brought his arms together, felt the metal hum in anticipation, thrumming over his skin. They touched and Eli yelped in shock as energy coursed through him, pulsing through his veins. His arms seemed to stick together by some force of

102

their own volition, and try as he might, he couldn't separate them.

"Focus," his mentor urged.

"Thanks, Alsair," Eli gritted out. "Wouldn't have thought of that."

Alsair shook his head and chuckled. "Old advice, but still true." Eli held his breath and eased his arms apart. As he separated them, there was a bright flash of light, as before, but he remained rooted to the spot. Eli frowned down at his feet, still very present in the world. His mentor's rumbling laughter was the only response. "Keep trying. Maybe use a little more force this time."

Eli scraped his vambraces across each other, the vibration now familiar. The world swirled about him and he fell into complete darkness, drifting, moving, aimless ...

Colours and sights reappeared.

As did the strange ticklish sensation. The feel of rough bark digging into his hands. The wind sighed around his ears as he opened his eyes wide. A vast expanse of Leranion spread before him, and the northern marches of mountains climbed higher until they disappeared beyond the clouds. Wind became a roar in his ears, bringing a deeper chill to his skin, particularly without a shirt. And his hands ... his hands were digging into the bark of a tree.

He looked down.

Alsair's cackles were faint, even to his enhanced ears. And back at the mouth of the cave, Jayne straightened with Amora. The young girl's delicate features stretched into a full grin, but Jayne wasn't smiling. Her eyes narrowed, as though every part of her was focused on him.

It was a long drop. He reached with one hand, back to the tree trunk, prepared to climb back down—the crack was deafening as the branch snapped and he plummeted into thin air. The wind sang through his hair and a hoarse cry ripped from his mouth, echoing the violent freefall.

The crack in his leg made him scream even louder. Scorching agony travelling along every nerve in his body.

His Mark flared and his magic flailed against the injury, reshaping bone and reforging tendon. His breathing laboured as that power pushed through the injury, dulling the pain and renewing his strength.

A shadow fell over him as Jayne leaned over, inspecting the wound. "I leave for a few minutes and look what you get yourself into," she murmured. The gleam faded from her eyes. "What is this power you have?"

He sighed heavily and gestured for her to bring Amora over. The girl was still grinning, and light danced in her night-black eyes. "You may as well get comfortable," he said. "It's a long tale."

And so he told them. The strange magic he possessed, the Mark on his hand, how it had healed him from a would-be fatal slash of a knife the first time it appeared.

"Perhaps the Order wants you dead because of this power. They've already said the ruler's Marks are Nestham's gifts. But a Marked with no throne ..." Jayne trailed off, her eyes flicking to Alsair.

Alsair's eyes glinted at the remark, and he leaned back against the tree bark. "They'd call it heresy, not something they take lightly."

"What's the penalty?" Eli asked.

Alsair pursed his lips. "Death most likely. And then ..."

Straight to the worst of the Five Hells. Then again, with the other sins deserving their own hells being Murder, Treason, Greed and Adultery, the Order wasn't looking too perfect these days. And with the Jinnam gone, the Eternal Order and the Musadim were the last of the four great faiths. Eli shook his head. What had he gotten himself into? He groaned as he hauled himself to his feet.

"Let's get to your hideout then, Jayne."

Chapter 15

The landscape stretched on, endless hills rising into mountains, the trees thinning and the temperature dropping. Eli trudged through the snow under the noonday sun, his nose running, the liquid cooling immediately. He continually wiped it on the back of his hand, much to Alsair's chagrin. The other hand carried the Eternal Torch, idly held by his side. Jayne led the way, plodding through the snow with a purpose he hadn't yet seen. She stopped at the edge of a sheer crevasse, which snaked through the gap between the mountains, bridged by arcing stone laden with snow.

"I hope nobody has a fear of heights," she said, noncommittally.

Eli coughed, his stomach churning. "It's not a fear of heights; it's just a healthy respect for the drop."

She smiled over her shoulder and scuffed the snow in front of her. When that didn't work, Eli dropped to his knees, the snow quickly dampening his pants. His knife chipped away at the packed snow as she dug beside him, his fingers stinging with the cold and soon losing feeling altogether. For minutes, the only sound was the scraping of steel on snow.

"What are you doing?" Amora asked. Jayne didn't answer immediately. Finally, she stood back and brushed the snow from her hands with a smile.

"Look." She pointed at the hole in the snow. Emblazoned on the stone beneath was the golden outline of a snow leopard, snarling in fury. The artist had drawn it impeccably, so much so that the lines brought it to life. The more he stared at it, it shimmered on the stone, roaring at an unseen foe. He tore his gaze from it with an effort.

"Are you sure this is a rebel hideout?" he asked.

Jayne's gaze snapped to his. Too fast. "Of course, why?"

"Because that's Leranion's seal," he pointed.

She pursed her lips appreciatively, and the silence stretched out. "Oh, don't worry. The Kingdom hasn't used it for centuries." She gazed at the snow-covered bridge stretching over the ravine, leading to a mountain with a peak that rose above the clouds. "Let's go."

Eli homed in on Jayne as she tentatively stepped towards the bridge, cautiously settled her weight on the deck. The crunch rang throughout the abyss. Eli shuffled to the edge and glanced down instinctively. The world tilted on its axis and he staggered back like a drunken man. Amora tugged on his shirt and her fringe fell to the side as she cocked her head, that little nose reddened by the cold.

"You all right, gruntah?"

He forced a smile. "Fine, I just need some air. You two go across."

Alsair shot him a pointed glance. "Be on your guard. There's always danger in these mountains."

"Cryptic as ever." Eli grinned, but staggered away and sat on the snow, forcing deep breaths. Out of the corner of his eye, he saw Alsair heft the Torch in his hand and, with Amora, walk easily across the bridge to join Jayne on the other side, standing by a rock wall beneath a looming mountain. Their voices floated across the windy ravine.

"Great. I feel so protected," Amora drawled.

"Can you help me get in?" Jayne asked.

Amora squared her shoulders, rising on her tiptoes to place her nose at Jayne's chin. "Because I'm an urchin?"

Alsair placed his hand on her shoulder. "I'm sure she meant no offence."

She dodged him. "Hands off, smoother."

Jayne ignored them, dropped a knee to the ground, and tapped the stone wall ahead of her.

A faint crunch in the snow alerted Eli, and he flicked his eyes back and forth. A single bird fluttered away, its song a dissonant note in the harmony of the world. He tensed, his hunter's instincts rising to the surface of his being, ones he had forged with Alsair, the monk now seated with Jayne, searching for the Sanctum's entrance. Far away from offering aid.

A dark blur rushed out from behind him, and steel gleamed in the sunlight. Eli scraped his sword from his scabbard, but even with his new power he would never have a chance. The blur leaped for him while his sword was still waving in the air.

A clap of thunder blasted through the valley, punched through his chest, pushed all the air out. His eyes flickered open to see a trembling warrior towering over him. Trembling, not in fear, but in an overwhelming effort to move. He had frozen in place, as if someone had placed an enchantment on him. Eli jumped back, levelled his sword at him. A silver tattoo gleamed on a deep bronze cheek, spiralling elegantly over the nape of the man's neck.

"You're a Vindicator, aren't you?" he said.

The man merely glared at him, solid as a stone wall. A Vindicator, the King's personal enforcers. All commanders of legions, and yet legendary warriors in their own right. Alsair hurried towards Eli, boots crunching on the snow.

"Alsair, what in the Hells is going on?" Eli asked, never looking away.

"Let's find out," Alsair replied. "Ask him his name."

"Who are you?" Eli ordered. The Vindicator just glared at him, lips pressed into a thin line. "Speak!" Eli yelled. The man trembled and grunted, straining to get free of whatever magic held him in place.

"My name is none of your concern, whelp," he rasped. "Once I get free, you're all coming back to Imbra."

"They sent you after us?" he asked. The man began to thrash again in the magic's grip. Eli reeled back. "They sent *a Vindicator* after us?" he roared. The Vindicator's face didn't change. Eli's anger deflated as quickly as it had come. "Wait. I recognise this bastard," he murmured. "Yes, you were the one I pulled back from the Citadel wall. How drunk were you, Vindicator?"

Alsair's eyes flashed, and his grey beard twitched in a smile. "You say you pulled him back from the ramparts, Eli?" A quick nod was all the confirmation he needed. "So, he would otherwise have fallen and died." The Vindicator stopped his fighting and stared at Eli, eyes like a dark abyss. "He owes you a life debt," Alsair continued. Eli lurched forward as something clicked in his core, a tether that connected him and the Vindicator, pulsing energy that bound them together.

"I've never heard of such magic," he protested.

"You really should have," Alsair said. "The Order doesn't like it existing, but it does nonetheless. It's ancient magic. Some say it's from Nestham himself. Regardless, he cannot harm you or anyone you tell him not to, and it compels him to help you until he saves your life, at which point he repays the debt."

Anger blazed in the Vindicator's eyes, burning with an intensity that chilled Eli to his core. He forced himself to grin like a fiend. "A Vindicator could be a useful ally." He then addressed his remarks as an order. "I forbid you from carrying out your mission or to harm me or my friends. You will keep us safe for as long as you can." A single muscle twitched in the man's square jaw. "What is your name?"

The Vindicator sighed and slumped, the strength gone from his stance. "Monsun. Monsun al-Iman," he murmured.

Eli motioned for Alsair to go on ahead, then turned back to the Vindicator. "I want you to carry me across the ravine. Try not to slip," he said.

"Are heights a weakness of yours?" Monsun snarled. Yet, even in such a horrible tone, his accent was rich and rolling.

Eli didn't answer. Monsun scooped him up easily and trudged across the bridge, while Eli sealed his eyes shut. Seconds later, he carefully set him down and Eli peered at the ground. As Eli scanned the members of the group, Jayne turned and her eyes widened before she snapped her gaze away. Amora was still prodding at the sheer stone.

"Trouble getting in?" Eli asked.

She shot an annoyed glare over her shoulder. "What does it look like?" He raised his hands in surrender. "It should be here somewhere," she hissed, then tapped another rock experimentally. Her entire body went rigid, and she smiled slowly. "Now, that's a lock I could crack."

They trudged over and crowded around a shape etched into the stone. Another snow leopard. Amora pressed her finger to the carving. Stone scraped, and the rock swung away, opening a dark hole into the mountainside. Eli picked up the torch from where Alsair had dropped it, its magical strength preventing it from burning out. It left the snow perfectly intact. Eli glanced around at all those assembled.

His smile was more a baring of fangs. "Welcome to Dawn Sanctum, Monsun."

Chapter 16

Eli held the Torch aloft and crossed the threshold, golden light spilling through the dark passageway. The air was musty—stagnant from being sealed for too long. The stone-finished grate on the floor was a masterwork, made by someone with greater skill than now walked across Ekra. Not only a memory of the past, but also a memorial.

Eli raised his brows at his companions and moved ahead, their footsteps pattering behind him. Monsun's heavy tread echoed above all the rest. As soon as the Vindicator entered, the door groaned again. They all whipped around, but it was too late, and Eli could only stare at the door as it swung shut.

"Wonderful," Amora said, giving words to the thought creeping in his mind.

He shot a look at Jayne. She shuddered, closing her eyes. "This doesn't feel right," he said. She opened her eyes, grabbed the Torch from him and swept past, reaching over her spine for her sword. Eli drew his own blade before following her. Amora tailed his heels and Alsair brought Monsun up, the big warrior still twitching, fighting off the life debt—the compulsion placed on him. If he broke it ... Eli had no idea, but it would likely be catastrophic.

"You'll want to be careful how you use that," Jayne murmured, without turning around, as if she knew exactly the thoughts floating through his mind. "The life debt. Just ... don't let it turn you into something you're not."

Eli grinned. "If prison couldn't do that, I doubt a life debt could."

She stopped and pivoted slowly, every inch of her a pure, lethal grace. "Power is dangerous, Eli. To the wielder and everyone else. Please ... be careful."

The smile dropped from Eli's face and he nodded. As they kept moving, he realised it wasn't as dark as it should have been. Somewhere, somehow, light was getting in. That, at least, was hopeful.

"So. Where's the gold?" Amora grinned.

Jayne glared back at her. "If you think there's gold here, then you really don't know the rebel movement."

"What happened to them?" Eli asked. The question went unanswered as the passage opened into a circular chamber, with walls of ancient carved stone, worn smooth with age. The familiarity of it pressed into Eli and he glanced at Alsair, the old monk nodding, confirming his suspicions. It was so similar to the halls of Mount Sancti—simple dwellings, worn from years of careful use.

With a few exceptions. Eli had studied many ancient texts by generals and architects of castles and other defences. His trained eye noted the twisting corridors, the choke points where only one could walk at a time. Even the passages forced them to walk in single file. Same with the bridge, with its lethal moat. No, Dawn Sanctum wasn't a rebel base.

It was a mukking fortress.

Jayne brushed the Torch against the ancient lamp brackets. Nothing. Without heat, that shouldn't have been surprising.

"I guess you can only create Eternal Flames from the wellspring itself," Jayne said.

Eli shrugged. It made sense, though his head still swam at the thought of *wielding* an Eternal Flame.

"Why did Leranion create this place?" he asked.

Jayne shrugged. "I don't know."

112

Eli whirled on Monsun, saw the intelligence in his eyes, quickly shuttered behind the Vindicator's mask.

"I think our Vindicator friend knows." Eli smiled. "Well, Monsun? Tell us what you know."

Eli's eyes narrowed on Monsun. He visualised the bond between them, the snapping energy, and he grabbed hold of it, sharpened his mind, every inch of his being thrown into the force of *compelling* him to tell the truth. The man's features tightened into a snarl and he groaned against the force of the compulsion, the magic tightening its grasp on him. The Vindicator had an impressive strength of will. But would it last?

"It's—" he uttered and clamped his mouth shut, right before a muffled scream emanated from his throat. Eli pushed harder, nothing but brute force tugging on that bond linking them.

"Eli!" Jayne yelled. "That's enough!" Monsun sagged to the floor, his breathing ragged as Eli let go of his mind.

"It's older than Imbra. The Queen and Prince of Leranion used it as a base in the demon war," Jayne said.

Eli cocked his head. "Demon war? That's nothing but a myth," he laughed. "It's an old folk story. Temero, the wicked demon, slain by our illustrious rulers."

Her eyes flashed once, swift anger replaced by neutrality. "The demon war was real," she insisted. "The Queen and Prince held the gates for days before the Sea-Kings arrived from the South and pushed them back."

"Look, I'm not arguing that there was a war. It's just, you can't honestly expect me to believe there were demons wandering around."

"Jayne, you should have told us this base was Leranion's. If there were troops here, they could have captured us." Alsair frowned, his whiskers twitching in disappointment. "If we're going to work together, we need to trust each other."

The girl glared at him, the picture of fierce defiance. "Would you have gone along with me if I had?"

Silence fell across the chamber and Eli shuffled his feet. When it stretched out, he drew breath to break it. "Well, it's clearly unused. We're stuck here now that the door has sealed, so the best we can do is explore this place, see what we can find," Eli said.

Immediately, Amora's night-dark eyes lit up. She charged off into the unknown, not even bothering to grab some light. Footsteps faded to silence unnaturally fast. Eli glanced around at the others, finding even Monsun looking nonplussed.

He chuckled and followed in her wake.

* * *

The girl was a whirlwind, tearing through the caverns, picking up and dropping everything that wasn't nailed down, and some stuff that was. Her footsteps rapped in the stone passage as she scoured through dusty books, and weapons covered in trailing cobwebs. She struggled to pick up an ancient sword, swaying under its weight. It was so covered in dust you couldn't tell what the original colour of the scabbard was.

"Not bad, huh?" she commented as she dropped it at Eli's feet. It fell to the floor with a clang, and when he looked up, she was gone. Eli picked up the sword and brushed the dust off almost reverently. It would be worthless to keep up with her, so he shook his head and strolled out, holding the Torch over his shoulder, to find Alsair. He found him in a circular chamber, complete with shelves reaching all the way to the roof. Each was covered in ancient books, even the leather covers crumbling to dust. Alsair leaned over a stack of parchment on a stone desk, worn from all the years weighing on it. "Ah, that's better. Low light is hard on these old eyes."

114

Eli leaned on the entrance port of the chamber, the rough stone scraping against his tunic. "How were you reading without this light, anyway?"

"Old eyes can still see," the monk chuckled. "It looks like some kind of library," he said, still scanning the parchment.

"Of course," Eli rolled his eyes. "We're in an ancient fortress complete with heaps of fascinating weapons, and you head straight to the library. I shouldn't even be surprised."

"Look at this," Alsair gestured. "The seal of the King. This was definitely one of Leranion's last hideouts during the war. A bastion against the demons."

Eli shrugged. The ancient myths that Alsair and Jayne believed, where demons walked across Ekra and fought against humans, really had nothing to do with him. His struggle was against more mortal opponents. His attention snagged on another scroll, strewn to the side. He picked it up and gently blew on it, dust scattering in the air. The parchment crunched in his hands, and he froze, not daring to move lest he destroy it. Alsair zoomed over to him, waving his hand frantically. "Careful."

Eli sighed. "You sound like an old grandmother clucking around her cottage."

"You should have more respect for age, Eli. This old grandmother still wiped the floor with you. Besides," he continued, reverently taking the parchment away from Eli's hands, "I doubt you'll be able to read this. It's in the High Language."

"And whose fault is that for not teaching me the High Language?" he retorted, racking his brain to decipher the words. Though the monks had taught him much over the years he had trained with them, this was still beyond him.

"Because if you actually listened to me, I would have told you that the High Language is one you get when you're a ruler. Apparently it goes with the powers. But you never were one for the ancient texts, were you, boy?"

Eli grinned in return. "No, I preferred you hitting me until I couldn't breathe."

"Always the masochist." Alsair kept reading the text in front of him until at last he spoke again. "Well, from the shape of the text, it's a poem."

"Who by?"

Alsair glanced up, raised his brows. "How should I know? I can't read it either." He scanned it further. "Wait, it was Prince Cayce." A crooked smile. "He signed his name at the bottom."

"Prince Cayce? Isn't he the one who lost the diadem?"

"You learned something in my lessons after all." Alsair chuckled, and placed the poem back on the table. "I'll make a copy for you, and once we find ourselves a ruler, I'll get that poem translated."

Eli raised his eyes to the stone ceiling and gestured at the monk. "Thanks. So, if we have finished the history lesson, shall we continue?"

"Yes, let's," he rumbled. "With Nestham's providence, we can find some food in this hole."

"You lived in a mountain for half your life. Who are you to judge?"

They left the chamber, following the tunnel as it wound endlessly upwards. Alsair's breathing was steady, the monk apparently not even tired despite his age. Eli mindlessly rapped his hand on the wall, banging out a rhythm on the spot. Rap-rap, rap. Rap-rap-raprap. Rap-rap-rap. Rap-rap, raprap. Alsair just let out a deep sigh, and Eli grinned to himself.

Eventually, a flicker of white appeared at the end, more than just the golden light Eli carried with him. At last, the tunnel opened into a wide circular chamber, decorated in rich murals depicting bright men and women in silver battle-armour. One man in the centre of a mural, with golden hair falling to his collar, rested his jewelled sword on his shoulder, his deep blue eyes staring through Eli.

Rays of light fell through the room from a crevice on the far side. But they weren't all coming from there. He glanced up and raised his brows in surprise. Suspended high on a rusty chain, a crystal swung from the ceiling, clear and beautiful. Every bit of light, it magnified tenfold, illuminating the room completely.

A small barrel by the other wall caught his attention. He knocked on it experimentally, then grunted as he pried the lid open. Salt lay piled in the ancient wooden slats, but as he rifled through it, his hand snagged on something leathery. He pulled out a strip of dried meat.

"Finally." He smiled. He checked the rest, but there wasn't much. "Doesn't look too promising," Eli commented, though something nagged at him. "Well, I've still got my bow, I'll go hunting in the morning." He glanced around the chamber. "Huh. Blankets as well. And new torches. You might want to gather everyone else. This looks like a decent spot to sleep, for now."

While Alsair nodded and ambled off in the sedate way that came with a lifetime of meditation and training, Eli wandered over to the crevice. He just stood in the rays, letting a peace wash over him. Peace that had been missing for many days, ever since Mount Sancti.

A gentle touch on his shoulder caused him to whip around. Every time that happened, his skin felt itchy, like someone was watching him.

But there was nothing there. The phantom hand moved to his chest, tugged at his shirt. He resisted, but it only grew more forceful. Insistent, even. Eli pursed his lips and reached out to the wall, tapping a small carving on the stone face. Another snow leopard. He pressed his hand against it. Stone rumbled, and the wall swung away. Sunlight spilled in and Eli gasped in delight. They'd climbed hundreds of metres high, and all of Leranion now stretched before him. The march of the mountains. The sweeping plains beyond, bathed in the setting sun to his left. Nestled within the hills, pillars of smoke rose into the reddened sky. Imbra. His shining capital caught in the grip of madness.

As if in a trance, he stepped through the breach. A grassy bluff awaited him, shielded from the relentless snow by a stone overhang. Eli grinned and sat near the edge, above a sheer drop, just staring at the horizon.

A gentle hubbub of noise sounded behind him, signalling the arrival of the others. He turned, and waved to Jayne, who smiled softly. They dumped the objects they were carrying on the ground and cautiously emerged through the hole. Each blinked with wonder at the sight that awaited them. Delight and longing warred across Monsun's face as he gazed at the city.

"Monsun, what did you find?" he asked.

A vein pulsed in the man's neck. "Nothing," the man replied, but he couldn't meet Eli's gaze. Eli glared at him, and cold anger crossed Monsun's face. Finally, he shuffled over and pulled out a mass of parchment, worn and tattered.

Eli scanned it for a moment. "Looks like you found a map to the whole of Dawn Sanctum. Well done, Monsun." He grinned. He looked at the young women. "Did you find any more food down there?"

"What's there has rotted away, not enough to last more than a few days," Jayne said.

"We found some blankets, but that's about it," Amora interjected. Eli noted her pockets were bulging with other objects, however.

Jayne chewed her lip. "And winter is at least a week from breaking."

"At least we can wait out the winter before we think about what to do next. Monsun can keep us company until then, can't he?"

The Vindicator grimaced in response, and Eli's smile was a dark beauty to behold. "I'll go hunting tomorrow morning."

"I'll go with you," Jayne volunteered.

He drew breath to argue. He worked better alone. But his heart sped up, and he relaxed into a smile. "Everyone get some sleep. I've got a double watch tonight." He stuck his tongue out at Alsair. The old monk smiled in satisfaction. Eli took his weapons out onto the bluff while the others used the bedding they had to lie down.

* * *

Eli's breath emerged as a gentle puff of mist escaping his lips. No cloud dared hide the stars tonight; they blazed in all of their glory. The moon was bright enough that his hand left a shadow on the ground, as he glanced back longingly at the sputtering, glowing fire, at the huddled shapes around it. The smoke didn't fill the chamber, in fact it vanished into the ceiling and somewhere into the stone. He turned back to stare at the surroundings, a shiver running through his body.

"You're not warm enough, are you?" Jayne's voice whispered behind him.

"I can manage," Eli said, through chattering teeth. A thick woollen blanket fell across his shoulders as Jayne settled

119

beside him. He wrapped it around himself and smiled at her gratefully.

"Couldn't sleep?" Eli breathed.

"No." Silence fell across the bluff. Then, Jayne shuffled closer and grabbed some blanket. "You can't have it all," she said indignantly in response to his glance. Eli grinned and let her steal some fabric as they watched the countryside, her presence a reassuring warmth at his side.

He knew what she suffered. He fought it too, since Mount Sancti's fall. After what she'd endured, Eli couldn't fathom what she must see at night. But their shared time in prison, listening to each other's screams of pain and suffering, had bonded them in more ways than he could have expected. This was all he could offer. Though ... perhaps there was more than just solidarity. Hesitantly, he reached out an arm around her, seeking to draw her into the safety and security he was fooling himself into thinking he could offer her. Her breath hitched just once, and she recoiled.

"Jayne?"

She shook her head. "It's nothing." She accepted it and leaned into his warmth. Her scent wrapped around him—rose, and the oil she used on her blades.

"Do you miss home?" he asked the silence.

She thought for a moment. "Sometimes. But it's people who make a home, and I miss them more."

"You left someone behind?" he said.

"Yes. Someone," she replied, her small mouth stretching into a sad, wistful smile. Despite his sympathy for the girl, his heart fell a little. The moon brightened slightly, and crystal light bathed the landscape. "But whenever I miss someone, I just look up," she said, pointing at the stars above them, glittering jewels in pure blackness. "They're beautiful," she breathed. "I'm entranced every time." He turned and met her gaze again, let the depths of her eyes sweep him away into oblivion.

"You used to stargaze?"

Her eyes glazed slightly, as if she had retreated into the deepest recesses of memory. "Oh yes. When I was younger, I used to sneak out onto the roof and just watch them all night. I nearly froze my back off on the cold stone, but it was worth it."

Eli snorted next to her, and she leaned a little closer, though she remained taut, ready to flee. His heart began to pound, and the desolate peaks before them were both reassuring and discouraging as the wind swirled through the ravines. "I just wish I could see them one more time," he breathed, "before all of this goes wrong."

"It may not go wrong," she answered.

"Even if the Order doesn't find us, we still have soldiers looking for us, and a Vindicator trying to bring us back in chains." The understanding in her eyes faded quickly, and she glided away in silence, leaving the blanket behind. The blanket. Of course. This fabric would have long rotted away in the last few hundred years. Yet not only were there blankets, there was *food and weapons.*

We weren't the first here. Yet they'd found no one in the Sanctum, living or dead.

He marched back inside several hours later, as the moon began its descent in the west. He noted Monsun quietly shuffling back to his bedroll, eyes widened. They narrowed in a glare when Eli met them.

Amora woke as he reclined on the empty pile of blankets.

"Is it time for my watch?" she whispered.

He shook his head. "I don't think there'll be anyone tonight. Go back to sleep."

* * *

121

A single ray of light burst through the gap in the southern wall, streaming into the crystal in the centre of the room. What had started as one beam now refracted throughout the room like a sunburst. When Eli opened his eyes, it had filled the chamber with brilliant light. The groans and mutters of the others gave an indication of their wakefulness. Alsair waited until all had arisen before nodding to Eli and Jayne.

"You two need to go hunting. But stay safe."

Eli nodded. His bow leaned against the wall where he had checked the string and arrows the night before. He now hefted it and extended a hand to Jayne. "At your leisure, milady." She rolled her eyes at him.

They marched in silence, Jayne with her sword and a knife, a fur hood covering her head. Eli forced his breath to come in even draughts, settling into his hunter's awareness, letting his instincts take over. Alsair had always taught him those instincts acted like a second person, always watching his back— though it seemed someone else would do that now.

They followed the map that Monsun had given them, opening a door on the northern side. The snow wasn't too bad, halfway up the peak. The tundra slopes stretched away as the mountain that held the Sanctum extended out into a vast range. Alsair had followed them outside and now waited on the threshold, his features creased into a frown. The Eternal Torch he clutched in his hand.

"Eli. A word if you please." Eli shrugged and strode to him, quiver strapped across his back.

"Watch your back out here, boy. It's a dangerous place. And listen out for the snarls."

"Snarls?" Eli raised a brow. "This isn't one of your tricks, is it?"

Alsair shook his head, his jade eyes hard. "There are worse things than Order soldiers out here."

122

Chapter 17

Eli and Jayne left Alsair in the Sanctum and headed north. As they passed over the nearest slope, they approached a gentle mountain creek, muttering as it wound its way down the hillside. Eli nodded to Jayne, and they followed parallel to the stream, as fast as the ice floes drifting aimlessly in its current. Despite his initial worries about how Jayne would handle the trip, her tread was as light as his own. They had agreed they would not speak in this place—there was no telling how far the sound could carry. Already, the wind was up and biting as it swirled in the valley. Eli drew his scarf tighter over his mouth and nose, and watched as Jayne did the same. Their footsteps crunched lightly in the snow, and Jayne moved to check behind them, covering his back instinctively. He hadn't realised how useful it was to have a partner on a hunt, to have someone you could rely on.

A gentle nudge to his side made him turn, meeting Jayne's deep blue eyes before she nodded to her left. Eli slowly drew an arrow from his quiver, packed tight and lined with felt so it wouldn't rattle. His fingers passed over the worn string and he nocked the arrow through muscle memory, surveying his prey. A young ibex knelt by the brook, long horns nodding up and down as he lapped the water.

As if it were a gift from Nestham himself, the wind died, making the shot child's play. Eli drew, felt the brush of the fletching on his cheek, and fired. Despite the bow's unfamiliarity, the arrow sank deep into the neck of his prey. The buck quivered once and collapsed.

"Dinner," he grinned before strolling forward.

A snarl ripped across the valley. Eli's heart stopped for an instant, but Jayne put her back to his and together they probed ceaselessly, searching, scanning for anything. The icy grass shimmered as the ground around the ibex slowly splotched red. Eli nudged Jayne, and she stood shoulder-to-shoulder with him. That was their first mistake.

Heavy breathing sounded behind them, and his limbs locked immediately. His limbs refused to obey him.

Beside him, Jayne's breaths fell silent. Steps padded away, and he sucked in a breath and risked a glance over his shoulder. A mottled, sleek shape slunk away down the valley. Jayne slowly let out her breath at the snow leopard's retreat, its tail dragging a furrow in the snow.

Ah, mukk. Not retreating.

No, it was gliding towards the ibex. It easily leaped the stream, its powerful limbs propelling it across the sparkling brook. It lowered its head to the ibex's neck and gripped tightly, before dragging it away, the arrow still protruding out of it. All that remained was bloodstained snow.

Eli cursed under his breath as the leopard dragged away their meal. Jayne nudged him. "You could go get it if you want." He glanced over at her pale face, but she was grinning at him. Her eyes caught the light, gleaming with terrified humour. He didn't think his mouth could get any drier. He was wrong. So Eli allowed himself to brush her hand and chuckle in reply. The grass crunched underfoot as they kept hunting, passing by a massive rock, on the lookout for prey ... and predators.

Muffled grunts echoed from down the valley. Eli and Jayne exchanged glances, and she shaded her eyes, squinting. She held up three fingers and he nodded, his heart stopping and starting again. He glanced around and gestured at a nearby rock. They crouched behind its bulk, peering over the stone. The thuds kept coming until three figures emerged, silhouetted against the misty skyline. Eli frowned at the girl next to him.

"I can't make out their insignias, but I bet they're soldiers," he breathed.

"You don't need their insignias. They're in red and black," she spat. "Eternal Guardsmen. There's no outpost in this area besides Dawn Sanctum. They wouldn't be out here unless ... they're hunting us."

Eli nodded grimly in response. "We can take them," he urged, but even the thought of a real fight with trained soldiers made his head swim.

She shook her head and dropped down, her back to the rock face. "Too risky. We'll wait until they leave and then tell Alsair. Even if you can get them with your bow, it's not worth it."

The soldiers approached. Eli shuffled around the corner, flicked a glance over the rock. "They're too close now. We'll have to stay here until they move on." Indeed, it was doubtful the soldiers would bother to make a decent search of the area, as they ambled with bowed heads and exhaustion in their steps. As they moved past on the other side, their uniforms became clearer. A deep red jerkin, black pants. Functional swords swung at their sides. Definitely Eternal Guardsmen. An entire mountain's obliteration, black smoke piling into the sky, an arrow tearing skin—the images all flashed into his mind.

Jayne gripped his arm, as if sensing his thoughts: *Don't you dare go out there.* Her nails dug into his flesh, blossoming into sharp pain, leaving pale crescents on his skin. Footsteps thumped closer. Eli tensed and wrapped a hand around his sword's hilt, preparing to draw it at a moment's notice. His heart hammered so loud it was a miracle the soldier couldn't hear it, even with his lungs begging for air.

The soldier paused on the other side.

A faint splashing echoed and Eli's mind worked frantically, trying to deduce it. He scrunched his nose as the tangy smell of urine drifted over, accompanied by the faint sigh of relief. Jayne rolled her eyes and her mouth twitched involuntarily, relief flooding her face. The soldier finished tending to his needs and ambled back down, utterly unaware of the prey lying behind the rock. The strangest urge to burst out laughing rushed through Eli, and he clamped his lips together.

He hadn't realised Jayne was clutching him so tightly until she let go. He raised a brow at her and was rewarded by a faint touch of colour on her cheeks. He shifted his weight, rising to peer over the rock.

Then the screaming started.

Eli plummeted back down behind the rock, wrapping an arm around Jayne to wait out the attack. The air filled with the coppery tang of blood as the snow leopard made its way through the three soldiers. When all was quiet again, Jayne rose and shuddered at the sight beyond.

The snow leopard had utterly wrecked the Guardsmen. It growled, a statue guarding three disembowelled corpses. As they watched, it turned and gazed at them, power and majesty and destruction in every part of its muscled body. A furry maw dipped slightly before it vanished.

Leaving nothing but death behind.

"Stay here," was all Eli said to her before he rose and lurched towards the carnage. The smell of death clogged his nose, bile filled his throat, and he retched into the grass. When he finished, he turned back to the scene. Their medals now lay stained with blood, but the design of one was visible. He trawled back through his memory, through the years of study with the monks. The Medal of Armentine. Given to those who had served with valour and strength, usually in the Leranion army.

He pulled his collar over his nose and made to turn away, but the glint of metal on snow caught his eye. A new symbol, thrown clear of the carnage. A dove, with its wings stretched in flight, pierced by a golden sword. Eli swore and grabbed the medal, stashed it in his pocket. The symbol of the Jinnam monks, men of peace and reflection, who had served

126

Nestham with all their heart. And this man had helped destroy them. Had been rewarded for *that*.

"I doubt Nestham will forgive you for that," Eli growled, before he stalked back to Jayne. Her bloodless lip trembled once. That was her only sign of horror. She'd held it better than he had. Despite Mount Sancti's emphatic destruction, he didn't at least witness any bloodshed. He could only imagine the slaughter. She had *lived* it, watched her friends die around her.

Alsair had done his best to protect him from the horrors of war, taught him to live with honour and to fight with it, not to take life unless it was in the defence of others. That was the warrior's call: to defend and protect.

Jayne must have seen the look on his face. She froze, then threw her arms around him. He staggered underneath the sudden weight, but she just held him in comfort, even if her arms were stiff, almost unwilling.

It was a long walk back to the entrance to Dawn Sanctum. They did not let go of each other the entire way. Above them, darkened clouds swept in from the north.

* * *

They stumbled back into the Sanctum, found Monsun's map and the Torch lying at the entrance, where Alsair must have left them for them. Neither spoke in the twisting maze. The sleeping chamber was silent, though Alsair and Monsun reclined on their bedrolls. Alsair's waking snuffles echoed through the chamber, whilst Monsun glanced up from where he had been polishing his axe, a glittering blade, in fading crystalline light.

"Where's Amora?" Jayne said as she entered.

"Probably ransacking the place," Eli whispered. Her brief snort was gratifying.

"What happened?" Alsair asked, his bushy eyebrows clumping together. "Did you get any food?"

127

"Well ..." Jayne began but trailed off, the normally confident act melting in the old man's stern face.

Eli finished it for her. "We found an ibex, but a snow leopard beat us to it." Monsun dropped his smooth-shaven face into his hands, his braids weaving behind him.

"It's worse," Jayne continued. That got their attention. "There were Order soldiers out here."

"Were?" Monsun caught, his tone harsh.

Jayne shrugged stiffly. "The snow leopard got them too."

Alsair sighed, his voice cracking. Eli pulled the medal out of his pocket and flicked it to Alsair, who deftly caught it in his remaining hand. Tears made silent tracks down the old man's cheeks.

"The Order is growing stronger if they can parade their slaughters out in the open." Eli glanced out to the south. Clouds flitted across the sky, spreading mass shadows over the landscape.

"There is more snow coming," Monsun said. "It will be here for a while."

Eli let out a small cough. "I really miss the flatlands. At least it wasn't so damn cold." Alsair nodded silently.

"Did you know the Order was coming?" Eli demanded of Monsun. The Vindicator shook his head, his dark eyes meeting Eli's with shining honesty. He could respect that, at least.

"But what I do know," Monsun said, "is that this snow will last at least a week, and none of us will survive if we go outside."

We'll be trapped here soon. Eli reached for the water canteen lying by Alsair's boots, gulping it down as he gazed around the chamber and took in the grim faces. A week of snow. With barely enough food in the ancient stores, and nothing to show for their hunting trip.

"How much water is there?" Eli asked Alsair.

"Aside from what you stole from me? Water's no problem, not with all that snow out there," the monk replied. "We'll seal the door to the bluff. There won't be anyone moving out there with the snow on the way."

"In the meantime, we can spend some time searching this place," Jayne said, before flashing a quick smile to Eli and leaving.

Monsun's eyes followed her out until he left a minute later.

Chapter 18

The stone was rough against Jayne's back, scraping her skin as she slid down the wall. Her breath came in ragged pants as she fought to maintain control. After that snow leopard had looked at her, she had worked hard to keep her composure. Seeing its ferocity and ... *majesty* had knocked her world off-balance. Particularly after it left the soldiers in pieces. A companion like that could turn the tide of any conflict. If only.

Monsun's footsteps slowed as he marched past her, arched his elegant brows. She shook her head, and he padded off silently.

She pushed herself off the ground and headed down to find Amora, the girl's name echoing off the stone passages. After half an hour of searching, she found her crouched over a wooden chest, the glitter of gold reflecting from the bottom. A single torch flickered in a bracket nearby, casting strange shadows on the wall.

"How long have you been down here?" she asked as she leaned against the wall.

The girl didn't look up. "No idea," she said. "It's amazing what people leave behind when they're in a hurry. If I sold this, I'd have enough to buy the entire poor quarter, back in Imbra."

It was a joke, but it left a sobering mark behind on Jayne. The slums were a harsh, brutal place inhabited by the urchins, night women and the crime lords who ran them. Sometimes, sons of noblemen and soldiers ventured in for an opportunity to get some fame or to prove themselves. Few returned intact. Some never returned at all.

"Anything of note?" she asked.

The younger girl nodded emphatically, her short hair bobbing. "I'm fond of this," she said, holding out a gleaming dagger, the blade engraved in a swirling font. Jayne reached out a hand and ran a finger along its surface. It shimmered faintly in the flickering light.

"I think that's one of the Sea-King's blades," Jayne said, "left after they came through the Sanctum. They had a special coating on their steel so it wouldn't rust. Unfortunately, they never wanted to share it with anyone. It'd be worth a lot"—she grinned—"unless you want to keep it. We'll be here a while, anyway. Snow's coming in."

The girl's dark eyes just twinkled in reply. "Perfect. More time to explore."

Jayne shook her head, smiling gently. "How will you carry all of this out?"

Amora shrugged, the motion full of the expected irreverence. "No idea. Guess I have time at least to work that out."

Jayne joined the girl in her explorations, collecting items and trinkets. After a while, she glanced at the young urchin.

"Why did you come with us?"

Amora sighed and tossed the gold back into the pile. "Because I wanted to get out of Imbra. And ... I like you and the gruntah. He's a weird one, that's for sure."

"Do you have nicknames for everyone?"

"Course." She winked. The girl was all over the place, one minute quiet and contemplative, the next bouncing on her tiptoes. "Actor."

Jayne froze, her mouth drying immediately. "I'm sorry?" she mumbled.

"Exactly." Amora grinned, her little fingers waggling.

"Warriors can't act, I'm afraid," Jayne smiled, her fingers tapping furiously against her leg.

"Then start talking like one." The girl winked back at her, then turned back to the glittering pile of blades. Jayne stumbled backwards and sprinted into the tunnel.

* * *

She lurched back into the sleeping chamber and set to checking her sword, polishing it until she could see her own reflection in the blade. Her heart wouldn't stop pounding as she settled onto her bedroll.

"You feeling okay?" Eli asked. She jumped and spun to face him, but he was already backing away, hands held in the open. Her heartbeat quickened when he sat down in front of her, silver eyes fixed intently on her own. She nodded, but her posture gave the lie to the motion as she sat with her knees drawn up to her chest. Her stomach roiled, a reminder of the demons living inside her.

"I tried to catch some sleep," she said, "but they came again." How long would it take before these scars healed?

"Go back to sleep," Eli said gently. "I'll stay here with you if you want." She looked up, her heartbeat fluttering. "If you don't think it's proper, I'll leave you to get some rest."

"I never cared about propriety," she mumbled. But days of exhaustion finally caught up with her, days of fear and mistrust. And, Nestham above, she just wanted to trust someone.

And when he held out his hand, her cheeks warmed as she took it and laid her head back onto the pillow, the hair she'd just untied spilling over her face. She fell into the confines of sleep for an instant.

Her eyes fluttered open again. A muscled body lay next to her, about to attack. Jayne drew her knife immediately and lunged. Cold blue light flared as Eli rolled away and stared at

132

her, muscles trembling in anticipation, as if watching the snow leopard all over again.

"So that's why you didn't want me around," he whispered. She nodded, barely a dip of her head, as her breathing slowed to normal, her heart rate dropping. The knife clattered from her grasp, a single sharp note ringing through the chamber. She collapsed back onto the bedroll, drained and unable to move. A featherlight touch ran through her hair and she stiffened in surprise, then her wire-taut muscles relaxed.

"You're safe," Eli whispered. "Nothing can hurt you now." She heaved a breath, forcing the mask back into place. "You can trust me," he said.

She bit her lip. "The last man I trusted killed my friends and threw me in my cell."

He closed his eyes, sorrow creasing his handsome face. And damn, he was handsome. Trayse had been handsome too. Her teeth began cutting deeper into her lip. He turned to leave the chamber, but she sat up, dared to ask, jumping out on the knife edge of trust. Yes, she'd been fooled once, but maybe ...

"Will you stay with me?"

He turned, and his eyes filled with moisture. "Of course." He shifted his pile of blankets to beside hers and lay down, just keeping her company. A feeling of companionship stole over Jayne for the first time in weeks of solitude.

"Please try not to kill me," he mumbled as she fell asleep.

Jayne's eyes fluttered open, and she breathed a quiet sigh. The crystal glittered in the room, but it was way too bright for dawn. The other bedrolls were empty already, just piles of blankets and weapons. A steady, rhythmic thump echoed through her body, getting faster and faster, and she glanced down. Eli coughed once beneath her. She flushed and reared back, realising she had been sprawled over him, her head resting

133

on his chest. She rolled off him immediately, and he hissed as she landed on his arm.

"Sorry." At least his heartbeat had sped up slightly; that was gratifying.

"It's okay," he gritted out. His smile made her shiver, for not a single flash of terror, of panic, crossed his face. "No nightmares."

"No nightmares," she confirmed, lying a nice, *proper* distance away. Five minutes later, he groaned as he got up and made his way to the door.

"How did they manage to take all of that food without waking us?" he mumbled.

"Food?" she perked up.

"I'll see what I can find." He popped back outside. "Salty meat again," he replied as he strode back in. "We're running low since our unsuccessful hunting trip."

"And with a week trapped in here ..." She didn't need to finish the sentence.

"The others are downstairs."

Jayne found them one floor beneath having finished breakfast. Alsair brushed a hand over his mouth, but when he removed it, he was still trying to hide a smile. Eli shot him a glare and the smile only widened. Amora coughed pointedly. When Eli glanced back at Jayne, she looked down at her food, but she couldn't hide the flush on her ears.

"Are you eating?" she asked him.

He shrugged. "I already ate." A rumble echoed through the chamber from the general direction of his stomach, and she glared at him.

"We won't have enough to make it to the end of the blizzard, will we?" he said to Alsair. The monk shook his head.

Her empty stomach dropped, but the look on Eli's face was even more worrying. Eli tugged Jayne aside, and the blood drained from her face at the blazing silver in his eyes. "I'm going back out there."

Her heart stopped. "Are you insane? The blizzard is still going outside."

Eli made a vague hand gesture at the exit to the bluff. "It seems to have slowed. Regardless, I failed to get food the first time around."

"That's not your fault," she said heatedly. "Besides, we can still survive on the rations." Her heart began to pound. Surely he wouldn't be so *stupid* as to go out there.

He flashed a mirthless grin at her. "I'll see you in a couple of hours." As he left with his weapons, she cradled her head in her hands.

Jayne paced in the uppermost chamber, restless as a caged beast. Sweat pooled on her forehead, as if the weather had shifted to a scorching day in the Southern Desert rather than a northern blizzard.

"He's been gone too long," she said to Monsun. Her companion nodded, his brows drawing together like an approaching storm. Concern flickered across his face, an emotion that took her by surprise, considering Eli's constant anger towards the Vindicator.

"So, what will you do?" he merely asked. Her head snapped around and she stilled. She hadn't really been expecting a response, merely looking to spiral deeper into gut-churning panic.

"I mean, there's not much I can do, is there?" she said.

He raised his brows, his face harsh. "You know exactly what you could do."

The words rattled in her mind. "Thanks for not telling the others," she said. He smiled briefly, dimples appearing on his cheeks. "Though I think Amora knows."

"She is an intelligent girl. I am unfamiliar with the word 'gruntah', however," he said. The wind howled again, and her stomach dropped in fear, accompanying the curse she whispered under her breath. Monsun sat up straight and froze.

"Is it the magic again?" she asked. His head twisted around, gaze fixed on the door. He grabbed the blanket he was lying on, arms as stiff as wood. He threw it around him, then bolted from the room.

She paused, doubt slamming into her. *Save him*, a voice seemed to whisper. That was all she needed to fling herself into action, grabbing furs and slinging her scarf around her face, before grabbing the Eternal Torch from its resting pace and following the bulky Vindicator down the twisting warren of tunnels, careful to keep the heatless flame from touching her.

Monsun moved like a born warrior, sprinting heedlessly throughout the maze, yet it was clear his body was no longer under his mind's control. No human could react as quickly as he did, turning the corners with a grace impossible with his bulk. It was all she could do to keep sight of him before he turned the next corner.

You could keep up if you wanted to. She forced that voice back down into the abyss where it belonged, focused on the door. All she could see was white as she threw herself out the northern entrance, breathing a prayer to Nestham.

She was instantly enveloped in snow. Flakes pelted her body, clung to her eyelashes. Her eyes watered and she blinked it away. The storm fought to wrench the Torch from her hand, but its magic kept it burning bright. Monsun was already a distant figure, a shadow amongst the stark white. With his superhuman strength, he had blazed a path through the snow and she barrelled after him before the blizzard wiped away his tracks.

Her legs burned, and she stumbled again, pushed back by the howling wind. The snow became a constant barrage across her entire body, while her breath rasped in her ears.

There was nothing.

Nothing but snow.

Nothing but hopelessness.

Nothing but death out here.

Where was Eli?

"Over here!" Monsun yelled. Jayne strained her eyes to make him out, gasping as she saw the dark silhouette against the blizzard. His arms moved frantically, but he was struggling. Jayne put on a final burst of speed, her legs aching as they laboured through the damp snow.

Her teeth chattered as she lurched up to his side. He was bundling something up in the blankets. A dark form, prone on the ground. She looked down at Eli and gasped. The boy must have been half-buried in snow when Monsun found him. He'd already removed the bow from Eli's frozen grip, the hunter's hands a deathly pallor. His fingers, cracked and bleeding. His eyes, glued shut by the snow. His lips, already a pale shade of blue.

His Mark flared, no doubt his magic trying to protect him from the certain death of the cold, but it was fading fast. Beside him, a young ibex, almost identical to the one he had brought down yesterday. Frozen stiff, blood around its neck.

"Can you carry him?" Jayne yelled.

A quick nod. He would have to. The magic wouldn't let him do anything else.

"But we need that food." He hauled up the frozen boy and reached for the animal with the other hand. Jayne reached for Eli's bow, but her fingers were already too numb to move. She tried to flex her fingers to bring back the feeling, so she could grab onto it with her left hand. The other held their beacon through the snow. If only it emitted heat, it could have melted the snow away in front of them.

The tracks were only visible a metre in front of her. Only the rasp of Monsun's breath ensured her he was behind her.

She pushed on, her throat closing up with thirst. Ice began to find its way down her collar and she shivered as the trail ran down her back.

It grew quiet.

Monsun wasn't behind her anymore.

* * *

Jayne whirled to find Monsun kneeling, his face a faint blur in the flurry of snow. He was trying to lift himself, but he couldn't. The magic had deserted him after working for so long. It seemed it wouldn't last indefinitely. Or maybe it was because he had divided his focus.

Monsun couldn't carry Eli and the ibex.

And Jayne couldn't carry either, not with the way she was trembling in the cold. Too much longer and she would be the one in the snow. Already her fingers and toes were tingling, even with the Torch in her hand.

The tracks faded from existence, filled in by the roaring snow. Stranded in the storm, with no hope of finding the Sanctum.

"I'm sorry, Jayne. I failed him." He tried to put Eli down, but his bones locked. He would have to take Eli back or the magic would kill him. But if he couldn't, they might both die out in this frozen wasteland.

"I'm the one who's sorry," she whispered. "I'm sorry I lied to him." A single tear coursed down her cheek, freezing in the chill. She merely glanced at Monsun, who nodded and bowed to her. She thanked Nestham that Eli was wearing his vambraces. Without them, she doubted this could work.

This was why she'd stayed far away from the Eternal Torch.

Why she'd never shared her knowledge of Eli's power.

Why she always wore black gloves, gloves she now shed. She reached out and clasped Eli's vambraces, felt the bite of chilled metal, chilled metal that warmed under her touch. There was no going back now.

That heat spread throughout her, a coursing, warming strength that shuddered through her whole body like a wildfire reawakened. Golden light spilled out across the valley and she screamed, a rapid torrent of words that rang throughout the world. Words not in the common tongue, but in the High Language, the ancient tongue of the rulers, the kings and queens of North, South, East and Sea. Those with the gift.

For only two things could reveal a Marked. The Eternal Flame—or Nesthamir. Strength blasted through her, renewing her fatigued body. Monsun beamed, but bowed his head.

As did the snow leopard which appeared behind them. *Thank Nestham.* Her heart hammered in her chest even as her strength rushed back, as light wreathed her hand. She held her breath and fell to a knee in the damp snow, stretching her hand out in front. Even as her pant leg became sodden in the ice, she waited. The wind howled, but she refused to open her eyes. She trusted Nestham.

Coarse fur scraped against her callused palm and she exhaled quickly, even as her heart continued to race. As she dared open her eyes, she met the snow leopard's intent gaze. Pale blue eyes gleamed, shifted to a powerful violet that trapped her, held her in its stare. The snow leopard—no, *her* snow leopard—nuzzled her hand, a throaty purr spilling from its maw.

"I need you to guide my friend back to our home. Can you do that?" she whispered into its ear, glanced at Eli. The leopard blinked once and stalked over to Monsun, stared him up and down. Jayne almost thought she saw a feline shrug. Monsun passed Eli to Jayne. She inhaled deeply and hefted the young man. The supernatural strength she hadn't used in a long time coursed through her and she tensed, the magic throbbing through her, replenishing her, invigorating her. Her leopard looked back at her reproachfully, then led the way.

Jayne's sob of relief was lost in the blizzard as snow lashed her eyes. It was merely minutes before the dark hole in the mountainside lit up, and the leopard didn't hesitate before marching in. Alsair and Amora's relieved cries dimly echoed in her ears. Alsair grabbed Eli from her and rushed him away, whilst Monsun and Jayne sagged on the floor. She nodded for Amora to go on ahead, and the girl barely hesitated before following Alsair.

Their voices dimly reached Jayne's ears in their rush to get him to the sleeping area.

"We don't have long," Alsair said. "I'll get the fire going."

"The smoke might kill him," Amora commented, as she strode alongside him.

"Better that than he freezes to death. His magic's almost depleted." Jayne wanted to follow them, but she couldn't. Not just yet.

Monsun reclined against the wall, vigorously warming himself up. "We need warmth almost as much as he does," the Vindicator said. He took the Torch and bow from her and staggered away, dragging the ibex with him. It was only Jayne and her leopard now, and she took a moment to study it. Study her, she realised. A mother, recently given birth. Thanks to her,

140

Jayne had saved Eli. But at the cost of something she hadn't been sure she was prepared to lose.

The leopard looked once over her shoulder at the blizzard. The bond between them strengthened, forged into a tight weave.

"Go. Go find your child." The leopard bowed and rushed into the blizzard. The white coat faded into the storm immediately as Jayne surged upstairs, golden light still pulsing from her clenched fist.

Her legs screamed in protest at the torment she had put them through, her gift fading too soon, muscles strained from the flight through the snow and now endless running through the Sanctum. At last, she burst into the sleeping chamber, her pulse racing. Alsair had already coaxed a fire in the hearth and they covered Eli in dry blankets beside it. Monsun lay nearby, enjoying the warmth, wrapped in a blanket, his wet shirt by the fire. Alsair gave Jayne a meaningful look, then he nudged Monsun, and they stepped outside. With them gone, she shed her outer layers, the furs, the soaked scarf.

Amora already wrapping a blanket around her. Jayne could barely do anything to prevent herself from sighing; it felt so *good*. She staggered to the boy on the ground, barely hesitating before wrapping her arms around him, lending her body heat, even as she fought to prevent her own shuddering.

This was all she could offer him now. She knew the others had many questions; whether she answered them was her choice. But for now, sleep tugged at her, and she fell into its depths.

Chapter 19

"You knew," Alsair murmured. He flicked his battered copy of the *Nesthamara* shut and glanced at Monsun, sitting rigidly next to him. Both kept their gazes on the young man and woman by the fireplace. Eli's form was unmoving, and Jayne—no, not Jayne, whatever her name was, it wasn't Jayne—wrapped her arms around him, fully clothed again. "You knew," he said again.

The Vindicator nodded, his elegant tattoo glinting in the firelight. "I knew. I am the Senior Vindicator of Leranion. I saw her many times at court, and I was responsible for her security on some outings. Though when she left on the mercy mission, the Musadim escorted her."

Alsair pondered that for the moment. "Why did she leave Leranion?"

Monsun shook his head. "According to the nobility, marauders from the Kingdom's south killed her, along with her entire escort, when she was a day out from Imbra. They found no bodies. The King was beside himself. Her naming ceremony was a year away."

"Did you believe the nobility?" Alsair said.

Monsun smiled grimly. "Not for a second. Neither did Hadrian."

Alsair chewed his lip and glanced around. "Hadrian didn't know his daughter was in the cells of the Cathedral."

"How could he?" Monsun breathed.

"Would that be why Finon placed her in solitary?"

Monsun brushed a hand over the stubble lining his face. "I imagine so. It would be too risky to put her with the others where she could talk, but I don't think he was prepared to kill her. Finon doesn't have the spine to do that. He would have seen the value in keeping her alive." A brilliant smile flashed in the Vindicator's face. "He underestimated her. Just like everyone else."

"You seem to know a lot about the Order leadership," Alsair commented. Perhaps he would prove a great ally.

Monsun shrugged. "Finon is a political animal. He tries to get involved at court as much as any minor landowner. He's eager for scandals, and any dirt on his opponents."

"How much influence does he have?"

Monsun raised his hands behind his head and stretched, his muscles rippling with the movement. "I expect he's gathered more by now, but there were rumours of an alliance with House Giara."

"And the King? How does he react to this?" Alsair asked.

"He tries his best, but he's struggling."

Time to test the Vindicator's patience. It was the best chance he had.

"It appears we might be allies, soon," Alsair ventured.

Monsun glared at him. "My mission is still to bring you in. However, I'm doing it for my King, not Finon." Alsair's brows shot up, and Monsun grinned.

"You would do that?" the elder said.

Monsun ignored the question. "But I'm not the only one with secrets, am I?" The question lingered in the air and the Vindicator shot him a look.

"Her powers, what are they besides calling the snow leopard?" Alsair needed to avoid the question, to pretend to hide the knowledge he had gleaned from hundreds of texts and his own mind.

"She's a Marked, so she has increased speed and strength, and would have wielded Leranion's Staff, but that never returned after the war."

Alsair's eyes fluttered shut, processing, thoughts churning, thinking over the possibilities. "I might know where it is."

Monsun hissed a laugh. "What are you, monk?"

"Someone who's trying to stop something terrible," Alsair breathed.

"And why do you need him?" Monsun pointed at Eli, as the young man lay prone, Jayne slumbering beside him. "What makes him so special?"

"Just a hunch. I believe Eli has a part to play in all of this. Jayne, too. Or is it 'Her Highness', now?"

Monsun frowned deeply. "You can try to call her that, but I doubt she'll want to hear a word of it." The Vindicator sighed. "She shouldn't have been able to activate her powers again. I expect she forced them dormant, and they normally stay that way unless they touch Nesthamir."

Alsair was silent, waited for Monsun to make the conclusion. The Vindicator rounded on him so quickly Alsair could barely breathe. Amora glanced up from where she was eating and gazed at them. Alsair winked at her and she went back to enjoying the food.

"You bastard," he hissed. "You found the Guardian's relic and didn't tell him what it was? The burden that lies on him?"

Alsair closed his eyes and inhaled deeply. When he opened them, Monsun's face was harsh, that silver tattoo gleaming. "How do you know what the relic is?" Alsair replied.

Monsun shrugged. "My former country isn't as stupid as to forget its entire history."

"Regardless, he needs to find out on his own," Alsair said. The guilt lay heavy upon him, but he had no choice.

"You're a piece of work, monk." Monsun swore. "You're lucky Her Highness saved your precious boy, or you'd all be halfway back to Imbra in chains."

Alsair's laughs rumbled from his burly frame. "Your life debt still holds, doesn't it?" The stony look Monsun threw him was confirmation enough. From what he guessed, there wouldn't be one between Eli and the girl either. The debt would belong to the leopard, as it didn't matter whether they could have carried him if they couldn't find their way out of the blizzard. Fortunately, life debts did not form with animals. "You don't have loyalty to the Heir of your adopted country?" he pressed.

Monsun stiffened. "She's being brought to Imbra. My King will protect her." Alsair understood. The way Monsun saw it, he was acting in the princess's best interests. But he was wrong.

"Your King?" Alsair hissed, and the violence in his eyes was like nothing he'd unleashed in twenty years. "Your King can't protect anyone. Did he lift a finger to stop the purges?"

Monsun dropped his head. "None of us knew how bad they were until I heard what happened to you and the boy. Finon keeps Hadrian in the dark. I know it is hard to believe, but it is true."

Alsair heaved himself to his feet, groaning as his old bones creaked against one another. "Once Eli wakes, we'll search this Sanctum. My heart tells me we still have more to do here. Besides, the storm will keep us indoors for a while still."

A mournful howl echoed off the stones and they shot up from their seats. Jayne stirred, her Mark flaring gold. A strange sight, but one he would have to get used to. Power to match the strength waking within Eli. Monsun and Alsair took one glance at each other and dashed out to the lower chamber. Drops of blood and blue ooze coated the ground. Alsair swore under his breath. He thought the fell beasts were all gone.

Jayne was behind them seconds later, still rubbing the sleep from her eyes. The snow leopard had returned. Gashes and gore covered it, and the strength in the violet eyes was fading fast. The leopard took one look at Jayne and bowed its head, lowering the cub to the ground. A delicate mewl rang out, and the cub shrank back into its mother's paws, seeking shelter.

Jayne's leopard, which she had bonded with for all of half an hour and which had saved Eli's life, collapsed to the floor and did not rise.

Chapter 20

Jayne's hand flew to her mouth at the sight of her leopard on the ground, blood leaking away onto the stone. It felt as if she had fallen into an icy river, immersed in the freezing cold. She sank into the numbness, the cold dark embrace.

"No." No, this couldn't be right. How could the leopard with whom she had just bonded, who had saved Eli's *life*–her muscles went slack, and she collapsed to the ground in front of her leopard. She choked back a sob. "Who. Who did this?" she whispered. " *Who!* " Her shock gave way to rage, that icy wrath she had kept trapped down in that abyss, mirroring the storm raging outside in all its power. A heavy hand fell upon her shoulder as the tears finally came, spilling like a dam bursting its banks.

Monsun squeezed her shaking shoulder, whispered in her ear. She nodded and hiccupped a breath, then began to hum a melody, the ancient lament of the kings, beseeching Nestham to care for the souls of the departed and watch over them. She began to sing.

It was neither tuneful nor worthy of performance. She didn't have a great voice at the best of times, but now sobs and coughs racked her song as she choked her way through it. Monsun and Alsair formed a vigil around her, heads bowed. Even Amora lingered in the shadows. Finally, the song came to its shuddering conclusion.

"For what you have given, we thank you," she choked.

"May we always remember your sacrifice," Monsun finished huskily. She glanced back at the stony warrior and saw his eyes puffy, tears glistening on a silver cheek.

The leopard's breathing grew shallower, raspy. She didn't have long. Jayne closed her eyes at the sight, but before she did, the leopard gave a mighty groan. She placed her paw on her cub's head, drawing a frightened mewl from it. The mewl cut off abruptly as eyes, closed since birth, opened wide, revealing vibrant, glowing purple eyes.

Jayne choked back another sob, torn between grief and joy. Grief at the sacrifice, relief it hadn't been wasted. She stayed on her knees and held out her hand. The cub took a step forward, wobbled. Amora's slight giggle mirrored Jayne's tear-stained smile.

Finally, its little paws padded on the hard stone, brushed its head against her hand. She smiled immediately at the soft fur butting her palm. A tiny purr enveloped her as she scooped it up, held it in her arms like a child.

"It's okay, little one," she murmured. "You're safe now, thanks to your mother." The cub snuggled deeper into her embrace and she had to fight the urge not to laugh, despite the tears still staining her cheeks.

"Welcome home, Nix."

Nix closed her eyes and purred. The room fell silent as everyone gazed at the leopard cub, at Nix.

"I'll give her the burial she deserves," Monsun whispered. Jayne nodded. As a citizen of Imbra, Monsun would understand the rites for burying such a warrior. For a warrior it was, who had fallen before them.

"You should get Nix back to the fire," Alsair echoed in the same whisper. Jayne wasted no time in taking the little cub back upstairs to the sleeping chamber.

The crystal reflected the light of the fire around the room as she made a beeline to the hearth and the body beside it. Eli's breaths were deep and even, finally entering the restorative sleep he needed. Outside, the wind howled past as the blizzard raged on, like a horde trying to force the door itself. Someone had sealed the stone wall to the bluff, and Jayne breathed a prayer of thanks. The chamber didn't need a mass of snow piling through it, not when they all needed to stay warm.

The isolation was chafing on her. Even in the Sanctum's safety, the loneliness enforced by the blizzard was a slow weight, beginning to crush her. But even up here, people could get injured. People could die.

She gazed upon the prone form of Eli, still unconscious by the fire. The colour had returned to his face, and his lips were now a healthy shade of pink. Yet he twitched in his sleep, as if whatever battle he had fought outside, fighting off his demons, was still being waged inside his mind. Jayne placed Nix down close to the fire, and curled up beside Eli.

Somehow, lying next to the young man had become the only way she could sleep, as if his presence gave her strength to fight off the shadows that came for her in the dark.

Not tonight, however.

She stood alone in the grassy valley where her second life had ended. The ruins of an ancient chapel still smoked behind her, leaving the sickly stench of charred flesh and scorched earth. The faces of the dead surrounded her. The loved ones who had died for her, even without knowing her identity. Died not in a heroic sacrifice, but from her carelessness and her mistakes.

Tonight, there was one more. Violet eyes stared at her reproachfully.

"You failed us."

"I did everything I could!" she yelled, but as usual, she couldn't stave off the inevitable. Jayne bolted awake, covered in sweat, muscles trembling in the night.

"Are you okay?" a voice whispered. Young, yet deep. Raspy from sleep. She looked down and her mouth curled up into a smile. Eli was awake, his eyes half-closed, but he was awake.

"I'm fine," she breathed.

Strong arms pulled her into a hug she didn't know she needed. The strength to hold herself together was like a single thread holding a chandelier. Every setback, every death, was like a file scraping on that thread. The chandelier came crashing down as she clutched his arms, sobbing into his blanket.

"I've got you."

She smiled softly, held him tighter, laid her head on his chest, right above the brand that marred his skin, the rapid beating of his heart pounding through her, too. Nix peeked up from the bedroll where she had been sleeping. Eli gasped at the sight of the tiny leopard as she narrowed her eyes at him. A tiny growl rumbled from the cub.

Eli smiled. "I guess I have her mother to thank for the ibex."

That jerked her attention to him. "Her mother brought you an ibex?"

He nodded. "After she tackled me to the ground." He trembled slightly at the memory, but she could see the recollection on his face. "When she sniffed my hands, her eyes flashed violet."

A sob caught in her throat. "The leopard's dead."

Eli's eyes opened wide. "How?"

She shook her head, the tears threatening to come free again. His eyes grew soft as he gently pressed his lips to her forehead, then held her tighter.

His throat bobbed once. "Thank you. I owe you everything."

She waved him off and slumped back onto his chest. "Monsun did most of the work," she murmured into his shirt. "He carried you so far back."

"I still would have died if not for you. His life debt didn't get repaid. I can still feel the bond."

"I'll bet Monsun's happy about that," she giggled.

He snorted in her ear. "Yes, the poor man seems to be stuck with us for a while." His eyes grew distant for a moment, then he pulled back. "It seems you have a lot to tell me," he said.

And so she did. Everything that had happened after he had left that chamber. How Monsun had felt the bond pull him and she had followed. How Monsun had carried him and the ibex so far through the mountains. How she summoned the leopard. Guilt clutched at her throat, made it hard to breathe. He noticed and brushed a hand down her hair, and she sucked in a breath.

How the leopard had died because of her actions.

"It wasn't your fault," he whispered. "She made her own choices." She shook her head, but was grateful for his comforting words. It still ran through her head. Her scream, the leopard's sudden appearance. Its collapse on the stone floor.

"Why didn't you tell me who you were?" he asked. And for the life of her, she had wanted to, but she hadn't.

"I couldn't. The world thinks I'm dead. So do my parents." King Hadrian and Queen Taera.

"How?"

Her mind flicked back to the day she had lost her old life. "I was being escorted south with a group of Musadim, spring last year. Even in the flatlands, it still gets rough. And when we were walking, the Order showed up and slaughtered my escort. The Guardsmen told me to die or jump into the Kinar. I jumped." She shivered, remembering the icy grip of the river, the plunging and torrential surge of water. "I made it to the banks and fell unconscious. When I woke up, I was in a warm bed, and a young man gave me dinner." Eli cocked his head. "His name was Luca. He was one of the few who knew the real me. I didn't know who to trust, but anyone could trust him."

Eli's smile turned wistful. "They had turned him out of the Royal Scouts, and he became a hunter in the wilderness."

"Why didn't you go back?"

"We were having dinner one night in an inn, and I heard that everyone thought marauders had killed me. I thought, if the Order wanted to kill me once, they'd do it again." She let out a heavy sigh. Did that make her a coward? *Yes*, whispered a small voice in her mind.

"Finon executed the soldiers who attacked me, for 'failing to keep the peace'." She could see the fiery rage that lit behind his eyes at those words, the set of the jaw that almost defined him. Eli would never stop fighting to protect people. That was just—him.

"He covered it up. Just like our imprisonment."

She nodded. "We ended up assembling a group that began to help people suffering from the Order's persecution."

Eli shook his head slowly. "I'm guessing that's why you called yourself the Ghost." She smiled and nodded. The Ghost. Nameless. A name she didn't need anymore. "How long has it been happening?"

"Almost a year," she said. "I first saw it in the outlying towns, when the local Order priests started removing non-believers. I—got people out, and persuaded some priests to change their ways. But Mount Sancti ... that was different altogether. My camp fell a few days later."

He fell silent and the tension in the room thickened. "I have two more questions," he said. She tensed slightly, but nodded for him to go ahead. "Can I see your Mark?"

She nodded and held up her right hand, clenched her fist. Nothing happened. She blinked, tried again, focusing on that core of energy inside her, the gift Nestham had placed in her. Nothing. The pit of power that had lain dormant was now untapped, inaccessible. She gave up and slammed her hands

152

onto his vambraces, let her power wrap around the Nesthamir. Golden light flared through the chamber as she sank into her gift, let the strength and speed course through her. Eli glanced at her wrist, at the small golden star on the knuckle of her forefinger.

"I forgot how good it felt," she said. "Is that how you feel all the time?"

"Most of the time. Sometimes it's like a fire just burning me up from the inside. Eventually, you just get used to it."

"How much of your magic do you use?" she pressed.

He held up his hands, one above the other, about a hand's width apart, palms parallel to the ground. "This is where I feel full, like I'm at my most powerful," he said, waggling the top hand. "This is where I am now," he said as he waved the bottom one. "It seems I used up a lot in the blizzard."

"What's your limit? How much power do you have altogether?"

He silently placed his bottom hand halfway down to the floor and her eyes widened. Nestham above, that sounded deadly. "What about you?" he asked.

"I don't know." At his inquiring look, she added, "I haven't checked. I only used it when I needed to summon the leopard, but I can't light the Mark or use my powers without touching Nesthamir." She frowned. "I think it's because I repressed them. I remember reading something about Mark suppression. The more you do it, the harder it is to access, even with Nesthamir. If I repressed my powers for a long time, I may never have regained them."

He raised his brows, contemplating. "Could you use my vambraces? Can you move around as I can?"

She shook her head. "I can't heal either. My magic isn't entirely the same as yours. From what I gathered from Alsair, you survived a slice across the neck and an arrow to the chest. That's some powerful magic." He nodded distantly.

She let the Mark brighten, just to see how powerful it was. Eli flicked his Mark, let his ice blue light play with her golden radiance. He was silent, though a single tear tracked down his cheek.

"It's beautiful," he breathed. She blushed and propped her head on her elbow, locked eyes with him.

"What was the second question?"

He grinned. "What's your real name?"

She sucked in a breath. Of course. Her name. Nobody would know it.

An Heir of Leranion was nameless until their eighteenth birthday, when they were fully named and acknowledged. Only she and her parents had known it. She'd disappeared when she was seventeen, become the Ghost. But in that year, she'd changed. A year of avoiding her identity, forgetting her past, had entrenched walls within her mind, stronger than any prison could tear down. But in Eli's silver gaze, they crumbled within seconds. Maybe she could trust him after all.

"Kyra Antarun."

Chapter 21

Eli settled in place besides Kyra, all of them in a circle, awaiting breakfast.

"We've still got at least a few more days of snow," Alsair said, and they all groaned. "Hopefully, we won't have any more shenanigans like last time." He pointedly looked at Eli.

Eli cringed but hastened the conversation along. "You sound like you have something in mind."

Alsair nodded as he passed him the breakfast. At least that was taken care of. "Some of us are getting a little rusty," he said precisely, to Eli.

Eli glared at Alsair. "One more annoying comment from you and I'm going to throw something."

The old man smiled. "Good. If you're up to throwing something, then you've recovered enough to train." Eli cursed under his breath and Alsair chuckled. "Don't worry. We need to get you using those vambraces so we're ready when Monsun tries to take us back to Imbra." Monsun coughed, nonplussed, and the greying monk beamed at him. Eli spluttered as he realised how far he had fallen into Alsair's trap. After ten years, the monk could still manipulate him so easily.

"We will need all the help we can get, and I'll work with Jay— ... Kyra, and Amora," Monsun said. "There's still a few tricks to learn, Princess." Eli shivered at the title. He shifted in his seat and Alsair winked at him.

"What are you going to teach me, Monsun?" Amora interjected. Monsun looked at her with a gentle smile Eli had never seen.

"How about some ways to put someone like Eli on the ground in a few seconds?" Eli spluttered again, but Amora's eyes positively glowed. Monsun's smile was quite disarming as he gazed upon the little one. Once they had finished eating, they gathered their weapons and descended into the depths of the Sanctum, where they found a nice circular chamber. Eli and Alsair stopped there, keeping the Eternal Torch, whilst the others kept looking for another space.

Before she disappeared, Jayne—no, Kyra—flicked her eyes over her shoulder and met Eli's smile. It was strange to think of her as a princess, rather than the strange, broken girl with a heart of steel he had met in prison. Alsair placed the Torch in a bracket on the wall and knelt down. Eli recognised the position. He'd seen it countless times at Mount Sancti. Alsair reached into his shirt, pulled out a worn wooden pendant in the shape of a dove. He closed his eyes and his lips moved silently.

A second later, Eli opened his mouth. "Feel like a rest, old man?"

"Hardly," Alsair said as he motioned for Eli to sit with him. "I want you to try again with the vambraces. Can you describe how it feels when you use them?"

"It's almost like I fall into this rift between our world and ..." He hesitated. "... something else."

"Rifting. That's a good name for it," Alsair commented.

Eli sighed and brought them back to the task at hand. "But do you have another way to do it this time? I don't want to end up in the wall."

"Possibly."

Eli waited. But Alsair had lapsed into silence, closing his eyes. Eli hesitated, then copied the motion.

"Focus your energy. Picture this room in your mind," Alsair murmured.

He thought of a dark stone chamber, illuminated by a single Eternal Torch. The image drifted in and out of focus.

"Clear your mind."

"I'm trying!" Eli hissed, but that only made things worse. The image tilted, became fuzzy.

"One more time," Alsair murmured.

Eli swore. "This isn't going to work."

Alsair snapped his fingers. "Of course. It's why you didn't really fit in at Mount Sancti."

"Alsair, that's not helping," Eli said through gritted teeth.

But Alsair pressed on. "You responded best when we fought. There are points where you have this singular focus I rarely see, but it only shows up in a fight. You're a born soldier, Eli."

Eli began to smile.

"So fight!" his mentor roared, flicking his sword from his sheath faster than Eli had ever seen.

Eli's magic flickered into being and he dropped into his power. His senses sharpened and every twitch of his muscles moved with controlled power. The strength coursed through his arms and he made a few gentle swings, relishing his strength. He grinned at his mentor, then circled him.

"Recovered yet from your little trip?" Alsair threw the opening barb.

Eli just smiled wider, so deep was he in his magic. Not today, he promised himself. Alsair couldn't damage his mood or throw him off balance.

"*Her Highness* seemed very eager to find you in the snow. She almost died trying to save your life. Isn't that something the Order would want to know?"

Immediately his mind began to tilt. *No.*

"If anyone finds out about the two of you, she'd never be safe. Not even as Queen." Alsair curled his lip, and it transformed his face from the jovial old monk to a battle-hardened and disgusted warrior. Eli's muscles tensed as he took the punch to his core. Alsair had never been this brutal. But the wounds just kept coming.

"You could never have her, you know," he spat. "These days will be just a dream when we leave this place. It's against every law we have. Even if we can return to Imbra, she'll choose a lord or a prince from another land. Prince Jalek of the Sea or Duke Stallor are both apparently good-looking." Eli struggled to clear the spots in his vision. It would just be another set of shackles. Even if she didn't choose him ... she should choose someone who she cared for. "You've got nothing. No family, no money, no choice."

"Enough!" Eli roared and swung. Again and again and again, wrath incarnate against his mentor, but it was just monstrous waves crashing on unyielding stone. Alsair was unbreakable. Eli let out a snarl that was practically inhuman and slammed his arms together. A burst of light filled the chamber.

He wandered through darkness, through shifting colour and smells. But an image floated back to him, a single circular chamber lit by a golden Torch. A man currently standing with closed eyes. He narrowed his focus even further to Alsair's unprotected, slightly stooped back. He surged back into the living world, back to the light, back into *existing*. His sword stabbed forwards, ready to plunge into Alsair's back.

But the monk was already moving and smashed it out of his hand. Eli stumbled forward and Alsair merely shifted his leg so Eli tripped over the outstretched foot. Eli hit the ground with a thud that knocked the wind out of him. Alsair pinned him, an unearthly gleam in his eyes beginning to fade.

"Well done, Eli." Eli heaved with all his strength and threw the monk off him. Alsair thudded to the ground, but Eli paid no heed. He was already bolting to the exit, intending to head straight to the upper chamber.

Footsteps rang behind him, and Kyra's voice echoed on the stone.

"Alsair! Monsun's injured." Alsair immediately left with her. Eli risked a glance after them, down the passageway. Alsair looked back, met his eyes and shook his head, and Eli sighed, continuing back up to the sleeping chamber.

Alsair was right, even if he was just trying to get under his skin. He was just a commoner. Worse, he was a criminal, with the entire Order ready to kill him at a moment's notice, a Mark on his hand and a brand on his heart. He had no future with her. Not when she would reclaim her throne one day.

Eli swore and began to pace. But that didn't even destroy the tension. He drew his sword, sank deep into his magic. Blue light pulsed around the room as he moved fluidly. He followed through his drills, never pausing, always moving from one to the other in a flowing movement born from years of training. As he relied on his magic more and more, his movements became faster, stronger, until his sword was a constant beam of light surrounding him. Sweat coursed down his body, but his breathing remained steady.

A small flame had begun to burn in his chest, no matter how much reality tried to smother it. Hope remained.

* * *

He was still training twenty minutes later when Kyra walked in, Nix under her arm. She set the cub down and watched her crawl into the blankets. He noted how her gaze rippled up and down his body, studying him and his form, but he kept at it, relaxing into the kata. A minute later, he made one final slice, dropped to one knee and slashed across an imaginary opponent's chest. He lifted his eyes to hers, which were reddened and bleary.

"I see your training session went almost as badly as mine," he said.

159

He plopped to the ground, released his hold on his magic. His exhaustion caught up with him and the world tilted. His muscles ached. Kyra sat down next to him, brushing her hands with his briefly. She let out a sharp gasp and withdrew, the barrier shooting back up, studying her hands.

They were stained with red that smudged otherwise golden skin. It took forever for her to meet his gaze. The blue of the deep ocean, once dancing with light, was now bloodshot and dull.

"Alsair also tried some baiting tactics on you, didn't he?" she said. He nodded slowly. "Well, how did you respond?"

He tried to muster a weak grin, but failed. "I managed to use my vambraces. Still ended up on the ground, though. You?"

Her grin was as feeble as a drought-stricken stream. "Summoned my Mark. Pinned Monsun, then Nix bit him on the leg. Alsair's patching him up now."

He nodded vaguely, but reached over and clasped her hand. "Can you do it again?"

She clenched her fist and breathed deeply, summoning her Mark. A star gleamed just beside the knuckle of her forefinger. Burning brilliant gold. Eli joined her, and crystal blue mingled with her light as they released their power. A hesitant hand touched his shoulder.

"I'm sure they're trying to help," she said.

"Maybe, but Alsair's still being a kratten." Horror crashed through him at swearing in front of royalty and he turned to her, apologies ready to spew forth— but she was wide-eyed, trembling with laughter. He hesitantly reached out, brushed a lock of dark hair that had escaped from the braid, so tightly wound, like the iron mask she kept in place. He saw a shiver run through her, and she swallowed quietly.

That night, the nightmares came again, but they were different. The forest was deathly silent, even the stars hidden from sight. Eli stood alone in a grassy clearing, moonbeams glittering off his naked blade. His vambraces, cracked and useless. His Mark, sputtering, drained of energy. In front of him, a man he had only seen once in the glow of a branding iron held Kyra in a vice-like grip, a knife at her throat, her hand devoid of light. The Vindicator's smile was a savage thing to behold as he drew the knife across her neck. Blood spurted from Kyra's throat. Eli lunged for the girl, yelled for Nestham to save her, but nothing could. He could only hold her as the light died from her eyes.

Eli sat up straight, breath coming in ragged gasps as the sweat glazing his body froze in the cold air. Beside him, Kyra stirred, twisting her lithe form on the bedroll, that braid falling across her cheek. They stayed with each other each night now, holding each other through the nightmares and terror. It seemed to be the only way to fight off the horrors attacking from the shadows. But how long would it last?

"What are you thinking about?" she whispered. The others were still prone on their bedrolls, Monsun's snores rumbling through the chamber—a rolling thunder, just like the warrior himself. Eli stared at the crystal overhead, holding a dim orange light, like the glow of the ember that had seared his skin.

"Nothing in particular." He turned over to his side to find Kyra gazing at him intently, and *Five Hells* it was too easy to fall into those blue depths. Yet he couldn't, haunted by what he had just witnessed.

"It was different this time, wasn't it?" she asked. He bit his lip.

"Usually it's either Mount Sancti or the brand, but this one was different."

She hesitated. "Was it about ... me?"

He nodded again, eyes moistening, not even attempting to keep the brave face. A lean arm latched on his shoulder, and as she enveloped him in her embrace, it made it so much easier to close his eyes again. A welcome weight dropped onto his chest as he fell back into the depths of blissful peace.

Chapter 22

Heavy clouds overhead stopped the morning rays from being drawn into the crystal, giving Eli a pang of disappointment as he awoke. And, yet again, it was Alsair's idea of how to spend the day that prevailed.

"I don't think training will kill time today," the monk said. He gathered his breath in a dramatic gesture. "The Staff of Leranion is somewhere within this Sanctum. We need to find it." Monsun's eyes widened, and he shifted, grimacing as his wound pulled. "Monsun, you need to rest and recover."

"I am fine," the Vindicator insisted, his face taut.

"Just sit down," Alsair said. "But the rest of you, we're off." Amora practically clapped her hands with glee.

Ten minutes later, Eli, already carrying the Torch aloft, scuffed his feet and shot a glance at Monsun. The seconds stretched out until the others understood and cleared the room, heading down into the Sanctum. Alsair carried spare torches, whilst Kyra clutched Monsun's map in her hands.

Eli shuffled his way over to Monsun, unable to look him in the eyes, the Vindicator's face inscrutable.

"Thank you," he said. "For saving my life. I know it was the life debt that compelled you, but ... I'm grateful."

Monsun said nothing, but his eyes crinkled slightly. Eli smiled in return and left. Four humans and one snow leopard descended into the depths of the Sanctum. Nix snuggled inside Kyra's jacket, a warm bundle just over her heart. Eli grinned at her and she smiled down at the ball of fluff popping her head outside.

Amora reached up eagerly to stroke her head. "She's so adorable," the girl piped. Nix narrowed her eyes and snarled at Amora, who quickly stepped back.

"Shh, Nix," Kyra murmured. "Friend."

Eli pursed his lips at the snow leopard cub. "She really doesn't like strangers," he commented.

"Look at it this way. She bonded with me, and she's supposed to protect me, but she's not old enough to tell friend from foe." Kyra laughed at Eli's expression. "Don't worry. Once she gets bigger, it'll be much easier."

"Once she gets bigger, she's more likely to look at me as food."

She snorted as they came to a junction, with four stone passages splitting their route. They crowded around the map.

"We haven't covered these passageways," Alsair said, doling out and lighting the extra torches. "Amora, take the one on the left. I'll take the one on the right. And you two"—he pointed at Eli and Kyra—"take the others. Meet back here in half an hour."

They all nodded. Eli made it only a few steps before he had to double back, thanks to a dead end. He quickly joined Kyra.

She glanced at him. "What happened to your route?"

"Dead end. And I'd rather be searching with you." He winked, and she rolled her eyes. They continued down the hall, but a chill settled in his bones as they did. "So, there's not much time until we'll be able to get out of here," he said, not sure where he was going with this.

"Yes." She gave him a quizzical look.

He took a deep breath and just said it. "Where do you think you'll go after the storm?" he asked, even as his heart beat faster and his palms began to sweat.

She shrugged. "I haven't quite decided yet." He let out a quiet sigh as she stepped ahead of him. That could have been worse. The chill magnified, as if something was *pushing* him back. Kyra extinguished her torch, dropped it, and unfolded the

164

map as he hefted the Eternal Torch higher. A stone wall faced them.

"Another dead end?" he asked of nobody in particular.

Kyra searched the map, creasing her brow. "This shouldn't be right. The drawing has this tunnel keeping going."

"So it's—" he began, but Kyra finished it for him.

"A fake, yes."

He raised the torch to the uppermost corners of the wall, traced the edges of the dark stone, letting the gold illuminate the wall.

"Nothing."

Kyra slumped against the wall. "This can't be it." She narrowed her eyes. "Cover the Torch," she said, and when he wrapped it in his cloak, she let her Mark flicker into being, bathing Eli in warmth. A golden hue almost identical to the Torch, but with its own power. Its energy whispered on his skin and he shivered at the touch. His magic surged, wanting to play, but he damped it back down.

She laughed. "I should have guessed."

Another snow leopard emblem was there, glowing in her light. She dropped the magic back down and it vanished. Let it out again and the symbol shone brightly. Eli had a bad feeling about where this was headed. Kyra reached out and pressed the symbol. The stone rumbled and rose into the roof, leaving a dark cavity behind.

He hefted the Torch higher, let the golden light flicker into the space.

They glanced at each other, not even needing to speak before swords scraped on sheaths and they edged around the corner. If something lurked in these caverns, it would have an easier fight in a Hell. The light flitted around the chamber and they gasped at the sight that lay before them. A painting stretched across the wall. In swirling colours, men and women in

165

luminous armour fought shadows across a grassy field. And in the centre, a man and a woman fought back to back, battling a horde of—

"Demons," Kyra breathed.

"It was real." Eli swallowed and reached over to grab her hand, found her palm slick in his grip. Something nagged at him as he swept the ancient painting. There. The man in the middle, holding a sword with two hands. His eyes glowed with fury, a burning passion of the fight. Eyes of pure silver.

Eli sagged slightly and Kyra took the Torch from him, edged forward. Studied it even more carefully. The woman to the silver-eyed man's left brandished a staff of a shimmering metal. A simple tiara rested upon her hair, tied back in a battle-ready braid. "Queen Eshe," she said. "In the stories, she led the war against the demons."

"I think we might be finding out the truth for the first time," Eli murmured.

Kyra's brows rose. "Look," she said. "This man is at the centre of the fight, yet I've heard nothing of a silver-eyed warrior in the war." Her eyes probed ceaselessly, snagged on the man's forearms. "Eli," she tapped his arms. "Your vambraces."

"That's impossible." He shook his head as he stepped closer. "Mine are too rare."

She levelled a stare at him. "You seriously believe that?" she asked.

"Not really." He sighed. "And what's this?" he pointed to the bottom of the frame.

Just beneath it, a single symbol glimmered there. A golden star. He didn't need to say a word. She understood. Whatever was waiting on the other side had been waiting a long time.

Waiting for *her.*

Kyra never hesitated. The warm hues of gold blazed through the chamber, brighter even than the Eternal Torch held in his hand. She sucked in a deep breath and pressed her glowing hand to the symbol. The painting shuddered and raised up on unseen cords, leaving shimmering light in a small tunnel behind. Kyra grinned at him, and *damn it,* his heart began to soar.

He could only beam back. Once the painting stopped, Kyra stared intently at the light at the tunnel's end. She moved forward as if she was in a trance, a dream. Eli followed behind her, retrieving the Torch, despite the sweat that coated his hands. A faint crackle echoed in his ears and he tensed. "Doesn't this feel familiar to you?" he murmured. Something nagged at him, a memory he couldn't access. A faint roar rang through the chambers and his breath caught.

The tunnel opened up into a vast chamber. Golden flames lined the walls, dancing on water. Another wellspring. Just like the Cathedral. Beside him, Kyra gasped and pointed. Behind the flaming arc, a single gleam of metal, a glittering diadem. A single, perfect sapphire glowed at the apex of the circlet. The same diadem that had graced the head of the Queen of Leranion in the painting. Lying beside it, a shimmering staff. The Queen's weapon.

Eli touched her arm, saw her eyes snap back into focus.

"It's behind a wall of fire," he said.

"*Eternal* Fire," she countered. "I have a hunch." She took another pace forward. The flames climbed higher, as if sensing her presence and guarding the treasure behind it. Eli's muscles locked up as Kyra stepped into the fire. A single cry of pain was quickly silenced. The flames swallowed her whole, hid her from his sight.

Eli stumbled backwards, mouth dropping open. "Kyra?
Kyra!" he roared, but there was nothing but the blazing fire, now reaching up to the stone ceiling.

She couldn't be gone. His lip quivered, as he stared at the stone floor. A phantom hand reached under his chin, pulled him to face the fire again, but he wouldn't. Couldn't.

A roaring wind rushed through the chamber, whipping the tears into a frenzy. The flames vanished, yet two hues of gold remained. He lifted his eyes and gasped. Kyra stood untouched, a diadem on her brow and the staff in her hand. She walked back towards him, but immediately he detected a change. Though she had always moved gracefully, she had walked like a warrior, lethality in her steps. Now she moved like a queen.

Eli was completely entranced at the sight, and she smiled demurely when she met his gaze. She ran a reverent hand over the staff and her Mark flared as the Nesthamir recognised her power. Kyra launched into a full swing of the staff, years of training evident in the motions. Two wickedly sharp blades flashed out of the ends, glowing gold, matching her Mark. Eli yelped and jumped back. Kyra's smile only widened.

* * *

"So, you found it." Alsair's voice was completely unsurprised.

Eli whirled and glared at the monk. "How did you get here so fast?"

Alsair ignored him. "I hoped it would be you who did." He surged past them, easily sidestepping Kyra in his path to the back of the dais, over the extinguished flames. He tapped the back of the wall, creating a ringing sound throughout the chamber. Seconds later, he let out a small noise of triumph as he stood brandishing an ancient scroll in his hand, still tied with crumbling ribbon. "Eli, did I teach you nothing? Always look past the obvious."

"How did you find that?" Kyra asked, her eyes narrowing. She shifted her leg, her arm dropping to her side, still holding the staff. Had she just assumed an attack stance with that weapon? Eli tensed, his fingers tapping on his leg, as the air seemed to crackle with energy.

"Experience, my dear." Alsair beamed at her. Eli just shook his head at the incorrigible monk, breathing a relieved sigh. "And now that we're finished here, shall we retire?" he asked, breezing past them. "If your Highness wishes, of course." He aimed the parting shot over his shoulder.

Kyra glared at his back, but Eli allowed himself a small smile as they stepped after him back through the twisting tunnels. As soon as Alsair rounded the next corner, Kyra yanked on Eli's hand, pulling him back around the wall where she pushed him against the stone.

"What?"

"I've got a bad feeling," she murmured. He strained his ears. Alsair's footsteps were virtually inaudible by now.

"About what?"

She pointed down the corridor. "Him."

Eli shook his head. "Absolutely not. I trust him with my life. He saved us back in the Cathedral."

Kyra nodded and shifted her staff in her hand. "That's exactly my point. Nobody knew where we were, but he did. How?"

Eli pursed his lips and shrugged. "I don't know. But I'm still trusting him." He pulled himself out of her grasp and took a step away.

"Eli." Something in her voice made him turn back and stare at her hard eyes. "I checked the back wall. There was no way I could have missed that." There was nothing else to say, but a shadow settled in his mind.

They hurried back to the upper chamber. Monsun sat on the floor, completely still with legs crossed. His silver tattoo glinted in the crystal's light, but he didn't open his eyes. Eli approached on hunter's feet, waved a hand in his face.

"Just because I'm in a life debt to you doesn't mean I can't throw things at you, Eli," the warrior commented, still with closed eyes.

Eli withdrew hurriedly. He jumped and clutched a hand to his chest in a dramatic gesture as Amora appeared beside him, her short hair bobbing with an excited energy. "Don't do that!"

They took seats on the blankets, forming a relaxed circle. Kyra dropped next to him, and a part of him beamed with her nearness. Alsair waggled the scroll in the air.

"Just to bring you two up to speed"—he nodded at Amora and Monsun—"we have here what they left after the Prince fell at the Sanctum. It was well guarded, none but the heir could have claimed it. And ..." He hesitated. "We might find something that answers why everything is going wrong back in Imbra."

"We already know why," Eli sighed. "It's the Order."

Alsair glared at him. "The Order has stood for a thousand years, ever since the demon war. I don't think it would turn evil immediately."

Kyra's head snapped to the monk, and she bared her teeth at the greying man.

"What did you just say?" she breathed. Golden light flared, and Eli could practically feel the power rolling off her, thrumming through his skin, a mighty magical maelstrom.

170

"I said I don't think it's entirely the Order's fault," the monk replied. Eli sensed the cold fury roiling off her like the blizzard roaring outside.

"The Order destroyed my life. Twice. I'm not letting it happen a third time." Her voice could have frozen Alsair's face completely.

The entire room tensed, rippling through the air. Monsun was gazing at Kyra, regret and agony written all over his face. Eli squeezed her fingers, and she glanced at him, the anger melting from her face. Seeing her rage vanish made it easier to control his own.

"Alsair, the Order has done terrible things to all of us," he said. "They destroyed your entire monastery. This isn't a time to be passive anymore."

Alsair included Eli in his stony expression. "As a Jinnam monk, I follow the *Nesthamara*. 'For in His grace, we find forgiveness'," he quoted. "Even if the Order has fallen, I must still have faith they can redeem themselves."

And yet the Order follows the Nesthamara, too, Eli thought.

Alsair unravelled the scroll and his eyes darted over the page, humming to himself. "It's in a strange form of dialect. Not the High Language, just old. It will take some time to decipher it." After a minute, he looked up. "I think it's Prince Cayce's diary, just before he died," he said. They waited. "I see parts here about some ... enemy? A demon and his hordes. They didn't know his true name, so they called him Temero."

"That explains the painting," Kyra said. "Demons. An army of them," she concluded with a shudder.

Alsair nodded, eyes still on the page. "Yes. Cayce fell three days before the end of the war, but the scroll doesn't stop there. The Queen kept writing in his stead. She has some impressive calligraphy." He hesitated. "One of my soldiers stepped up. A man with eyes of ... silver," he said. Kyra's grip tightened on Eli's hand. "He called himself Jaser Cathom and said something about Nestham. I followed him and we fought against Temero, along with representatives from Biralam, Valmor and Amerin."

"Amerin?" Amora asked.

Alsair glanced up. "I guess it was the name of what is now the Plains, before it split." Biralam, the Southern Desert, past the Severed Peaks splitting the continent. And Valmor, better known as the Golden Isles. The Kingdom of the Sea.

"Let me guess," Eli interjected. "They slew his dark carcass and went home happily ever after."

Alsair looked up from the text, his eyes grim. "Almost. The Queen notes that Jaser was an incredible warrior, the likes of which nobody had ever seen. Temero badly wounded him, but he slew the demon. And then ... it was if a ... wind? Gale? I don't know that word ... rushed through, ripping Temero's body into dust. Temero had broken his back, and still Jaser stood, his wounds vanishing without a trace, a Mark like that of the four rulers appearing on his skin, a cold blue. The wind picked up again, and eight items and five animals appeared around Jaser. The rulers approached Jaser, but he merely sheathed his sword and walked away. One animal, a hawk, flew after him. When I called after him, he merely said he had failed as Guardian." Alsair paused. *Guardian.* A quiet calm settled inside Eli. Finally, he had a name for his magic.

"When the rulers met, they found each item forged of a strange metal, strong yet light, a likeness never seen in Ekra. Four weapons and four relics appeared on the ground. Each ruling representative took one of each. For Biralam, the king took an axe and a necklace. For Amerin, the Prince took a bow and a quiver full of the strangest arrows, and an armlet. For the

Sea, the Princess took a rapier and an anklet. For the North, the Queen took a staff and a ring."

Alsair paused for a breath. "At this moment, four great animals pledged their service to a ruler. A wolf, a sea eagle, a lion and a snow leopard." Kyra instinctively glanced at Nix, curled up asleep in the chamber's corner.

"We later received reports of three pillars of this metal, hidden across the continent, that hummed and were warm to the touch. They were hidden in Talon Reach, Aurimia and ... Mount Sancti," Alsair sighed. Eli cocked his head and kept listening. "It was theorised that these great pillars were part of an immensely powerful spell which kept Temero out of these lands. Yet, others believe his spirit still walks the earth, and if any of these pillars should fall, he could rise again."

Eli's heart beat even faster as sweat broke out along his brow. "The Order destroyed Mount Sancti. There's no wreckage and no pillar to be found," he breathed.

It was Monsun who spoke the final words, even as all of Eli's mind was screaming at him to be silent, that ignorance was bliss. "Temero is free."

Nobody spoke for a long moment.

"So where is he?" Amora asked.

"Imbra," Kyra said. "He would go straight to the seat of power in the Kingdom."

Eli asked the obvious question. "Can we kill him?"

Alsair pursed his lips. "I don't know. Clearly, the Queen thought Jaser had killed him, but look how that turned out. I don't think that will work this time."

Eli steeled himself, glanced around at everyone. Kyra nodded, even as the blood drained from her face. Monsun was focused and intent. Alsair unnaturally grave. Amora ... his heart broke as her eyes bored into his. She'd seen so much at such a young age. Yet her look was harder than steel.

"I think it's time we made an agreement," Eli said. He reached over and grasped the Vindicator's callused hand.

"We get Kyra to Imbra and find out more about Temero," he said, a chill creeping over him. A demon—a creature of shadow and nightmares walked their land. Monsun's night-dark eyes held steady, and that tattoo seemed more prominent than ever. A Vindicator would always obey his commands. "This enemy is bigger than all of us." Monsun's grip was limp, belying the strength in his body. "Will you help?"

A firm grip squeezed back.

Chapter 23

Eli couldn't do anything but stare at the lightless crystal. The noonday sun was lost in the blizzard. The wind shrieked like a mournful prisoner, even shaking the stone of the Sanctum. Or prison, as it seemed to have become.

The patter of feet that slipped into his senses warned him, and he smiled as Kyra joined him. With a disgruntled mewl, Nix wormed her way out of Kyra's thick jacket and rolled to the floor, letting out a delicate sneeze. Eli's chest lightened at the innocent sound, and Kyra smothered a laugh behind her hand. The cub rolled onto her legs. Violet eyes opened wide and fixed on Kyra.

Eli leaned forward as if in a trance, fixated on the sight. Kyra gasped as Nix pressed herself up on her legs and began to wander towards the hearth, straining towards the heat. The cub let out a delicate mewl, almost a squeak.

"How did she learn to walk so quickly?" Eli whispered.

"It's strong magic," she breathed, not daring to talk loudly lest she break the spell. "When an animal bonds to a ruler, they grow much quicker than usual, and much bigger. At least, that's what I've read." She shrugged. "No Leranion ruler has bonded with a snow leopard in several generations." Impressive. The young woman had claimed two out of three of Leranion's blessings.

"There's one thing that's bothering me," he said.

"If it's just one, you're doing better than I expected." She laughed softly.

"Did you know what I was?"

She pursed her lips. "No. I guessed that you had a similar magic, but had never heard of any Guardian."

"What if—" He hesitated. "What if that's on purpose?" His palms turned clammy at the thought. She raised a brow, and he pressed on. "It makes sense, doesn't it? If no other source has any information, and not even that man is mentioned in the other accounts, then that must be it. Someone tried to erase the existence of the Guardians, and I'm betting it's the Order."

"If it is the Order," she said, and raised her hands to ward off his protests, "and you're probably right, it sounds likely, they must not want any opposition to their claim to Nestham. And the one thing that would make people want a Guardian ... is a demon." That would be it. The Guardian—one of Nestham's Chosen, and a threat. What other lies had the Order told them over centuries? Claiming Temero wasn't a threat?

"How are you holding up?" Kyra asked. He found himself wanting to lean into her warmth, but restrained himself. Not a good idea. And not with the crown as a new barrier.

"I'm—I'm not. I didn't expect any of this," Eli said, throwing his hands out. "After Mount Sancti, I thought of nothing but revenge. I even tried to get into the Archbishop's chambers before they put me into prison. But since then, I've done nothing but run."

The crackling fire was the only sound for a moment. "We're all running from something, even when we say we're not," she replied. "What matters is whether you turn and face it."

He stared at her, at the way she bit her lip and kept her eyes trained on him.

"Then what are you running from, Princess?" he breathed. She blinked away the tears and shook her head. He let out a sigh and met her gaze, and even the firelight sparkling in her eyes couldn't move him. "It's like there's this crushing weight on me, and no matter what I do, I can't get rid of it."

Silent tears began to course down his cheeks. "I don't know who he is or how I can defeat him."

"What makes you think the burden rests on you alone?" she whispered. His churning thoughts stilled. "You're not alone, Eli, nor are you the only Marked. I'm with you. We're with you," she added with a gentle smile. She brushed a callused hand over the tears on his cheeks. "And I will not let you face him alone, regardless of who he is."

A faint blush crept up the back of his neck, mirroring the one on her cheeks. His bloodshot eyes began to droop.

"What's that?" she asked. She nodded her head at his chest, at the pendant fallen out of his shirt. Eli fished it out of his jerkin and held it up in the flickering light. Not the dove that Alsair wore, but his own symbol, worn wood and a childlike carving. *ES.* He caressed the engraving with his thumb.

"It's an old trinket. My sister Miriel gave it to me when she was little." Surprise glittered in her eyes, yet it vanished quickly, her court-trained mask sliding back into place.

"What happened to her?" she asked, almost hesitantly.

"We were out exploring," he began. Immediately a lump formed in his throat. "We snuck out of the house at night and went to the river at the back of the farm. Our parents told us never to go there. I jumped to a rock in the middle, and she followed. She saw something in the water and reached for it, but she—she fell in. I never found her body." The tears began anew. "She was practically my shadow," he whimpered. "And then I lost her."

Kyra laid a comforting arm on his shoulder as the tears welled again. "I'm so sorry," she said into the fire.

He took in a shuddering breath. "How do you do it? How do you just pick up the pieces and keep marching on? What if this is it? And we have no chance of stopping Temero?"

177

Kyra's eyes glimmered, but she didn't waver. "Because I don't have any choice," she said. "I have to believe that we have a chance, regardless of what it looks like. If we believe we have no hope, then we don't."

"I just wish that someone else could bear this burden," he said at last.

"I know. I know," she whispered. Even then, those fears, those horrible smells and sounds began to overwhelm him again. The roaring in his head swelled, and for the life of him he couldn't drown it out. Kyra faintly brushed her lips on his cheek, and the roaring faded. He tried to speak, but no sound would come out of his mouth. Kyra's fair skin flushed even deeper, but her smile was mocking him.

"You look like you need a distraction," she grinned.

"How am I supposed to do that?" he gestured helplessly.

"Follow me. That is, if you're not too tired." She winked. The challenge stirred his soul, and he rose with her.

* * *

"Are you sure about this?" he said, muscles already tensing. His body was practically thrumming, his mind dropping into that other plane, that other consciousness. His heart hammered at her answering grin, at the same energy that ran through her. They stood paces apart, surrounded by stone in one of the countless chambers. But the walls faded away, irrelevant, as they circled.

For the first time, he knew exactly how to use his magic. He saw the roiling storm of power inside him, and he dropped into it as it swept him away, consumed him. The increased awareness took him, the heightened senses, as if he could practically hear her heart leaping out of her chest as her own fire raged through her. Kyra moved like a hurricane given flesh. She lunged at him, staff already sweeping at his head. A flick of her wrist, and those wicked blades flashed out, ready to slice, to maim.

Steel rang on Nesthamir as Eli blocked with his sword. Kyra withdrew for one moment. He glanced at his sword and swore at the large notch in the blade. Gold and blue flared throughout the chamber as they sparred, moving at inhuman speeds. But they were human no longer.

The Marks on their hands signified a greater purpose, a greater power, a greater destiny. But for now, there was only the two of them—and their magic. Eli flicked his blade to the side, and she fell for the feint, blocking to the left. Despite her experience with the staff, one made of pure Nesthamir apparently took some getting used to. Yet it was clear it was made for her, and she for it.

Eli's smile was one of battle joy, fierce and deadly. He leaped into the air and crashed his arms together, dropping into the familiar abyss. Finding his place in the world was quicker each time, and he appeared behind her, sword already seeking a target.

He had forgotten one crucial detail. That staff gave her a much greater reach than his sword could ever have. The gleaming metal was a solid blur as she spun it in an endless barrage of strokes. Time and time again, he could barely block the shimmering blades. He plummeted into the core of his magic, allowed it to replenish the strength rapidly leaving his body. The humming reverberated through the chamber as he threw himself into the abyss of the Rift, becoming a non-stop flicker of light and sword. He blinked around her until his head began to spin, but she took no heed of his position. She merely continued with her blocking, as if she was going through one of her drills.

Finally, an opening. His sword flickered out and caught under her staff. He twisted it to the side, and it spun away, flashing end over end until it clattered on the stone, blades retracting immediately. Even with her magic, Kyra's breathing was ragged and sweat poured off her brow.

"Surrender?" he smirked.

"Never to you," she said, though he could have sworn she flushed slightly. Her glowing hand, rife with power, flashed forward and caught him in the chest. He staggered back, letting out an *oomph* of pain. Kyra showed him no mercy and barrelled forward, sweeping up with a booted foot he barely saw coming. He dropped his hand and only just blocked it.

His magic thrashed, replenishing his energy, but he was reaching the dregs now. His fingers tingled, then grew numb, his tongue stuck to the roof of his mouth. White nudged at the corner of his vision. He hadn't even tried to conserve his power. It would be exhausted soon. Much more, and he risked complete collapse. He flew into that raging fire, the battle fury.

Yet his senses pricked. It wasn't just the fire, but something else lived there, in *him*. Something powerful, like some untapped wellspring of energy.

It happened eventually. Kyra began to slow, and in her exhaustion, she overstepped her punch. Her momentum was enough to carry her into his hold. When he released her, Kyra's glare did nothing to sully his joy in winning their little contest. Joy, and something else. Something danced in her eyes, and he knew the same light sparked in his own. *Beautiful.* She tossed her head, her braid whipping around the other side. His eyes dropped to her lips, and he swallowed once, tried to calm his heartbeat.

"That's enough for now," she said, though she couldn't contain her smile. They strolled down, grinning, to find the others. Alsair raised a brow at their flushed faces and damp hair.

"You two feeling okay?" he asked mildly. Eli couldn't wipe that stupid grin off his face.

Chapter 24

Eli jerked awake to complete silence. His eyes strained to penetrate the blackness. The fire had died to sputtering embers. A phantom hand gripped his, yanked it so his arm stretched fully. He clamped his lips to avoid crying out, glanced downward. Kyra merely rolled over from where she lay beside him, muttering something in her sleep, words he couldn't understand, yet he felt he should. Nix's eyes fluttered open, gleaming violet in the night. He froze, but she put her furry head back on the ground and slumbered. The hand yanked again, and he clambered up, smoothing his rumpled jerkin. He shivered as his feet met the biting chill of the mountain stone that stretched around the sleeping bodies of the others, and paced quietly to the sealed door to the bluff, unopened since the blizzard had struck.

Four days and nights in this stone tomb, and he was going mad. And yet, some of the best times he'd had. The touch lifted from his hand and he flicked it in the air as if it was still clinging, like an insect, not a mystery. His skin prickled as he sensed the ghostlike presence moving away. Yet he resisted the call of the magic, now replenished after a restful sleep. The snow leopard engraving gleamed as the wall receded into the ground, leaving a gap in the wall. A breach. Eli tensed, fingers flexed, reaching for a sword lying metres away. A flurry of snow burst through the small gap in the wall and swirled around him, faster and faster. The flakes never reached the ground, instead dipping and rising, fluctuating inward. This was no natural event. They stuck together, shifting in the air. Forming a human outline.

He gasped as a human stepped out of those snowflakes. Tall, broad-shouldered, with muscled arms. He moved with controlled power as if he could become a raging animal if he wanted to, yet he kept it damped down beneath a warrior's grace. He faced Eli, a strange calm written on his features. Eli's arms tensed, preparing to attack unarmed should the man pose a threat.

"You don't need to fight me," the man said, face blank. He merely sat down across from Eli, crossed long, muscled legs. He cocked his head as the firelight caught his eyes. Glowing silver eyes. Eli's arm slackened and his mouth dropped.

"Have a seat," the man motioned. When Eli hesitated, the stranger frowned and pointed again until Eli shuffled onto the ground, settled into place.

He surveyed the man, clad in gleaming armour. "You've been watching me," he said. Glowing silver eyes, always observing him. It was a sure bet that strange, phantom grip was him as well. The stranger nodded.

"I'm sure you have a lot of questions," he began, but Eli was already shaking his head.

"Not as many as you might think. But your name is at the top of that list."

"It's Jaser," he said. "Jaser Cathom."

"You shouldn't be here." Eli scratched his jaw, an itch that wouldn't go away. "You died centuries ago."

"It's simple, really," Jaser said and rolled his shoulders. The dead didn't care about tight muscles. At least, that was what everyone had taught him. "Nestham sent me."

Eli raised a brow. "Nestham sent you." Doubt coloured his voice, but Jaser nodded all the same. "Really? What does the all-powerful, all-knowing God want with me?"

"You're one of His Marked, Eli. And He would want to know you even if you weren't."

Eli just sighed. "Frankly, I have no idea what you're talking about."

"The Marked—the four royal bloodlines and the Guardians, of which I was the first." Jaser kept speaking but the roaring in Eli's ears drowned it all out. He shook his head, tried to clear it. "The relics are for the rulers as well. Each of the four royal bloodlines that answered the call in the war received their gifts from Nestham."

"You've missed a bit. There are only three nations," Eli said. "The Plains don't have a king."

"Yes, that's true," Jaser said, his eyes flicking to the side.

"So why send you?"

A pause. "You haven't believed in Nestham for a long while, have you?" Jaser breathed.

"No." The wind outside was the chamber's only sound.

"What happened?" Jaser asked. He was, for the first time, open and honest, as the stony mask slipped from his face. As if the war hadn't changed him at all, as if years of fighting, watching comrades die beside him, hadn't left scars on his soul.

Eli let out a mirthless laugh. "You lived in a different time, Jaser. A different world. I don't know if you've kept an eye on what's happened since then, but Ekra ..." He faltered. "Ekra has changed. Five Hells, I don't even know if the Order believes anymore. Nestham knows they haven't kept His teachings."

Jaser's eyes shifted to silver flame, and he straightened, nostrils flaring. "Be careful when you use His Name. Are you not one of His Marked?"

Eli couldn't keep the laughter from his face anymore. "You keep using that word, but I don't even know if this is what I want. All this Mark has brought me is pain. Pain and torture." He hefted up the hem of his shirt, revealed the ugly brand marring his skin. "Was this Nestham's will?" he hissed.

Jaser blinked rapidly. "You've endured a lot, but that's what it means to answer Nestham's call." He hesitated. "I am truly sorry for what you've gone through."

Eli waved a dismissive hand. "The sorrow of a dead man means nothing to me."

Jaser's face tightened even further. "Nestham sent me to give you advice, but if you're just going to insult me, I'm leaving."

"Fine. Say your piece." Eli glared.

"Do you know what the star on your hand means?" Eli's stony expression said he didn't, so Jaser hurried on. "It's a part of Nestham's Shield."

Eli raised a brow. "And Kyra's?" he said.

Jaser nodded. *The same.* "A Guardian should only have loyalty to Nestham," Jaser pressed. "You are an instrument of His Will."

Eli's blood began to boil. He would never let Nestham use him like that. "After everything the Order has done, should you really expect me to have loyalty to Nestham? Forgive me if I don't take the word of a dead man as living proof."

"I left a young lady in my village when I joined the Queen's army. When Nestham chose me, I swore to have no allegiance to anyone but Him." His lips narrowed further. "We heard my village was under attack. I disobeyed Nestham's command and ran home as fast as I could." Jaser swallowed hard. "They were all slaughtered. And then, while I was away, Temero destroyed my legion as well because I wasn't there to lead them."

"That was why you said you failed," Eli breathed. Jaser's eyes froze on him and he swallowed before nodding. Eli's gaze slipped downward, but a second later a gentle hand lifted his chin. Silver eyes raged with frozen flame, trapped inside a calm expression.

"I don't want the same thing to happen to you. Because if you don't put her aside, she will die. You need to be prepared to do whatever it takes to defeat Temero." Eli drew a shuddering breath, but Jaser's next words were the killing blow. "You're leaving tomorrow. Remember where your loyalties lie."

The blizzard howled again, and the snowflakes dispersed, leaving Eli staring at a stony wall.

* * *

Remember where your loyalties lie.

He pondered it. A sole call to Nestham, setting aside all others. Jaser had been a Guardian, whatever that was. Whatever Eli was. The magic stirred inside him, almost purring as it sensed his recognition. A Guardian stood alone. Jaser had tried love, and his had died.

He couldn't make the same mistake. Not with Kyra so crucial to the coming fight. Not with her inevitable march to reclaim her throne. She'd already claimed her heirloom and her companion. Despite Eli's defiance, Alsair had been right. He had always doubted his own chances. He couldn't protect her if he got close to her. He'd failed enough people.

In his heart, he knew Kyra was far too high for him, Guardian or no. She had her own duty to her people. Not to him. There was no Mark, no sign they ever had a destiny together. Not even their powers meant that. A soft voice carried from behind him and he winced. A glance over his shoulder revealed Kyra's sleepy smile, still wrapped in her blankets. And the faint blush on her cheek, her eyes alight with the joy of *life,* of the peace that settled over her while they were snowed in ...

It was nothing more than a dream.

"Eli?" she asked, the smile now gone, her frown appearing. And that little frown, that had once made him laugh when he saw it, made him turn away even further. He couldn't have her. Would never have her. But at least he could still be her protector. Not that she needed much protecting, from what

185

he had seen. Inwardly, it began to crash, like waves breaking on him. So powerful. So powerless.

"What's wrong?" she breathed.

"Nothing." He smiled. Suspicion flickered over her face, but she smiled instead. *Duty. Honour. Sacrifice.* The words reverberated in his mind, as he took in her beauty once more. As her scent filled his senses again. As he forced his mind not to go down that road. It never could.

"You can trust me," she said.

He heaved a sigh. "I saw that man from the painting," he began, and her eyes widened, the only sign of her surprise. "He told me Nestham sent him." Each sentence increased the shock on her face.

"What did he say?" He had to admire her for ignoring the impossibility of it all, not bothering to question it.

"He questioned my loyalties. Said that this Mark," he said, clenching his fist in front of him, "means my duty is to Nestham alone. Anything else is just a distraction I can't afford."

Anger burned in her eyes. "A distraction?" she hissed.

He tried to be gentle, he really tried. "I don't think I have much of a choice in my life now." Taken from him by a cold-eyed god and his undead servant.

"We always have a choice, Eli. What matters is what we choose." He sighed and left, feeling winter's bite now more than ever. As he left the room, Eli brushed his hand over misted eyes. Leaving Kyra stony-faced behind.

* * *

Alsair and Monsun sat side-by-side outside the sleeping chamber, Monsun drowsily rubbing his eyes. The Vindicator was still barefoot, but at least he hadn't bumped into the wall on his walk this time, thanks to the monk following him out. Alsair rubbed his stump and heaved a sigh. Rushing footsteps ringing

186

on cold stone made them jerk their heads up. Kyra froze when she saw them, Nix peeping from her arms. The princess blinked once and vanished in a heartbeat.

"What happened there?" Monsun murmured.

"I guess he told her what he thinks will happen," Alsair replied.

"What, that he will face Temero and be victorious in a glorious battle?" Monsun said sardonically.

"They're too unpredictable," Alsair sighed. "Both of them. At first, I thought it was just Eli, but Kyra is just as wild in her own way."

"He is dangerous, that one," Monsun murmured. The tone in his voice—he'd already thought of Eli as a threat to his kingdom. As an opponent. As a target.

Alsair needed to persuade him otherwise. "I know. He's a living flame, and she's a rock. I thought the two of them would have been enough to win, but I guess they're too volatile."

"I guess even you can be fooled."

"It's hard to fool me," Alsair murmured as he twisted, staring into Monsun's night-dark eyes. "The one you seek isn't in Imbra. They were once, but not anymore."

Monsun's chuckle rang hollow. "I sought all of you, remember? I lost my horse along the way. And now I am trapped here until Eli releases me."

"That's not who I'm talking about," Alsair continued.

Monsun's eyes widened. "They still live?"

"Yes."

The Vindicator exhaled slowly. "Then so does hope."

Chapter 25

Eli crept back into the chamber as the dawn's rays splintered through the glittering crystal. Dark rings underlined bloodshot eyes in a haggard face. Though he did his best not to look, he noted how Kyra sat, with her knees drawn in, eyes on the floor. Another pang of guilt sliced into his heart.

Monsun was still dozing as he stalked past. Out of the corner of his eye, Amora stirred, her boyish hair tousled from sleep. As he glanced at her, a wicked gleam flickered in her dark eyes, the mischief of a born urchin, and she threw off the blankets and leaped onto Monsun. Eli inhaled swiftly, freezing in place. But the Vindicator merely smiled and let the young girl crawl onto him, tucking her head into his neck. A callused hand the size of Amora's face gently clasped around her own. Eli's breath hissed in a smile and he raised a brow. Apparently, the girl had been working her magic on the Vindicator whilst they had been trapped here, going from a stony warrior to a gentle giant.

He reached forward to the stone wall where Jaser had been not hours ago. The snow leopard glimmered in the crystal's light, a shimmering gold on grey stone. He sucked in a breath and pressed his hand on the stone. The earth rumbled, and the wall retracted away, vanished into the ground.

Nothing but clear blue skies above a whitened landscape. Jaser was right. "Finally," he breathed, a prayer into the endless blue. But with that, a pang of worry. Where would they go next? When he turned back around, all had awoken and faced him.

"I—I guess we can leave now," he stammered. After all this time, after all the joy and terror. The past days had shaped him in ways he couldn't understand.

188

"Where will you go?" Alsair asked him. And that was it. He could leave, couldn't he? He had no part to play.

No. That was the doubt talking. The fear. His Mark said otherwise. The same magic his predecessor had used to kill a demon. He could do the same, even if it meant losing everything.

"Imbra, I suppose," he said. "If Temero really has returned, it may be a good place to look."

"We need to get back as soon as possible, even if the Order is looking for us," Kyra said, without so much as a glance at him.

"We should not return immediately. Not without more information," Monsun said. "I expect much has changed whilst we have been here." Kyra glared at him, and the steel in her eyes was like a knife to the gut. Monsun raised his hands in supplication. "There is a town just a little out of our way, about half a day east of the route, called Rankil. I have a contact who was meant to pass through there soon. We should stop by and see what we can find out."

"But first," Amora said with gusto, "breakfast." Eli and Kyra were statues as the others smiled slightly.

The group was silent as they filed down the winding passageways, Eli hefting the Eternal Torch. Monsun walked beside him, scanning the map. The sound of clinking metal signalled Amora's steps behind him, with absurd amounts of finery stashed in a bag she had found. It was almost bigger than her. Alsair paced beside her and Kyra brought up the rear, the diadem now stashed in a pack and the staff in her hand.

Eli stumbled as a ball of fur wound between his legs, violet eyes gleaming in the shadows. He swore as Nix prowled off. "Can't you control your animal?" he hissed under his breath.

"Who says I'm not?" Kyra yelled from behind him.

189

The others stopped and glanced between them. Eli met Alsair's eyes, the concern and questions written across them. He shook his head a fraction. The monk's nod of understanding made his heart break further. At last they approached the entrance door, the one they had entered too many days ago, as fugitives and soldiers.

Eli heaved himself at the door, gritted his teeth and yanked the ancient stone towards him. Nothing.

"It must be stuck with all of that snow." Monsun joined him in pulling. They grunted with the exertion, but nothing. Kyra grimaced and stepped forward, putting her strength behind the movement. With a squeal, the door slid towards them.

Snow piled onto them, burying Eli under the frigid weight, filling his mouth and forcing the breath from his lungs. The cold bit at his senses, like a familiar touch he would do anything to forget. Minutes of exposure, horrible, racking chills ... the descent into darkness. His heartbeat pounded wildly, and he thrashed in the snow. A horrible screech rang throughout the chamber.

A hand pushed through the snow and grabbed his own. Without thinking, he latched onto it with all his strength and let it yank him from the freezing embrace, the white death. He placed his hands on his knees, begging his flailing heart to restore itself. Minutes later, when he finally looked up, Kyra's steely gaze met his own before she marched off to join Amora. The staff was taut in her right hand, whilst her sword remained strapped over her right shoulder. Eli's hands gradually grew numb from the constant touch of the snow as they scooped out the blockage on the door.

Once they finished, he shoved his hands into his jerkin and glanced at Monsun.

"Which—which way to Rankil?" he said through chattering teeth. The burly man didn't remove his hands from

190

his pockets, instead nodded back the way they had come, the twisting mountain paths.

* * *

With every stride, Eli's calves sank into the snow's numbing embrace. Soon his legs and shoes were sodden, and each miserable step strained his muscles. The sun's rays did nothing to help as his breath misted over at midday. Amora struggled most of all, with considerably shorter legs. Within minutes, Monsun had removed his axe from over his shoulder and hefted the girl up so she slipped her arms around his neck and rode on his back. Hour upon hour they trekked, until Monsun halted them.

Kyra sniffed the air once, twice. "Wood smoke." Eli did the same and swore. How had he missed that? The sun was already racing for the horizon, as brilliant golden rays scattered over the west.

The pillar of smoke rose into the sky to the east, just on the edge of a thickly forested valley. Eli nudged Alsair and pointed, hardly daring to whisper into his ear as his eyes landed on the familiar, hated, red and black uniform. "Order soldiers." His stomach churned, as the utter wreckage and destruction the Order had left in its wake flickered through his mind. He could tell Alsair's thoughts were drifting the same way, as jade eyes glazed over, and the monk staggered on, not his usual stride.

"Put the Torch down or you'll get us all killed," Kyra hissed. Eli startled and lowered the Torch out of sight.

"This route has become a lot more dangerous," Monsun rumbled. Eli glanced at him, noted the intense gaze and the sagging shoulders supporting precious cargo. "We go south-west, then circle around. We are too tired to engage right now and cannot risk an open confrontation."

191

"That would mean we'd need to cross the Kinar River. We won't have long if spring is almost here," Alsair said.

The wind picked up again, rippling over Eli's skin, biting through the jerkin. The men in the distance stirred. One looked over his shoulder in their direction, away from their fire flickering in the breeze. A low snarl cut through the air as Nix dropped to the ground, violet eyes already narrowed in anticipation. Kyra merely stooped and picked her up, muttering soothing words under her breath.

Without speaking, they crouched low, seeking cover behind the scattered trees and headed in the opposite direction. Every crunch on the snow, every stumbled step, made Eli's head spin. Once they were out of earshot, his muscles relaxed, but they still moved with caution. After some time, Monsun placed Amora back on the ground to continue on her own legs, and they moved even slower.

An hour later, the landscape shifted, as the snowy earth became dotted with trees, though they were mere shadows in the winter. Another few weeks, and life would bloom once again. Eli wondered if they would even live to see it. A wet plop sounded on Eli's hair as melting snow ran through it, and Amora let out a tiny giggle. He forced a grin at her and smeared the snow across her face. She jumped back, vigorously rubbing her skin to warm it up. The smile she wore was brighter than any he'd ever seen before, and something lifted in his chest.

At last, they stopped at the shimmering course of ice gleaming in the noonday sun, winding all the way from the northern mountains and cutting through Imbra. The Kinar River.

"We're lucky," Alsair said. "Another day and spring might be too near to risk the crossing." He noticed Amora was shuddering slightly and moved to put an arm around her protectively, but Monsun was already there. The girl leaned into his bulk and warmth. "Even so," the monk continued, "one at a time."

"There has to be another way," Kyra demanded. Alsair rebuffed her with a gentle shake of the head, but she jerked her head at Eli. "What about his vambraces?"

He shook his head. "I don't know if I can carry people into the Rift, but it doesn't matter, anyway. I wouldn't be able to make the distance multiple times. One way or another we have to cross this river on foot."

"I will go first," Monsun said. "If it holds for me, it will hold for the rest of you." The Vindicator ruffled Amora's short hair and smiled widely, though his eyes betrayed his fear. The burly man paced away from them to the frozen banks of the river, and Eli's throat closed over. He let out a quiet cough, tried not to show his nerves.

Monsun froze at the bank, bowed his head. A muttering of a strange language reached Eli's ears. His mind worked to decipher it.

Of course. Khaavi, the language of Biralam, the Southern Desert. Monsun's homeland. The Vindicator was praying. Despite his calm stance, he was worried.

The thought knocked the breath out of Eli's lungs and he took a step forward, as if to pull Monsun back. There could be another way, they could turn back—Monsun took his first step onto the frozen water. A creak ripped through the air and Kyra gasped softly next to Eli. A single tear fell to the icy ground beneath her, but when he glanced at her, the fiery gleam had lit behind her eyes. The fierce determination that had carried her through prison and the mountains. Monsun slowly but surely made it to the other side and the knot in Eli's stomach loosened slightly.

Amora steeled herself and marched forward, the kingdom's worth of treasure in the sack on her back clinking with every step. The girl's small size helped her, and she pattered across the ice. Alsair followed Monsun's example and muttered some words under his breath. Before he took his first step, he glanced at Eli, then flicked his eyes to the steely figure of the young woman next to him. Eli sighed and waited until the monk was across before turning to Kyra. The princess glared at him, anger lining every core of her being.

"Are you going to be okay?" he murmured. His hand twitched once, but he clenched it into a fist, stepped back, damped it back down. Duty over his heart. That was the lesson Jaser had taught him.

"I'm fine," she hissed and stalked away, the staff clenched in her hand. She motioned for Nix to go and the cub scampered over the river, skittering on the ice before reaching the other side. Alone on the northern bank, he could only watch the retreating figure on the frozen water, the fury clear in her taut muscles. He had caused this.

He had never felt a deeper shame, for getting close to her, protecting her and then turning tail and running. Beyond her, Alsair had his head bowed in a posture Eli had seen countless times, yet something nagged at him.

Silence. His flesh rippling, his mind sharpening, his Mark flickering, his power growing. A phantom hand tapped his shoulder. Alsair's eyes opened wide, and he opened his mouth to yell.

But it was already too late. In Kyra's anger, she moved carelessly. One part of the ice had taken too many injuries over the last few minutes to sustain her.

And as she stepped onto it, it smashed open. A large hole ripped open in the ice as if Nestham himself had torn it in two. Kyra's scream shattered through the frozen air, to be cut off abruptly as she plunged into the icy depths. Leaving nothing but raging water behind.

It was that quick. One moment she was there, the next, gone. The phantom hand pushed Eli forth, and he sprinted across the ice, slamming into the frozen surface, cracks spreading behind him, the ice snapping and snapping and snapping under his weight. He didn't care.

He hurled his bow and Eternal Torch over the rest of the river to Alsair and leaped, hands outstretched, breath sucked in. He arced into the hole.

Darkness swallowed him completely. The cold was a punch to the gut, sapping all the energy from him, draining his very life. Almost immediately his muscles lost their strength, spirit stolen by the chill's inevitable onslaught.

His arms gave out, the numbness pushing through his entire body, his breathing slowing.

Perhaps it wouldn't be so bad just to sleep here, to rest and let the others keep going.

After all he'd seen, couldn't he just stop?

Please?

No. He wouldn't accept that. His duty was to protect everyone, and Kyra was part of that. Anything else was irrelevant. His magic flared, a beacon in the river's night. His lungs ached, begging for more air that he couldn't give them. An answering flash of gold lit up the bank, and his arms found new strength. He swam towards the light, the one he'd been searching for all his life. What he wished he could have.

The light flickered, then vanished, just in front of him. His crystal light illuminated Kyra's face, frozen in fear, her eyes wide and swollen. His pulse roared in his ears, blocking out everything else that could possibly be part of this world. There was no way he could swim back up there with her.

Kyra's eyes closed, and the last remnants of breath bubbled away, escaping to the surface. A silent scream rang through Eli's mind. He pulled her into a tight grip, praying to Nestham for the first time in months, and crossed his arms.

* * *

Alsair's hand was trembling as the seconds passed. He should have done something, should have *seen* better. A flash of light and Kyra and Eli appeared at his feet, the latter gasping for breath. The former ... nothing. She didn't move.

"No ..." Eli gasped as he knelt over her, shivering with cold as freezing water dripped off him. "Nestham, please. Don't take her yet," he pleaded. Whether the water clinging to his face was from the river or tears, Alsair did not know. Perhaps it was a gift from Nestham, but Kyra's Mark flared. Only a pulse of light. But her chest began to rise and fall.

Eli's gasp of relief echoed Monsun's, but by the time Kyra opened her eyes, he stood with Alsair, many steps away.

* * *

Kyra's vision blurred, from water or tears, she didn't know. However, she recognised the towering figure looming over her, the gleaming silver tattoo shimmering in the weak sun.

"How are you feeling?" Monsun rumbled. It was strange how such a deep voice, utterly used to barking orders, could be so soothing. Kyra tried to sit up, but her head swam and she dropped back to the snow.

"I think I'm going to vomit," she muttered. Seconds later, bile scorched up the back of her throat. Monsun leaned out of the way as partially-digested ibex and water landed in what was once pristine snow. Once she finished retching, she lay back on the snow, but her wandering gaze fell on Eli. A brief flash of something like pity flickered into his eyes, but before she could check, he was already looking away, anywhere but at her.

"What—" She breathed. "What—" She coughed again. A pitiful noise for a princess to make, a cold voice hissed inside her. She began shivering violently, but before she could cry out, Monsun was there with his cloak. He wrapped it around her, and together he and Amora rubbed the dry cloth over her sodden and frozen clothes. She sank gratefully against the Vindicator's side and leaned into his warmth.

"Eli got you out," Alsair said. The young man shot a glare at the old Jinnam monk. But seconds later, Kyra knew it. A bond snapped into place between them, magic that crackled silently with power, incredible power. Unbreakable save for death. Another life debt owed to the young Guardian. Eli felt it too, she saw. The sudden intake of breath as the energy thrummed through them, as it connected him with Monsun.

But he turned instead to Alsair. "I don't want this," he said. "I shouldn't have this." He met the monk's green eyes, eyes of the now-scorched grass around Mount Sancti. And then he spoke the words that chilled Kyra's heart, weak as she was. "How do I get rid of it?"

Despite the struggle to keep her mask, she couldn't keep her eyes from pricking. Alsair's silence was almost condemning. He beckoned the Guardian closer. The brutal words were uttered behind her, as much as she ached to turn and stop him.

"Princess Kyra, I absolve you of this life debt. I have no claim on you save that of my responsibilities as Guardian. Do you accept?" A cough caught in her throat, so she tried to shake her head into Monsun's shoulder. A reassuring arm wrapped around her shoulders, a Vindicator comforting his Princess. But her refusal was irrelevant. The bond snapped and withered away as if it had never been.

And then the cold set in for real. Her chills came again. A callused hand lifted her chin, and a muffled curse rang by her ear as she slipped into unconsciousness.

197

Chapter 26

Monsun scooped up Kyra's limp form, and her staff clattered to the ground, released at last. Not even the river had been enough to tear it from her grip.

"We don't have enough time to walk to Rankil, and we can't stay here. The cold will kill her," he said.

Eli's breath caught in his throat. "But Rankil is still three hours away," he said.

"Three hours for a normal person," Alsair interjected. They all looked at him. He hesitated, but lifted his head high. "How is your magic?"

Eli closed his eyes and peered inside himself to the stirring fire of his gift. It snapped, ready for him to unleash. "I can manage." He tightened his belt and nodded, passed his bow and quiver to Alsair. Somehow, his arrows had stayed in the quiver when he went in, though he'd need to check them later. Monsun passed Kyra to him and he hefted her over one shoulder. She seemed so small now, so frail, as she was nothing but dead weight. Her breathing was so quiet. He plummeted into his magic, the strength that would allow him to sprint while carrying her.

"Rankil is in a valley due south," Alsair instructed him. Despite the urge to run, Alsair's piercing green eyes held him fast while he explained. "If you go straight, you'll fall off a cliff. Once you reach the cliffs, head right to make it down to the valley floor."

"Understood," he said through gritted teeth.

"Be safe," Monsun said. A tenderness crossed his face before he locked it away.

Eli turned south. Blue light glittered off the river once more as he took off, leaving three humans and one snow leopard long behind.

His legs churned, thudding over the snow, as he did his best to hold Kyra steady, regretting any bump he gave her. In another time, he would have enjoyed the incredible speed with which he ran. Trees flew past as he neatly sidestepped roots and sprinted south, heading for Rankil. He ducked under a tree branch and pivoted to the side, leaping over an icy ditch.

About half an hour passed before he halted for breath, taking down gulps of air as his magic worked to keep him upright. His power was growing. Either that, or some skills burnt through it more quickly than others. He checked Kyra, but her breathing was already so faint. He swore and kept running, prayers escaping his lips along the way.

Before long, he was clattering across icy rock and he skidded to a stop barely a step away from the drop. The world stretched out before him, pale and cold, and Rankil nestled in the shadow of the cliffs—nothing but a few houses. He glanced to his right. Sure enough, the path got easier, winding down to the valley floor. Kyra's breathing fell to a rasp, and her magic, which had been sustaining her all this time, died.

He swore and his head whipped back and forth, analysing his options. There was no way she could survive the trip across the cliffs; it would take too long. But he couldn't jump or climb down the cliffs. Unless—he glanced at his hands. One numb, drained. The other glowing blue, flickering as his power dimmed. He didn't know if he could carry people into the Rift.

Well, now there was nothing but to try. He summoned a deep breath and closed his eyes. Crashed his vambraces together. He fell through darkness, through drifting sights and smells, but one picture remained clear in his mind—the snowy floor. When he opened his eyes, he was standing on the ground, Kyra still balanced on his shoulder.

His magic sputtered and died, but he staggered up to the most brightly lit building, his hands shaking with the loss of power. Black nudged at the corners of his vision, but he forced his way inside the tavern. The laughter and discussions fell silent as thirty men and women looked at him. He took one more stumbling step.

A matronly woman bustled up to him and pinched his skin. He grimaced, but she was already checking Kyra. Her mouth tightened.

"Give me a hand here," she said. Two men rose from the tables and knelt next to Kyra, picking her up. Eli snarled and rose, but the matron waved him down.

"It's okay, I'll take care of her. Come with me." She held her hand out, and he took it and followed her into a quiet room, complete with blankets and a roaring fire. The men placed Kyra by the fire and left the room. The matron checked her one last time, then nodded.

"Keep her warm and yell if you need me." Eli collapsed next to Kyra.

He was barely coherent enough to hear when the outer door banged open again some hours later and the other three filed into the tavern.

"Where is the boy with silver eyes?" Monsun rumbled.

"Nobody of that description here," the matron said.

"He came here with a girl. They would have been exhausted."

"Nope, nobody springs to mind. Can I get you anything?"

"We're their friends." Footsteps came closer. "And I expect you left them, right about here." The door opened, revealing Alsair's smiling face. He stepped in, turned, and immediately ducked under a stout club. "I keep telling you, we're their friends," he smiled.

The matron paused and glanced at Eli. He nodded weakly. "Oh well, alright. Soup for the lot of you then?"

Alsair nodded once, and she headed off. Monsun, after a nudge and passing of coins, followed her. Eli's head spun, but he pushed to keep himself awake.

"How are you feeling?" Alsair murmured.

"Tired," Eli breathed. He couldn't offer anything else.

The monk gave him a smile. "Well done."

Monsun trudged in, exhaustion in his steps yet joy on his face. "I spoke to the landlady. Kyra will be fine. However, she will be tired for a while." They all breathed a collective sigh of relief. Eli drifted back off to sleep.

When he awoke, Alsair, Monsun and Amora were holding conference around bowls of soup by the fire. Their voices were low, and his magic was too weak to allow him to hear that far.

He turned to Kyra's prone form. Her skin was so pale it reflected the firelight, but her breathing was steady.

"This never should have happened," he breathed. "I'm so sorry. I wish I could do what I want, but I don't think I have that choice anymore. I'm sorry." He knew she could never hear the words, and this was the only way he could say them. "I really messed up. Duty is a hard thing to live with, apparently."

Footsteps sounded behind him and he met Alsair's eyes again. "Mind if I sit?" Alsair asked. Eli nodded, and the man dropped to the ground with a grunt and massaged his legs.

"Ah, that's better," he chuckled. "Too long on these old legs is getting to be a pain." His gaze settled on Eli and he frowned. "How are you holding up, boy?"

"Not great," Eli muttered.

"And how's your *duty*?"

Eli just dropped his head into his hands. "Terrible. Is this what it's like? To have nothing but the mission? It just seems like, no matter what I do, I end up hurting someone."

"Well, what do you think Nestham is about?" Alsair asked.

Eli blinked in confusion. "He's a God. The Order said he's all about judgement and justice. And you cannot see him without dying."

"Why are you using the Order's teachings? You lived as a Jinnam. Did I teach you nothing at Mount Sancti?" Alsair demanded with a soft smile. "Tell me—what's the first lesson I gave you when you picked up a sword?"

"Careful, it's sharp," Eli quoted, in an impression of the old soldier-turned-monk.

Alsair chuckled. "After that."

A sharp intake of breath as realisation dawned on Eli. "A man uses a weapon for two reasons. Killing what he hates—or protecting those he loves."

Alsair nodded slowly, and for once Eli understood.

"Nestham is love, Eli, even if you can't look at Him. Love and forgiveness and so much more. Yes, the Order says judgement and justice. But the Order is just one faith of many. The Eternal Order was born out of the Demon War. Portraying Nestham's strength. But the Jinnam focus on his love and forgiveness. And peace, Eli." Alsair's eyes were kind, gentle.

"I mean, He sent Jaser, and Jaser preached just the opposite."

"Jaser Cathom? The Guardian?" Alsair let out a bark of laughter, and for the first time, Eli met his eyes which danced with amusement, yet shadows lurked there. "Jaser was a fool to think he knew what it was to be a Guardian."

"But he was a hero!" Eli exclaimed. "He saved the four kingdoms!"

202

"Oh yes," Alsair said. "Yes, he did. But he had already lost everything because of his own pride and arrogance. Jaser is as biased as all mortals are, whether living or dead. We can't cut ourselves off, Eli. Otherwise, we have nothing to fight for. You didn't jump into a freezing river because of your duty. Just as she"—he inclined his head at Kyra—"didn't run into a blizzard because of duty. She revealed her identity as a princess for *you,* Eli. Not even for her own throne did she do that."

Kyra stirred, and he nudged Eli with his stump. "You shouldn't be here when she wakes," he said.

With a last tender look at Kyra, Eli unbuckled his sword. Even if he shouldn't deny his feelings, this would be a bad time for any sort of talk. He needed fresh air. Needed to run, to remind himself why he was here, what he was doing. Needed to feel the blood pound in his ears until he couldn't think, until there was only one thing left.

It was pitch-black outside by the time he left the inn, ignoring the bustle of people who took one look at him and moved aside hurriedly. He moved like a warrior. Not with the swagger of the dangerous, but the quiet confidence of the deadly. Once the streets were clear, an irrepressible smile crept over his face. The magic, drained to the last drop on his flight here, had replenished in his deep sleep, nourished by food. He dropped into his power and *ran,* shedding any pretence he was just like the townspeople who had walked past. His legs churned as the magic within him ebbed and flowed, responding to his needs and filling him with the energy to press on. Trees blurred past him and he revelled in the euphoria.

One log remained in his path and he merely leaped, carrying far over the fallen tree and skidding on the snow. He drew to a halt, panting in the midnight air. He'd never been a fan of the nights. Too many issues with sleeping. No, it was the mornings when he found his joy. The early fog dissipating in the creeping sun, and the way the forest creatures appeared in peace, with gentle song and breath. Until he selected one for dinner.

He slumped on a fallen log, relished the feeling of the bark beneath his fingers. The new moon, Nestham's Shadow, was nowhere to be seen.

Only the stars kept him company now. But he refused to look at the glittering jewels above him. Since Miriel, they were as foreign to him as the depths of the ocean. Even as a child he'd never enjoyed them, and even less so when he'd arrived at the mountain monastery where he was forged.

Where a part of him had died in that explosion.

But Kyra had. She'd stared into the night sky and asked the stars their secrets. He kept his face turned to the ground until snow stirred around him and a figure sat next to him on the log. He didn't even need to look before sighing.

"What now?" he asked Jaser.

The dead Guardian merely stared at him. "You cut her off completely. I must say, I didn't expect that."

"You practically told me to. Your surprise means nothing to me," Eli snapped back.

Jaser's eyes almost appeared hurt and his outline flickered slightly.

"What, no comebacks this time?" Eli asked bitterly. "You were practically bursting to tell me to leave her, last we spoke."

Jaser's hand reached to Eli's shoulder and rested there, but it had no physical feeling. Not this time. "Strange," Jaser breathed.

Eli glanced at him. "What?"

"Your power, it's weaker than I expected," the Guardian said. "Exactly half of mine."

"Do you have any nice things to say?" Eli shot back.

Jaser merely ignored him, glowing silver eyes looking beyond the horizon.

"Can you see the future?" Eli asked, much softer.

Jaser's focus snapped back to him. "No," he said after a pause. "Besides Nestham, there is only one who has that power, but I am forbidden to talk to them until the appointed time." Eli nodded beside him, trying to contain the whirling emotions inside his mind. "Happy Lanmane, Eli." The festival of spring. Eli's brows shot up in surprise. He hadn't known it was so close. This time last year, the monks would have celebrated with wine and the food they had made over winter. He dropped into his memory, the familiar sights and smells. But they were all gone. His eyes began to mist over at the thought. So entrenched he was in his thoughts, he barely heard what Jaser said. "—keep an eye out," Jaser continued, as if he hadn't noticed Eli's distraction.

"For what?" Eli asked. But Jaser had vanished, back to whatever abyss he inhabited. Eli swore under his breath, the curse emerging as just a puff of mist. Time to head back. But the wild run from the river to Rankil had put warnings in his mind, deep, powerful ones. He wouldn't stand a chance if he didn't know his limits. How far could he really Rift? He crossed his vambraces and leaped into the darkness, keeping the image of the tavern in his mind, bright and cheerful and bursting with life. When he emerged, he had jumped about a hundred paces.

Good enough for short distances or a surprise attack. But nothing more. He crossed the threshold twice more, each time spending even more time in the Rift, before keeling over and gasping for breath, hands tingling with that familiar numbness of being sapped of power. It had drained him dry, and would take a few hours to replenish. But it seemed it was not how many times he jumped, but how far. After all, he had Rifted countless times around Kyra the last time they sparred.

Eli shook his head and began the long walk back to the inn. When he re-entered the tavern, the matron glanced at him and pointed at the stairs. He nodded and found Amora and Monsun in a dingy room, the former fast asleep, the latter doing press-ups on the floor.

"Am I interrupting something?" Eli asked. Monsun scowled, and with a glance at Amora motioned for him to be quiet. Eli hurriedly waved an apology and dropped his voice to a whisper. "Any trace of your army?" he asked.

Monsun sighed and sat back on his legs. "Nothing. They should have had a few scouts here at least, before they patrolled north and then east. Barbarians sometimes raid across the Eastern border, rovers from the Plains, so perhaps they went to check there."

"And you're sure they will still recognise you as their leader? You've been gone a while. At best, they think you're delayed. And at worst ..." he trailed off. *A traitor.*

Monsun nodded. "They're loyal men."

He nodded and closed the door, found an empty room. He curled up on the mattress, too exhausted to notice how lumpy it was. The morning found him gasping for breath and drenched in sweat. He went down to the taproom, finding only Alsair there.

"Good sleep, boy?" Alsair asked, and although his eyes betrayed the lie there, Eli nodded.

"We can stay here one more night," Alsair continued. "Monsun needs to scout the remaining area, Kyra won't be able to travel long distances yet, and I think the celebration would do us all good."

Jaser's words snapped back into his mind and he jerked. "Yes, the celebration. Sounds good." He brushed down his jerkin and went to grab his bow.

"Where are you going?"

"Hunting. Should make a few coins to spend tonight."

He returned a few hours later to find the town already set in motion. The day had fined up, and the sun shone bright, even if it was still a little cold. Smiles abounded as unlit lanterns decorated the square, hoisted above the outskirts, and tables were already being raised full of food. And despite the festivity, he had never felt so empty.

Chapter 27

Eli bustled into the inn and blended into the crowd, eyes darting around until he alighted on the table where his companions sat assembled. "Well, ready for a party?" he grinned, though it didn't reach his eyes. Kyra didn't even look at him.

"I will not be joining you," Monsun said. "My contact is meeting me here tonight. He should have information on whatever the hells has happened since we left."

Eli nodded. Kyra shoved her chair away from the table, her face stony. He winced as it grated across the floor, a deep groan that set his teeth on edge. "Excuse us," she said, nodding to Amora. "We need to get ready."

"For what?" Eli said with a raised brow.

"The party," she said, in a tone that matched the mountain wind's chill. Kyra ushered the urchin ahead of her and they disappeared upstairs.

"That could have gone better." Alsair shook his head. "That said, she's hurt."

Eli just hung his face in his hands. "I don't know what to do," he mumbled. "I know what you said, and I'm trying, but I feel like I may have just done too much damage." His voice quietened. "I miss her, Alsair."

"Then tell her. But it won't be easy," his mentor warned. "Heartbreak is not easily forgiven, but she's strong. Nestham knows, she's been through enough."

"I don't deserve her forgiveness," Eli mused. "She offered me everything, and I turned her away."

The corners of Alsair's mouth quirked. Eli tensed at the sight, but Alsair waved his aggression down.

"You have more of a chance than you think, boy."

Eli excused himself and found time to help in the celebrations. Even though he was an unfamiliar face, an open smile and an offer of help were always welcome in backwater towns. He should know. How long had it been since he was in these same festivities in Laif? Before his family had died and his mother had brought him to the Jinnam. He must have been a boy then. According to Alsair, he was still one.

The skies shifted to a shimmering red as the sun dipped below the horizon. The lanterns burst into flames and flickering light bathed the square. Noise swelled from the musicians on the simple wooden stage. Belatedly, Eli realised he was still in his travel-stained clothes, but it was too late now. He dipped his hand in a nearby bucket of water and brushed the grime off his face as best he could, smiling at a matronly woman. She nudged the young daughter beside her, wide-eyed and unsure. Eli stepped away hurriedly. That was one aspect of small-town life he hadn't missed.

A hand clapped him on the shoulder, and Alsair thrust a mug of drink in his hands. "Just one," he warned the boy with a warm smile. Eli grinned and took a sip. And promptly spat it out, the bitter taste lingering on his tongue.

"What the hells was that?" he demanded.

"I see my work here is done," Alsair grinned. "You won't want to drink for years."

"What did you do?" Eli snorted.

"An old concoction us monks used to use on each other to have some fun."

"You used to have fun? Seems I was missing out on it all."

"Aye, we had fun. But parties like these," he said, his gaze turning wistful, "aren't to be missed." He closed his eyes, almost waiting for something. He clapped his hand on Eli's shoulder. "Go have fun tonight," he said.

"You not going to stay?"

"I'm not feeling too well," he said. "I think I might just take a nap." He disappeared into the tavern before Eli could protest. Suddenly, he was the only single person in the square, and he hurriedly stepped back to the edge of the circle.

Eli hung around the food tables, watching how these people blended and melded together, laughing and dancing. The band on the raised dais struck a merry tune, and they changed partners. Out of the corner of his eye, a group of several pretty girls flicked occasional glances his way, and he smiled at them, but also noticed an opposite group of young men shooting him slightly more hostile looks, sizing him up.

He had just decided this party was not for him when Amora appeared at his side, clad in a beautiful green gown. Her short hair remained the same, still as boyish as ever, yet joy sparkled in her eyes. He smiled at her, yet something nagged at him. Something was different. Those eyes. Was that—makeup?

"I'm not hiding anymore," she said and his heart swelled at the thought. That she felt safe enough, despite the danger, to be herself. Far from the urchin who had tried to steal his gold, less than two weeks ago.

"Enjoying the party?" she asked.

"Of course," he smiled.

"You're still a terrible liar, gruntah." He ducked his head so she wouldn't see the red blooming on his cheeks.

"Maybe I can make this evening better," she smiled and pointed to the right, to the steps leading down from the tavern.

His breath caught in his throat as he beheld Kyra standing on the dais. Her lithe form, cut with muscle, showed through the shimmering blue dress. She stood tall, proud, and utterly beautiful. Her imperious gaze swung down over the entire square. Even as he stood stunned, he could make out the swinging gazes of several young men. One grinned as if he were a wolf hunting prey, and lurched off his seat to make his way towards her, all broad shoulders and narrow hips.

"She doesn't want to speak to me," he said, even though he wished the opposite was true.

"Oh, Eli," Amora sighed. "So powerful, and you can't even see what's in front of your face."

"What?" he said.

Her little grin became fierce. "She *likes* you, gruntah." The world stopped around Eli and his heart, once chained behind *duty* and *sacrifice* burst free. Unshackled, unchained, untethered. Free.

"So go get her," Amora said and jumped behind him, grunting as she pushed him forward. He resisted, and she scrabbled on the snow to move him. He took a hesitant step, then another, like he was in a daze, until he was stumbling forward, only intent on Kyra.

As he got closer, he noticed even more details. Like the way her dress made her eyes shine, or the way she went slack as she met his gaze. He smiled at her, his heart rising into his chest, the thump turning into a marcher's drum. Her returning smile stretched too wide, but her eyes were pure ice. Then she took the arm of the wolfish boy and spun into the middle of the circle.

Eli sagged back to the post, the breath knocked out of him. He could only watch as she danced them all to shame, never once fumbling on the footwork or the timing. He shouldn't have been surprised, considering her royal upbringing and combat training.

Even so, the way the other boy's brown gaze roved over her made his hands clench, to the point his fingers left indents on his palms. Her gaze she fixed firmly on her partner's eyes, and it would be impossible to miss his wandering view.

She just didn't care anymore.

The music finished with a sweet final note, cheers and applause breaking out across the crowd. He stirred and marched towards her, each step taking him too close and yet nowhere at all. Kyra detached herself from the young man, took two steps away from him, but he began to pull at her, demanding another round. She looked at the young man for the first time, really looked at him, and pulled away. He grabbed her around the waist and pulled her back into the circle.

Tried to, at least. Kyra couldn't have lashed out, not in a place where a woman fighting like a storm would start rumours. So she did it subtly, a neat trip to his leg. Eli did the rest, elbowing him in the ribs and wrapping his arms around Kyra just as the music began again. Though he tried not to notice her lithe muscle, he was impressed. She stiffened, arms locking by her side, and his heart began to crack, a tiny fragment splintering off into the night. They faltered until her arms wrapped around his waist and they stepped together. His breath, held for an eternity, began to relax. The music increased in tempo, not a mere backyard dance, but the band showing skills, driving rhythms and a wild beat.

"You shouldn't be doing this," she muttered. He glanced down at her, met those depthless eyes glaring at him.

"What? Defending your honour?" he shot back, immediately regretting it as she bared her teeth.

"No, you don't need to defend my honour. I mean dancing with me at all," she said. "I thought it interfered with your *duty*. Don't you need to remain unattached?" she hissed.

"Kyra, I'm sorry," he said. And he meant it. Nestham above, he meant it from the bottom of his heart. Vaguely, he was aware of how fast they were moving, how utterly matched they were in footwork and style, despite their upbringings. But the rest of the world had faded away, and there was only the two of them. She stepped back into a perfect spin, and he could only marvel at how effortlessly she moved.

"What for? For pushing me away, or forcing me to dance with you?"

He winced. "I pushed you away for a reason. I'm following Jaser's instructions—"

"*Jaser's instructions?*" she spat, stepping forward with him. "Alsair told me all about this resurrected bastard, and you want to follow his advice? He was a lonely man who died horribly." He spun her once, twice. She leaned back as he leaned forward, just centimetres away, and smoothly dropped her into a dip. "I just don't want you to make the same mistake," she breathed. Her breath misted into the air as they paused, parallel to the stones.

"I need to do this, Kyra. And I don't think I'll come back. So there's no point in getting close to me when I will probably die, anyway." They pulled back upright.

"I think just the opposite—" she began to say, and her attention snagged and she stiffened again.

"What?" he asked, but she ignored him. Instead, she pivoted them away from the whirling circle, still gracefully keeping step with the dance. The music seemed to fade away as she peered over his shoulder.

"I thought I'd never see him again ..." she murmured. Eli followed her glance, twisting over his shoulder, but all he saw was a hood being raised over a shock of red hair, just as a tightly wound black braid fell out from the hood. The figure disappeared into the tavern.

"Who?" he asked, but she swallowed. Once. Twice. Her face paled, and her eyes widened, as if whatever fear had hold of her was rooted deep within her.

"Trayse," she coughed out. His heart stopped. The man who had betrayed her and caused the deaths of her second

213

family. He reached within, brushed the roiling storm of power—but he wouldn't let it flare. Not yet.

"He's here?"

She couldn't nod, but the way her skin had paled told him everything. "But different," she breathed. He bit his lip. Why?

"Then we need to find out why." They pushed their way through the revellers and marched towards the tavern, but it was too much like they had a purpose beyond that of ... celebration.

"Put your arm around me," Kyra whispered. Eli frowned. *"Do it now,"* she hissed. Eli wrapped his arm around her shoulder and smiled, about to press a kiss to her forehead. He paused, pulled himself back. It was too easy to lapse into the familiar rhythms, the blissful days in the Sanctum. He wondered if she noticed. Her entire body was rigid with tension as their steps carried them to the porch, ignoring the elderly couple chatting beside them. As one, they pressed their faces to smudged glass.

Eli's jaw dropped, and beside him, Kyra's soft gasp carried over the cold air. Monsun waited at the bar, the only one without a drink in his hand. Trayse slithered towards him, and the Vindicator caught sight of him. Spots began to appear at the edge of Eli's vision as a friendly smile crept over the Vindicator's face.

* * *

Two drinks thudded on the bar as soon as Monsun raised his hand. He kept his eyes on his contact, stalking towards him. Over the man's shoulder, the Vindicator noted two dark shapes at the window. He narrowed his eyes, but as his contact sat by the bar, he dismissed it from his mind. This man would be his second-in-command had he not volunteered to spy for the

214

legion. A sweeper—the preferred term—to scout out territory and information.

"Good to see you, Haman," he said, clasping hands with his old friend. The grip was weaker than it once was, but then the years hadn't been kind to them all. Haman's hood covered most of his face, yet the long braid winding out from it was the same. The same golden ring glimmered on his finger, the only sign of status he would ever wear.

"It's good to see you too, Monsun." A lucky miss at the throat in a campaign years ago had left Haman's voice permanently damaged, so now he spoke with a chilling rasp that always made others turn away. It was a sight Monsun used to enjoy. Haman turned to the drinks in front of them and produced a small vial from his pocket, placed a few drops in his own tankard.

"Too bitter for me," he rasped, at Monsun's questioning glance. "Recently I've preferred the sweeter stuff."

Monsun frowned, but placed his drink to his lips. It was indeed very bitter. "I wish I had some of that," he coughed. No sooner had the words left his lips before Haman passed him the vial and Monsun dropped some in. He took a pull and smacked his lips in appreciation. His chuckle rumbled through the crowded tavern before he leaned closer. "Any news of the Seventh?" he asked.

"Don't you know?" Haman said. "Finon has been on the warpath ever since you left. Monsun, he convinced Hadrian to disband the Seventh."

There seemed to be a lump in Monsun's throat, something he couldn't get past.

"And—and the men?" He drained his mug to get some defence, found no consolation in the sweetened taste.

"Your Second and Third are 'on leave' and he transferred most of the rankers to the border legions."

"How did they get away with this?" he whispered. "Hadrian would have stopped it."

"Hadrian would have, but you left us," Haman said. "You left us at the mercy of Finon." He almost seemed to be enjoying this, but this wasn't like Haman at all. Monsun remembered him as a kind and gentle man, deeply protective of those he loved. A brother.

"What?" the Vindicator hissed. "No. No, I didn't leave. I was on a mission the King gave me—"

"Monsun, you know you've switched sides. You're helping the two that the King told you to bring in!"

Monsun raised his finger accusingly. "That was not my fault, and it is not relevant."

"Believe it all you want," Haman said. "But we all know the truth." Haman stood, and any measure of friendship between the two of them vanished. "Farewell. I hope we don't meet on the battlefield," he said, but for an instant, the rasp faltered, replaced by honeyed tones.

Haman swept to the door and flung it open. Just as he did, his hood slipped, falling to his shoulders, revealing a distinctive shock of flaming red hair. A long black braid dangled from it. Just where it would have peeked out from his hood ...

The noise of merriment floated through from the square. As Monsun turned back to the bar, he had time to notice Haman's tankard was still full, still untouched.

The two shapes—or four shapes, he couldn't tell—ducked away from the window. He swayed, mouth opening, perhaps to say something.

Then he crashed to the floor.

Chapter 28

As Trayse slammed the door, Kyra tugged Eli around the corner, ducking down into the shadows. The Orderman stalked off into the night, ignoring the townspeople who glared at him as he shoved his way through. Kyra pushed down the fear that threatened to choke her, and she whispered into Eli's ears.

"We need to take him." She'd sworn once what she'd do to him. Time to fulfil her promise.

Eli nodded. "Wait here." He took two steps and leaped into the air, slamming his vambraces together and disappearing. As Kyra watched intently, he fell back into the world right behind Trayse, wrapped one muscled arm around his neck, while the other smashed against his vambrace. He flashed back to Kyra's side and flung Trayse to the ground, following with a kick to the head that sent him unconscious immediately. A black braid tied to the familiar red hair flew out of the hood. What was that for?

"You've been practising," Kyra commented. That at least was easy to say. His grin didn't reach his eyes. He must have used up most of his magic—he sagged against the wall, sucking in rapid breaths to recover.

"Let's get him into the tree line," Eli said.

They dragged him through the snow, his legs leaving a long groove—easily traceable. Kyra kept an eye open for any revellers seeking privacy, though in this cold it wouldn't be that fun, anyway. The trees loomed overhead when they finally dropped Trayse's limp body onto the snow. The cold must have woken him, as he let out grunts and began to stir. Eli clapped his hand over his mouth.

"No sudden noises," he warned him.

It was too dark to see anything properly, with the new moon so dim. In the night, it made it easier to summon the warrior's irreverence, where Trayse wouldn't be able to read her so easily.

"Hello Trayse," Kyra said. "Remember me?" She waited, her heart hammering in her chest.

His voice quivered once, then regained its honeyed drawl. "Jayne Farer. The pleasure is all mine."

* * *

"What are you doing here, you piece of filth?" she hissed. The vague outlines of Trayse's smooth face became visible as Kyra's eyes adjusted to the darkness of the forest. It reeked of trained charisma, a power as strong as any sword. Once upon a time she had fallen for it.

Never again.

"You know, just saw a nice party and figured I might have a good time." Trayse's grin was as practised as ever.

"Don't lie to me, traitor," she snarled, her hand dropping to her side, to the dagger. Damn. She'd forgotten she was still in the dress. "Why were you meeting with Monsun?" Beside her, Eli bared his teeth. Between that and the silver eyes, the young Guardian cut an imposing figure.

"You saw my little chat with the *loyal general?* You should be careful with that one. He leaves palaces in pieces wherever he goes. Too bad he won't remember."

"What did you do?" Eli roared.

"I was playing a role, same as I was back in the valley," Trayse grinned. "He's just out of action for a little while." A flash of white teeth in inky blackness. "Which is more than I can say for *you.*" He let out a piercing whistle into the night and gold ignited in the night, a light brighter than any flame. Just as in the valley. Several soldiers rushed them, bearing naked steel.

218

Eli grabbed Kyra's hand and crashed his vambraces together, obviously expecting to fall into the Rift—but nothing happened. He cursed under his breath and reached for his dagger, while she spun to cover his back, stumbling in her dress shoes.

Ten soldiers. One knife. Useless odds. Not even a Princess and a Guardian, bearers of mighty gifts, could last against that many trained soldiers without proper weapons. Not as the fear threatened to choke her again. As Trayse gained the upper hand. Again. Trayse stood and brushed the snow off his cloak with a smug grin. He reached out an indifferent hand and one of his soldiers immediately handed him an amulet, which he donned, the metal glinting in the moonlight.

"Now let's see just who you are," Trayse murmured and reached up to Eli. "Who are you?" he murmured, hand brushing Eli's cheek. The young Guardian didn't react.

"Nobody of consequence," Eli replied tonelessly. Kyra flushed. He should know that wouldn't work on Trayse, he was too smart, too cunning—no sooner had the thought crossed her mind before Trayse slapped Eli across the face, the glimmer of gold shining on his finger as he did so. Eli's quiet hiss of pain cleaved her heart, but they remained silent.

"I will ask one more time."

Eli didn't answer. Kyra's heart became a rapid pulse in her throat. Trayse might not have noticed the small swallow Eli made, but Kyra did. "Or what?" Eli breathed quietly. Her heart sank as he pushed the madman too far. Trayse unsheathed his sword in the blink of an eye and her throat pricked. She glanced down and instantly stiffened as the blade rested lightly on her neck. The threat was obvious. "Eli Serae," the Guardian rushed.

Trayse's chest puffed out in victory. "There, that wasn't so hard, was it? Tell me, Eli, what are you doing with this beautiful thing?" he waved a hand at Kyra. Her knees locked, and a cold sweat broke out across her neck.

Eli's eyes became flinty as he stared down at the smaller man, but he forced a smile. "Why, are you jealous?"

Stop taunting him, she silently pleaded. You'll only make it worse.

"Not for much longer, I imagine," Trayse smiled. He reached into his pocket and produced two small fruits. "Now, as you two might have guessed, I know a thing or two about poisons and drugs." Eli's swift intake of breath made the lieutenant's snake-like eyes glimmer ferociously. "You're going to eat this, and then we'll march like a happy little family all the way back to Imbra." He reached for Eli first. The Guardian clamped his mouth shut and took a step back, but two soldiers held him in a vice whilst Trayse merely pinched his nose. Eli flailed, but eventually opened his mouth to gasp for air. Trayse shoved the fruit into his mouth and slammed it shut, forcing him to bite down. Eli coughed once, then stood still.

"Good," Trayse murmured.

He moved to Kyra, and she forced down the bile that rose into her throat, as the bodies fell once more in her mind.

"So pretty," he whispered. "I wish I wasn't on duty right now." He chuckled and brushed her throat. "I will admit, when I realised the Ghost was an eighteen-year-old girl ..." He let out a breathy laugh. "Well, I'd rather not say." The shiver that ran across her skin seemed to amuse him, and when he gripped her jaw, her mouth opened on instinct, despite her mind screaming otherwise.

He smiled. "Actually. You don't need it." He let go and she stumbled back. "You know to do as you're told." And she did.

There was no point in fighting anymore. Actually, she never should have fought. No matter how much she did, he always won. Perhaps it was time to give in. To obey him. He wouldn't want to hurt her anyway. Her mind clouded, stuck in the same whirling circle of thoughts. Trayse flicked his eyes over Kyra's shoulder and rough hands bound her hands behind her back. The cold metal bit into her skin, the familiar ache right on her old wounds, but the numbness that crept through her was unmistakable. After all her progress, he'd destroyed it all in an instant. He would always win.

No. A small voice inside her head began to yell, push, demand.

No. Trayse was her enemy. He was her hunter. She would never let him win. But the fear pushed back, smothered her in nothingness.

No. You will never surrender. That voice—it was not her own, but so, so similar. It had the power of a blizzard, the roaring gale of eternity that drowned out any haze Trayse put her under. Her mind swirled, strength fighting manipulation.

You will never surrender.

And at that, her mind snapped open again, her eyes cleared and she could feel the familiar bite of her shackles. Beside her, Eli did not resist as they stripped him of his vambraces. Clapped irons around his wrists. Ankles. Neck. Dragged the two of them back up and hauled them northward.

Kyra retreated inside herself, into the dark pit of nightmares she was sure she had escaped. The days she had paced the Sanctum just to remind herself that she was no longer in a cell. Her shoes sank into the melting snow, as unfit for walking as her beautiful dress. *You will never surrender,* that voice whispered. Despite herself, a small glow of hope began to burn in her chest, fragile and yet powerful.

An hour later, Trayse called a halt in a nearby cave, sheltered from the cold wind. At once, several men marched to the perimeter and assumed the watch, while others made a fire nearby. They shoved Kyra to the cave wall, Eli beside her. With no hope of escape. Not while Eli was still under Trayse's influence.

At least they were near the fire. That was some small mercy. Kyra just watched the dismal flames crackle, hoping for some distraction. Eli's solid bulk next to her was less of a reassurance than it once was, the young man still drugged from whatever Trayse had done to them. His breathing was deep, but he never looked at her, only gazing at Trayse in adoration.

"Are you happy now?" a voice jumped across the flames. That voice—she'd heard it before. Too high to be a man's voice, and she was the only woman in the camp.

Until she wasn't. The dim outline of a woman flickered on the wall a metre away. Age lined her elegant face and grey streaked her hair, but Kyra could have recognised it anywhere. The curve of the brow, the proud chin—that was her own. She would know royalty even without the crown. "Do you know me?" the woman asked.

"You're Eshe. Queen of Leranion, mother of Prince Cayce. I've read the stories."

"The stories are not the truth," Eshe countered. "Not anymore."

Kyra smiled. "I saw the painting. I know what you were to this land." Kyra's gaze flicked around the cave, unsure of who could hear.

"Don't worry, they can't see me. Or hear you, for that matter," the woman said. On her brow, an elegant circlet gleamed, a single sapphire set in silver. "Are you happy now?" she asked again.

Kyra coughed and cocked her head, unable to believe what she was hearing. "Why in the Five Hells should I be happy?"

"Why not? You've reclaimed your birthright, you've found the staff I left in the Sanctum, you've bonded to a snow

222

leopard in a way no ruler of Leranion has done for four generations, and you have a very handsome boy to call your own." Eyes glistened with moisture, but she smiled fondly. "I remember when I used to have the same thing."

Kyra sighed. "He's not my own, that's for sure. Have you chatted to Jaser lately?"

The queen waved a flippant hand. "Oh, I don't talk to him much. Ever since he died he's been a lot more grumpy." She reminded Kyra of Queen Taera, her own mother, even though she'd married into the Antarun line and didn't carry the Mark. Who she had barely thought of in the past year, refusing to acknowledge the past and her old life. "Why are you still here?" Eshe asked with a royally arched brow.

"Because I'm chained to the floor," Kyra replied. Couldn't she *see* that?

"Your gift has regained its power. You could probably escape from those chains if you really wanted to, though that might be beyond your skill at the moment. You would have left unless you had another reason to stay." Kyra couldn't help it. Her eyes flicked to Eli, his expression still vacant. Trayse knew how she worked. He knew that even if she could leave, she wouldn't if it meant it would hurt someone. Especially Eli.

"Are you afraid?" Eshe pressed.

Kyra bowed her head. "Yes," she quivered.

"You have every right to be, my dear. But you're letting that fear control you. You must *never* let that happen." Something like rage glimmered in her eyes, for just a moment, then the weariness returned. "How do you expect to rule a kingdom while you live in fear?"

Kyra's focused demeanour, the one she showed the world all the time, finally cracked. That icy rage spilled to the surface. "I don't expect you to know either, since you ran off to fight a war that got your son killed. Was that the asking price?"

223

Her voice dropped to a furious whisper. "The blood of your firstborn? Did you think there would be no consequences to your actions?"

Her ancestor's face, once soft and loving, morphed into steel, harsh and unbreaking. The face of the warrior who'd led her people in a battle against the greatest evil the world had known. "I don't think you're talking about me here." Kyra faltered for a moment and the queen pressed her advantage. "I remember the girl who survived the Order's attempt to kill her by jumping into a raging river. The girl abandoned by the nobility, forging her own survival. The girl who ran off to create a rebel movement because she was so *angry* she could have torn down the castle walls with her bare hands. I remember the princess who reforged herself into a soldier. Kyra, wars cost lives. I—I know that better than anyone else. But you need to stop blaming yourself for what happened. No one could have seen what Trayse would do. Not even you. Leaders can make mistakes, and there are some things that will always remain hidden, even in death."

"Why are you telling me this?"

Those tears crept back into Eshe's eyes. "So you don't make the same mistake I did. Kyra, your duty is to your kingdom. But that doesn't mean you need to sacrifice your soul. You have found someone you can trust, someone you can rely on. I know many people who wished for that same thing. And it's gone."

Kyra let out a weary sigh. "What must I do?"

"Forgive him, and trust him," the queen smiled. "After all, we're all running from something." A ghost of a smile touched Kyra's lips as her own words echoed in her ears. "You've had some tough choices, and some haven't always gone the way you wanted. But the important thing is, you don't stop making them. That's the only true mistake you can make."

"We will have our work cut out for us," Kyra breathed, even as she glanced at Eli.

"Yes. Temero's power is growing. With only one pillar destroyed, he cannot yet take physical form, but if he destroys another, then more horrors will advance, enough to make the Order's attack on the Jinnam look like a tea party." The chain turned slimy in Kyra's hand. "You need to act fast. Trust your family."

"My family doesn't even know I'm alive," she laughed bitterly.

Eshe's smile was warm, but something else gleamed in her eyes. "Family is more than blood, Kyra," the Queen said. "Trust them, trust Nestham, and trust yourself."

"Will—will you be here?" *With me,* she silently added.

The queen nodded. "I'll always be with you." Kyra nodded, and the Queen smiled. "You will never surrender." She vanished.

Kyra closed her eyes and pressed the back of her hand into the rock. The golden gleam was barely noticeable beside the firelight. *Nix. Nix.* She let the call go out to her cub, sweeping across snow-covered forest. *Nix.* She tried to let the image of her situation filter through the bond, then thought of Amora. Of Alsair. Of Monsun, wherever he was. The vigorous energy that snapped back through the bond made her recoil, though she wasn't sure Nix had gotten the message.

When she opened her eyes, Eli was still slack-jawed. A phantom hand brushed her chin, as if reminding her it was okay to want this so badly it hurt. *Beautiful,* he'd mouthed when they sparred. He didn't know how easily she could read it. But that word had slipped inside her heart, shredding every wall she'd ever built in the last year. So she'd break his walls down, break his prison. She brushed her lips against his forehead, wrapped her arms around him. Whispered a prayer to Nestham that Eli

225

could be freed. Nothing. The hope rushed out of her as sure as the breath left her chest, the sigh of defeat.

Muscles stiffened beneath her as Eli gasped for breath. She opened her eyes and met his gaze. A soft smile crept over his face.

"Kyra," he breathed. He glanced around the room and the fear crept into his eyes. The vulnerability he rarely showed anyone. Because he believed a Guardian had to be strong all the time.

"Keep your eyes still and listen to me," she said. Eli just stared at her as words from their previous *discussion* came back to haunt her. "I never expected to have a choice either," Kyra began in a whisper. "I knew my life would be one of duty. I thought I would grow up, marry a prince whom I didn't love, and keep my people safe." Her voice cracked a little.

"But then you came along." His eyes widened at that. "And it changed me. More than I could hope to tell. And I know you think you have this all figured out." He opened his mouth, but she shook her head. She needed to say this, whatever happened after.

"You think a Guardian has no feelings. He's unflinching. All he does is defend and protect. And that's noble. But that's all you want your life to be. Sacrifice." She lingered on that word. "But it doesn't sound like much of a life to me. I think it's okay to let someone in."

* * *

Truth lingered in those words. Truth he hadn't let himself see, despite Alsair's words. And he marvelled at the strength of the young woman beside him, the courage it had taken to say those words and *mean* them. To offer herself in a manner that he had never offered her. Ever since Jaser had opened his blasted mouth, he had become guarded, isolating himself behind *duty*

226

and *the mission*. But Alsair's words echoed in his mind. Without her, he had nothing to fight for. *Remember where your loyalties lie.* Words from the First Guardian. He knew where they lay.

They lay with the woman facing him.

"I am so sorry," he whispered. "I hurt you in a way I never wished to." A single tear coursed down her cheek. But as he reached over and brushed her hand, her smile widened.

"Get some rest before this all goes to the Hells," he said.

She blinked at him. "We have our gifts. We could get out of here."

"No," he shook his head. "I—I can't reach my gift. I can't run or Rift without it." He tried to drop into his magic, but the power—the fire subsided, nothing like the raging might it was earlier. Whatever Trayse had given him had sapped its strength. As if Trayse knew the Guardian's powers better than he did. He glanced down at his arms and swore.

"Where are my vambraces?"

"Trayse has them," she said.

"Five Hells." He chewed his lip. "All right, we'll wait a little while. They'll get tired soon."

Several soldiers were already leaning against the cave wall, well out of earshot. She settled down onto his chest, ignoring the shackles. It wasn't long before her breathing was deep and steady. A small part of him smiled, but he couldn't focus on that right now. He gobbled down every detail of the situation. The cave, twenty paces long. They would take at least a few seconds to escape, even without shackles or fighting the soldiers.

He swore as the glint of steel in the moonlight signalled the archers waiting outside. They'd have no chance against them. Unless ... his attention snagged on Trayse. The spy leaned against the wall, his chin on his chest, Eli's vambraces glittering on his forearms. Just on the other side of the fire.

He nudged Kyra, and she stirred, her breath catching once. He gently explained his plan to her, breathing it into her ear, a mockery of the lover's whisper he wished to be having right now. She nodded once. She didn't ask him to be careful. She understood the risks.

Kyra began to convulse horribly, her eyes rolling up into her head. Despite the strain in his heart to go to her, he forced himself to stare straight ahead, kept his face a blank mask. A soldier shouted and Trayse jerked awake. His eyes snapped open, and he grabbed a half-burnt log from the fire before approaching them, the flame flickering over the wood. Despite his rage, Eli had to admire the man's focus. He leaned over Kyra, checked her over, hand on her neck. She merely twitched, her breathing shallow, but he remained cautious, wary of some trick. His gaze shifted to Eli, and though his fear spiked, Eli winked at the spy. Powerless, and yet prompted by something, he reached for Trayse's forearms and *pulled*. The vambraces gleamed and faded through his arms, as if they were eager to return, merging onto his arms immediately.

"*Goodbye, bastard,*" Eli whispered to him. Trayse reacted with inhuman speed, slashed at him with the burning log. Eli and Kyra faded into the darkness as flames connected with Eli's chest. He screamed as the flame rushed over his clothes, searing his skin as the two of them fell onto the snow. He couldn't move, couldn't think. He'd felt this pain before. The heat had destroyed all his thoughts and only left a wasteland in his mind.

Kyra. She was saying something, words he couldn't quite make out in the flame's frenzy. *I'm sorry.* The words, over and over. "I'm sorry, Eli," Kyra whispered, and rolled him over, smothered the flames in the damp snow.

His magic roared back into existence and his Mark flared, brilliant blue light flickering through the clearing. Kyra clamped down on his hand, cut off the glare. "Finally," he groaned.

"Save your energy," she murmured, one hand idly tousling his hair. "You'll need it for healing. Don't try to Rift. We can wait this out." She heaved him behind a log and they clung to each other, hardly daring to breathe. *They could not wait this out.* Every bone screamed at him to run, to Rift. But he was in no shape to run, and they were still unarmed.

"You should go," he breathed. "Run. They won't catch you."

"I'm not leaving you," she hissed, the snow coating her hair and her dress, her eyes burning. "Not again."

Trayse's voice rang over the hills. "Send word to the Chosen. The Guardian and the Ghost have escaped. We need a legion up here now. *Go!*"

A horse galloped away into the night. Eli shook, but not from the cold. An entire legion to intercept them.

Footsteps crunched on snow near them and they froze. Eli gritted his teeth at the burns on his back, even as Kyra pressed a quiet kiss to his cheek and crouched, tunnelling into her magic. To protect them both. If this was to be their end, he wanted it to be the last thing he remembered.

"Boy?"

Eli sagged at Alsair's rough voice. At the flicker of golden light as he hefted the Eternal Torch higher. Kyra sighed as violet eyes peeked at her from the ground. Nix bounded to the princess and leaped for her, nuzzling into her neck. Kyra grinned and her eyes met his. A faint blush rose to her cheeks and his heart soared for the first time in days. But another concern pressed in on him.

"Monsun?"

"Alive. He woke up cursing and told me to come out here," he said.

"Thanks," Kyra said.

"Don't thank me. Thank your leopard."

Eli groaned and tried to sit up, but Kyra was already adding her strength to his. He leaned on her and they stood together. "We need to get Monsun and get the Hells out of here," Eli said. "They're aware of who I am and they'll stop at nothing to hunt us down now."

Alsair merely gestured for him to lead the way.

Chapter 29

The expensive bedsheets rustled, and Lucial stalked across the elegantly furnished room as the sun shone through the window of the Eastern Spire. He threw his blue shirt over the chair and shrugged on the white uniform he'd requested. As he buttoned up the jacket, also a pristine white, his gaze landed on the young woman still slumbering on the other side of the bed, pale shoulders hidden under the sheets. His grin was the fierce one of a conqueror as he dressed and armed himself.

Lucial blinked as he caught his own reflection in the mirror. He brushed a stray shadow from his cheek and idly remembered when it had been light. He shut the door of the suite behind him, and checked Monsun's room. Still empty. Good.

The morning rays glittered in the cascading waterfall as he emerged onto the castle battlements. He grinned, inhaling the cold air swirling from the northern mountains. Spring had finally arrived, and none too soon. He'd need the snow to clear before he could begin.

Underneath the castle, on the walkway above the roaring abyss, he found Finon contemplating the drop in the darkness. Just the two of them. Finon jerked up when he approached. Fear was ugly on the old man.

"Is everything in position?" Lucial breathed. A sharp nod was the only response he received, and he held up two fingers in response. *Two days.* With Monsun gone, the King had lost one of his last outspoken allies at court. The other Vindicators he could quietly deal with, though likely Raylene would be tricky.

Unfortunately, their loyalty to the King was as irritating as it had been last time.

Finon nodded once more, the sagging skin at his throat creasing with the motion. Lucial made to leave, but Finon's eyes held a question. "What?" the Vindicator hissed.

"Rumours have spread," Finon said. "Rumours of Mount Sancti's destruction."

"You know what to tell them," he replied. "Act of Nestham." The name tasted like poison on his tongue. He turned a muscled back on the Archbishop and marched away. Finon didn't know what he was getting into, but he was a master politician. Lucial would regain that skill soon, too, once he understood what had changed.

Lucial resumed his storming pace towards the chamber, ignoring the lethal drop less than two paces away. The waterfall's roar echoed off the stone ceiling as he swept into the antechamber. His rich white cloak and stark tattoo were enough to force the sentries to remove their barring spears. Two salutes were offered, neither of them returned, as they opened the gilded door. He took a deep breath and glided in, clenching his jaw at the courtiers nearby. In the early morning, few were present, as the nobility preferred to sleep in before enjoying the fruits of others' labours.

Each looked at him as though he was the scum on their tailored and impractical shoes. His glare faded away as he threw a wink at a beautiful young lady, her night-dark hair and eyes marking her as from the Plains. She raised a brow and glanced at the woman next to her, who frowned at him, her face framed by golden tresses. But he had another mission today.

His boots clicked on the lustrous floor as he bowed before the throne. Before the king who sat upon it. For now.

"Majesty," he straightened and smiled.

King Hadrian's mask of royal boredom didn't slip. "Vindicator Cedwin. A rare sight to note you at court today, though all of my Vindicators are welcome here." Robes rustled behind him. Perhaps that wasn't the case.

He smiled, gleaming white as pure as his cloak. "I was bringing a report on the fugitives."

At last, Hadrian's mask broke, and he showed interest for the first time. "You have news?"

Lucial's smirk widened. "Monsun has failed to capture them. I'm requesting the opportunity to go after them myself. I'll take a troop and bring them all in."

Hadrian's glare wiped the smirk off his face. "And you think you need an entire troop to do what Monsun—your Senior Vindicator—could do alone."

"Yes, Your Majesty. Monsun has failed."

The King raised a brow. "Be mindful of your tone, *Vindicator*."

Ire rose, his chest constricted by an ancient beast stirring from its sleep. But not yet. Not here. He could allow it. Could allow the king his power. "Perhaps a few more days, Majesty. The offer remains open," he said. He bowed and turned away.

"Vindicator." Not a question. He glanced back over his shoulder.

"I don't know what's happened to you, but ever since you got back from the valleys, you haven't been yourself. Sort it out." The valleys. A small part of him wanted to smile victoriously. The Vindicator had been unlucky, but now he was suffering a fate worse than death. But to publicly chastise a Vindicator in this way, to scorn *him—*

"Yes, Majesty." He bowed, deeper than earlier, and turned on his heel. The sun now gleamed over the eastern wall, reflecting from every droplet arcing across the bridge that joined the keep to the rest of the castle. He turned back to the route to his chambers, ready to return and wake his companion, but the clatter of hooves in the courtyard echoed in his ears. He glanced out and noted the red and black uniform. An Eternal Guardsman. He strode down to the soldier, who let out a grunt as he dropped to the ground.

"Do you bring a message?"

"Yes Vindicator, but my orders are to deliver it solely to Archbishop Finon."

"I'll get it to the Archbishop, don't worry." The soldier opened his mouth to protest, but Lucial let out a single breath and the man's eyes widened.

"Lieutenant Trayse apprehended the heretic, but he escaped with a woman. We believe her to be the Ghost. The Lieutenant believes we can catch them heading south."

Lucial's brows shot up. "Send word to my personal troop. Tell them we leave in an hour." His special guard, put together in the two weeks he'd gained control of this body, was a force unlike any belonging to the kingdom.

He wasn't stupid enough to face down a Guardian without proper reinforcements. A legion would suffice. Hadrian wasn't stupid either, though. Another Order legion, after Finon's movements, would draw his attention too much. Better to use a Kingdom legion. The so-called general was too old to stop him. As it happened, he'd put a man in place the moment Monsun left. "And have Commander Omun meet me in the courtyard in ten minutes." The soldier sighed as he bobbed his head and left.

Lucial hummed as he strode back into his chamber, and his smile widened at the sight before him. Ash brown hair cascaded over the shoulders of the woman clad in form-fitting black. She stared out the window as he approached and brushed a kiss over the back of her neck, prompting a delightful gasp. She twisted and captured his lips, pulled back and smiled at him. The smile dropped rapidly at his expression.

234

"Is something wrong, my love?" she murmured, gazing up at him from under her lashes. He skimmed a hand over her cheek, and she purred at the touch.

"Trouble's stirring out in the mountains, Alondra. We need to get ready." Her eyes cleared, narrowed. She reached back over to the desk, began tying back her hair into a braid. He could only watch as she strapped on her weapons to the armour he had commissioned, similar to what his own body sometimes wore. Flexible yet strong, it coated her like a second skin and would protect her from most attacks. On the torso, she slid several knives into their sheaths. Twin sabres, light and deadly, she fastened in place over her supple shoulders. Perhaps most wicked were the throwing spikes strapped to each wrist. Once finished, she began to glance around the room. He knew what she hunted for, and held out the dark hood.

"I still don't like this," she murmured as she took it from him. He pressed a kiss to the top of her head. She needed the hood, though not for her protection.

"I know. But you know why you need to wear it," he said.

"But why should we care what they think?" Alondra glanced at him, and the smokiness in her eyes was enough to make him almost forget about Omun and spend the day in the suite instead, as much as he'd allowed himself to indulge during the time she'd been here.

He forced himself to huff a laugh. "It's not that way, dearest."

She sighed, almost childlike, and put the hood on, tying it behind her neck in a motion that bespoke months—years—of practice. As she did so, a brilliant bracelet gleamed on her ivory skin, and fierce joy rose in his heart at the sight, the reminder of his victory. Her eyes gleamed out from beneath the hood.

"How do I look?" she asked.

They found Commander Omun in the courtyard. The Leranion soldier paced anxiously, his uniform decorated with a score of medals hard won through battles across the kingdom. New on his chest, the gleaming symbol of command of the Seventh Legion of Leranion. A short nod was all he received from the commander. Lucial raised a tattooed brow, and Omun threw a crisp salute. The soldier glanced at Alondra and his face paled slightly.

"Ready your new legion," Lucial said curtly. "We march north at noon."

Surprise and fear crossed Omun's face. "Sir," he stammered, "Are you sure you can trust these men? I doubt many will follow my orders. They still believe Vindicator Monsun will return."

"Your Second and Third are loyal to you," Lucial replied. Yes, Monsun's former officers were gone. Though they were on leave, he doubted anyone would retrieve their bodies from the Kinar River. "Omun"—he placed a hand on the commander's shoulder—"when I recommended you for this position, I thought I could count on you." He shook his head and made to walk off, Alondra half a step behind.

"Wait!" the call went out after him. Hidden from view, his smile stretched, twisted and victorious. "We'll be ready at noon."

"Excellent," Lucial grinned. He needed to rest. Regain his strength to fight off the attacks of this feeble human's body. That was something he could not allow. Not until he discovered how he had been given a second chance. A shot at redemption.

He closed his eyes and let his mind shift towards the last token he'd implanted to confirm his suspicions. That young thief was not who he said he was. To think he'd had the Guardian in his grasp and let him free ... he'd grown sloppy. He wouldn't make the same mistake again.

Chapter 30

Dawn saw them stumbling back into Rankil. The mess from the Lanmane celebration still lay on the ground, but the square was empty. Eli plodded into the tavern, his legs strained—but his magic curled inside him, nearly replenished, though not worth using now. His gaze landed on the matron. Somehow, she was already awake and working despite her long night at the bar during Lanmane.

She sighed and pointed upstairs. "Room three."

He nodded his thanks and headed up the creaking stairs, his heart thrumming in his throat. What had become of the Vindicator? The door swung open, and he charged into the room, Kyra right on his heels. Deep, rumbling snores emanated from the prone body on the bed. Monsun breathed deeply, though his skin had a sheen to it that made Eli's skin crawl. Amora slowly re-sheathed her knife, dark circles under her eyes, as she stretched from the armchair beside the bed.

"Monsun," Eli gasped. He reached forward and grabbed the man's shoulder. "Wake up." Nothing. "Please," his voice cracked. And in the ensuing moments, the hole in his heart opened wider. And he realised he regarded the Vindicator—his hunter—as a friend.

Monsun groaned, and, heart-stopping seconds later, blearily opened his eyes. "You're alive," he ground out.

Eli's smile didn't show the rush of relief in his heart, as Kyra sighed beside him. Amora blinked quietly from her armchair.

"No thanks to you." Eli forced a grin. "This life debt isn't very helpful when you're unconscious, is it?"

Monsun managed a weak grin. "Actually, as soon as I told Alsair about what happened, it stopped pulling on me." He frowned. "It is still there, though. It seems I will continue to serve." His smile widened as Amora shuffled off the chair and stepped to his side. She reached for him, and his scarred and callused hand enveloped her own.

"How are you feeling?" she murmured.

He smiled gently at her. "I'm fine."

"Are you sure?" Kyra said. "Trayse was bragging about his poison skills. You may not be up to this."

"I said I'm fine," he said. They all froze at his tone. "And what is '*this*'?"

"We need to get to Imbra before an entire legion blocks our path," Eli blurted, and winced. Just saying it made it sound so much more impossible.

Monsun grunted as he gathered his strength and pushed himself off the bed, but floundered. Amora ran to his side, and he pretended to lean on her, surreptitiously stretching a hand to the wall. Eli restrained a grin at the massive man leaning on the small girl. By the other wall lay the weapons they had abandoned over the past day. Eli belted on his sword, the familiar weight balancing him out. He eased it from its sheath, wiped the blade down. They grabbed the rest of their gear, ancient parchment crinkling in his bag, and he hefted the Torch over his shoulder. There was no need to keep it balanced or held high. It would burn forever.

Kyra finished strapping her sword over her shoulder, and she snatched up the staff. When they re-entered the taproom, he nudged her and pointed over to the bar where Alsair's remaining hand caressed the matron's. Kyra chuckled and Eli raised a brow at him, but the monk's brilliant green eyes stayed fixed on the woman as he spoke to her. He pressed some coin into her hand and murmured something that made her blush.

"What happened there?" Eli grinned, as the monk returned to them.

Alsair's returning smile warmed his heart. "Absolutely nothing. But she did a lot more for us than we deserved, that's for sure."

They gathered outside the tavern. For the first time in what felt like an eternity, Eli surveyed them all as a group. Alsair, tired yet firm. Amora, the gleam in her eyes fierce. Between that and the knives belted at her side, she was almost intimidating, despite her youth and the massive pack of finery on her back. She might have to use those weapons soon. Eli's heart cleaved at the thought. Monsun stood on his own feet, yet his breathing was a rasp and his skin pale. Kyra–Kyra's eyes were blazing, an ancient staff resting in her hands, the blades retracted–for now. Nix growled low, her violet eyes entrancing.

The princess was coming home. And he'd do all he could to get her there. Jaser be damned.

"Are there any horses we can acquire?" Amora asked too innocently.

Ten minutes later, Alsair and Monsun sat astride a pair of sorry-looking nags they had bought for too high a price. Amora gripped Monsun's waist tightly–to support which of them, Eli didn't know. But there weren't any more horses for Eli and Kyra. No, there was only one option for them. He shifted the pack on his shoulder, the clink of gold overly loud. He drew a deep breath, accepted the roiling power of his gift.

"We draw out our magic, slow and steady," Eli said. Kyra nodded. They wouldn't want to move too fast. They could only move as fast as the horses, but their power would conserve their strength as long as it could. Gold and blue light flickered over the land as they moved. Alternating between a canter, then a fast trot. From time to time, Amora and Alsair would swing down to give the horses a break, yet Monsun's condition worsened. Worried looks flickered between the others. The bond between Eli and Monsun wavered for a moment, flickering, straining, and then strengthened.

The landscape changed once more as they made their way south, the peaks becoming gentler into the familiar foothills. Finally, they paused for breath atop a low hill in the shadow of an ancient stone fort.

"We can't move any further until the horses have had a rest," Alsair said. Monsun swung down from the saddle and groaned, covering his face with a gloved hand. He swayed, his breathing too quick.

Kyra frowned. "Are you okay, Monsun?"

"Just a little tired is all. I'll be fine," he said and staggered over, sitting against a tree. He was asleep in seconds.

Kyra turned and met Eli's eyes. "I don't like this," she said. "He shouldn't be this tired."

"Well, maybe Trayse's drug was a little more potent than we realised." Eli couldn't clear the doubts from his mind either.

Eli glanced around at the landscape. Behind him, the frozen peaks. And beneath, the rolling foothills. Now that he had a chance to catch his breath, he surveyed the crumbling ruins at his back. "This is Raven's Watch," he whispered.

The ancient fortress located halfway between the capital and the northern mountains. Before the great kingdom had shrunk, its borders stretched to the northern coast. Now, for all intents and purposes, it held nothing north of the capital. Places like Rankil were essentially self-governing, answering to no one.

But Raven's Watch, the site of the famous battle of the north—he'd read the texts in Mount Sancti. The Jinnam monks had a massive collection of ancient chronicles—tales of warriors of legend, now all lost to history. "This is where your father crushed the barbarians," he said. "It's a legend."

Her smile grew, and she shook her head, laughing softly. "The battle was a lot smaller than the tales say," she said. "It was a small raiding party that they surrounded. My father was touring the area and sought to reclaim more glory."

"And the rest, as they say, is history." Eli grinned. He relished the blush that crept up over her cheeks. She just hugged him fiercely. "What's this for?" he asked into her hair.

"Just for being you," she breathed. He pressed a kiss to the top of her head. Drew her face up to meet his.

"We're going to make it to Imbra, you know," he said. She bit her lip and her eyes flicked over his face, his lips.

"Time to go," Alsair called. Eli shot a glare at him. Kyra giggled in response and broke the contact.

Her eyes turned serious. "How's your magic?"

He closed his eyes and peered inside himself. The magic swirled within him, depleted but with fight left.

"Good enough. Yours?"

She glanced down, focusing her power. The golden light flickered once, then faded. She swore under her breath.

"We're going to be moving a lot slower from now on." Eli held up his hand and watched as the blue light swelled. "I can't Rift us over long distances. You'll need to run without your gift."

"If we need to, then I'll do it," she said staunchly. He winked at her.

"Eli! We really need to go," Alsair yelled.

Eli stalked over to him. "Kyra's magic is almost depleted," he hissed. "She won't be able to keep going at the same speed as earlier."

Alsair's face tightened. "Then we go slower. But we cannot stop."

Monsun gritted his teeth and swung up into the saddle, Amora settling behind him.

Alsair frowned. "Kyra, on the horse."

She raised a brow. "You sure you can keep up, old man?"

"Before I was a monk, I was a soldier. Trust me, I can keep up," he grinned. He took off at a run, left stump resting on his sword pommel. Eli glanced around and met the others' eyes.

"I guess that's our cue." He dropped into his magic and ran ahead, as if Nestham himself pushed them on. He supposed He was.

* * *

Alsair guided them to a cave hidden in the rocks just as night fell. Eli pressed the Torch to the wall, let it burn for their light. Kyra had urged to press on, but Alsair had merely shaken his head.

"It's cloudy, and there'd be no chance to move fast enough without stumbling. Not even the Torch can give us enough light for that. If one horse falls, we'll be in a much worse situation. No, we need to stay in shelter."

Eli sat just inside the cave mouth, back against the stone wall, hood raised over his head. He stared out at the dark hills, eyes roaming ceaselessly. A light flickered to his right, but before he could get a good look, steps echoed behind him. Kyra wrapped her arm around his waist and laid her head on his shoulder. His heart stilled, and an overwhelming sense of peace washed over him.

"What are you thinking about?" she whispered into the dark.

"I'm thinking about how next time I see Jaser, I'm going to kick his teeth in for lying to me." He grinned, but sobered. "I was so wrong. *He* was so wrong. And I'm so glad you convinced me otherwise."

"If you do something so stupid again..." she trailed off with a grin. A clang of weapons and steel echoed outside the cliffs, down in the valley below. And a single flame flared into life. Followed by another. And another. Eli swore and rose onto his knee, crawling to the edge of the bluff. Kyra ran back and brought out Alsair to see what lay before them.

Alsair paled. "It's an entire legion."

"Leranion troops, though, right? There's no way the Order would send that many soldiers," Eli said, forcing down the fear. "Maybe they're on our side."

"You're right about one thing," Alsair nodded. "This is a Leranion battalion. But I don't think they're with us. Best guess, they're hunting us."

"What can we do? We can't take on an army and win," Eli said.

Alsair motioned for calm. "They don't know we're here yet. We must retreat north and go around."

Amora dropped in from the slope and heaved a breath. "There's a hundred soldiers camped on the other side." Eli's gut churned as they hurried back into the cave, noting Monsun still fast asleep in the corner.

"They definitely know we're here," Alsair sighed. But how? A faint tickling sensation crept up on Eli, morphing into a burning pain. It launched into a flame of agony, as if he was swallowing liquid fire. A deep red glow lit on his chest, a pulsing, living thing.

Kyra's gasp echoed through the cavern. Eli's hands shook as he hefted the hem of his shirt, revealed the brand on his chest. He drew breath to scream, loud enough to wake the camp beneath them, but Kyra clapped her hand over his mouth, muffling the cry so it was a mere hiss. Monsun came to. Bloodshot eyes fell on the brand and widened, but Eli collapsed to the ground, writhing in the dust.

"He got this brand back in the Cathedral. What caused it to glow?" Kyra asked.

"I—I don't know. I've never seen that in my life," Monsun replied.

Kyra sucked in a breath, her hand clutching Eli's. He whipped his head back to see her gritting her teeth. Another round of agony engulfed him and he hissed, tears pooling in his eyes.

"Who's out there?" Monsun asked.

"A troop of Leranion soldiers," Alsair replied. His eyes were grim.

Finally, the glow faded, and the pain vanished. Eli's breathing was a mere rasp as he settled against the wall. Kyra rubbed her hand along his shoulder, and he leaned into her touch.

"I don't know how to play this one," Eli breathed.

"I do," Monsun said. "Trayse said they had disbanded my legion, but maybe there's someone loyal to me, if I go out there and show my face."

"Absolutely not," Kyra said. "They'll put an arrow in you from a hundred paces."

"Well, what if you showed your Mark?" Eli asked. "Every soldier in Leranion recognises the royal Mark. If you prove your identity, they must protect you."

"No, the Order had strict orders not to let me live," Kyra muttered. "My father still thinks I'm dead. And Temero would gain a lot if he killed me. He could just kill me and claim I was an impostor."

"We need to run for it," Alsair said.

"How? We're surrounded," Eli gasped.

The elder man pointed at the back of the cave. "There's a tunnel back there. We could get out that way."

"Eli and Monsun aren't fit to travel," Kyra pointed out.

Amora had turned away from their conversation, petting Nix by the light of the Torch. "What if we left as soon as it got light?" she asked.

Kyra considered the idea, then nodded. Eli groaned, then let out a wet, rattling breath. Pain-wracked eyes homed in on Kyra. "This must have been Temero."

"Another thing he'll pay for," she vowed, running her hand through his hair. Nix butted her leg and growled at the mouth of the cavern. A man clad in dark, supple armour stood in the torchlight. His gaze swept over all of them and his eyes tightened when they landed on Monsun.

"Who are you?" Kyra hissed. She jumped to her feet, her staff in her hand in an instant. She stepped in front of Eli, not even bothering to hide it. He did his best to stand, but collapsed, strength and magic drained.

"Haman," Monsun sighed. "Is it really you?"

The man's smile was a welcome relief. "It's me, old friend." The group lowered their weapons. Even Amora, the little urchin hiding her blade behind her back.

"What happened to the legion?" Monsun asked.

Haman pointed at the army down the hill.

"It's out there."

* * *

Monsun's jaw dropped. "They brought my legion? How did Commander Aran allow that to happen?" His voice was barely a rasp.

"Aran's dead." Even in Eli's state, he could see the crushing blow Haman had dealt. Monsun swallowed, his face haggard and disturbed. "So are most of the top staff," Haman said. The punches kept coming, and Monsun blinked furiously, fighting to keep a straight face, even when it was already too late. "But we're still loyal."

"Who's serving as Commander now?"

"Some lackey Vindicator Cedwin appointed," Haman waved a flippant hand. "He's loyal to the Vindicator and will go along with this entire scheme. But the rank and file still recognise you as our leader."

"Cedwin's out there?" Monsun asked. "I must speak with him."

"Don't even think about it," Haman said. "Cedwin's changed. He was a good man, but now he's ... strange. Cruel and vile. Best we can do is get you out of here."

A plan began to form in Eli's mind. "Haman," he said and the man's gaze swung to him. "Does anyone know you're here?" Haman glared at him.

"I'd be a poor sweeper if they did."

Eli's grin slashed through the torchlight. "Then get back to the camp. Let everyone know Vindicator Monsun is working undercover and they can't expose him."

"No lies there," Monsun grunted. "That's what I would have done if not for this life debt."

"You have a life debt to this boy?" Haman said, almost an accusation.

"Blame the sleep-walking." Monsun grimaced.

"Fine," he sighed. "Hopefully, the legion will refuse to attack. But you still must get out of here."

"We have a plan for that," Kyra said.

Haman pursed his lips. "Don't tell me," he said. "Best if I don't know."

"It's two hours until sun-up," Eli said. "Good luck."

"You too." Haman bowed, and disappeared from the mouth of the cave.

They fell silent, hardly daring to breathe. The camp outside was quiet, barely a trace of noise coming from the hundreds of soldiers outside. After several minutes, Kyra shifted against Eli. "Have we made a mistake?"

He contemplated it, sighing softly.

"If we have, it's too late to worry about it." Eli said. They'd be dead soon if they had. And there was nothing to do but wait. Wait for the army to engage with them tomorrow. If they ran, the archers would pick them off with ease; if they stayed and fought it would be just as suicidal.

The group lapsed into silence, each left in their own thoughts. Kyra sharpened her sword, and checked her staff, but the Nesthamir held strong, and would keep its edge. How long before blood would stain those blades? Would stain her clothes? Nix, for once, was silent, as if she sensed the weight on each of them. Eli's gut roiled, a cold sweat beading along his forehead. Real battle against trained soldiers. A lifetime spent training, and yet without killing.

Would he kill tomorrow? Or would he be one of the bodies on bloodied snow?

A shimmering outline appeared in the cave mouth.

"How did you manage to mess this up?" Jaser demanded.

Eli groaned. "I really didn't want to deal with you again," he said. "I was hoping you wouldn't make another appearance."

Jaser's expression could have matched Monsun's stony face when they had first met. "I see you didn't take my advice with Kyra."

"Actually, I did. But then I realised how stupid it was and fixed the situation, no thanks to you."

Jaser's mouth cracked into a sardonic grin, and Eli did a double take.

"I wasn't aware you had the ability to smile," Eli deadpanned.

Jaser heaved a sigh. "Are you done?"

Eli hesitated, as if sensing something, but nodded.

"If you won't be persuaded," Jaser said, "then I guess we must make do with what we can. But I warn you, there will be consequences for your actions." Eli raised a brow. "You were right about one thing. You can't do this alone. What you have chosen will make you stronger. Having someone to lean on, someone to fight for—that makes it all worth it."

Eli's heart soared, persuaded by the stirring words.

"But you may find that it will not be worth it in the end. This gift comes at a price. You must be ready to pay it."

Eli swallowed, but the anger, the wrath, refused to be denied. He knew his eyes were gleaming with war as he stared Jaser down. "I'll pay *whatever* price, but I'm not leaving her. You're dead. Why do you care at all?"

"Because Temero poses a grave threat. Nestham's Marked must stand against him, or this world will fall."

Eli just looked down, and his bottom lip trembled. "I'm afraid, Jaser."

"So was I, the first time. The important thing is not to let it control you. Stop running, and face tomorrow as a Guardian."

A comforting pair of arms slid around his waist and Kyra rested her chin on his shoulder. "Jaser, you better have something good to say, or you can stay dead."

"You can see him?" Eli asked in surprise. She nodded, smiling. The smile died when she looked back at Jaser's shimmering figure, to be replaced by a steely gaze that suggested she was contemplating kicking a ghost in the jaw.

"I see the two of you are well suited." Jaser sighed. "Well, if this is what you want, don't let me stop you." His outline shimmered, fading, and he turned away from Eli.

But the young man couldn't let this rest. "Wait!" Eli blurted. Jaser glanced over his shoulder, cocked a brow. "Thank you."

Jaser smiled sadly. "No Eli, thank you."

The first rays of dawn began to steal over the land. It was time. Eli turned as Monsun heaved a breath and staggered to his feet, a faint sheen of sweat glistening on his pale face.

"We need to get moving," the Vindicator said, but fished in his pockets and passed out a small sphere to Eli. "Hurl this in the air—make sure it doesn't land anywhere near us. And close your eyes," he added with a weak grin. Seeing Eli's questioning glance, he added, "It's my signal. In case they need any more proof."

A commanding officer's signal. A very useful tool, coloured to each commanding officer, to warn others they were in the vicinity. Monsun shuffled to the back of the cave and began tapping at the wall.

Eli crept to the mouth of the cave and surveyed the encroaching army. Waves of blue and white, of morning light on gleaming shield and steel. On the banner in the centre, the snarling snow leopard.

He sucked in a breath and hurled the sphere high into the crisp dawn sky. A faint whistling noise echoed through the air as it plummeted down. It hit with a deafening bang and purple smoke poured out from the crash site. The army stilled. Where once it had been a uniform line, the right flank began to shift, a ripple of swords and shields moving in a new direction.

A small portion of the army trembled. Like a monster devouring itself from the inside, the fabled Seventh Legion turned. A crash rattled over the hill as the right flank dropped their shields.

Eli knew he should turn and run, but he was entranced, forgoing his safety to watch the change of heart. This could determine the future of Ekra. The shields parted and one man strode out, clad in black armour, and faced the army. Eli couldn't make out his words, but he didn't need to. The swinging black braid and the glimmer of gold on his finger were enough. Haman.

An arrow shot out from behind the banner and caught Haman in the chest. He plunged to the floor. The world around Eli stilled as the blood roared into his ears. No. Haman couldn't be dead. Not after he had promised an army and safe passage to Imbra.

The world blinked back into being and simmering rage replaced ice-cold shock. Another sin for Temero to suffer for.

"Eli," Amora tugged at him. "We have to go."

"Then go," he said, for he couldn't leave just yet. "I need to see this play out."

"Monsun can't stay here," Amora breathed. "He's too weak."

He shrugged out of her grip. His Mark flashed, as brilliant as ever before. Kyra glanced at him and ignited hers as well. He brushed her fingertips, letting gold and blue mingle as one.

"Boy, don't even think about it," Monsun gritted out.

"Eli. We need to go!" Alsair ordered.

"Fine!" he said.

Alsair led the way to the tunnel, now illuminated by the sun's rays. "Hopefully we'll have a good head start."

Now that the tunnel was fully visible, Eli could appreciate how small it was. "There's no way we can fit through that." It was barely wide enough to fit Amora.

"Get in," Alsair ordered. He bit his lip and hurried forward, but the thought of stone pressing in on him made his gut churn. "I can't do this," he whispered to the rock. A hand warmed on his shoulder and his gift flared again, and he grabbed the torch, held it in front of him and began to crawl. Just a little. His scabbard caught and he jerked to a halt. He scrabbled to free it, tossed the Torch ahead of him.

It fell out of sight a metre in front of him. The crack in the rocks opened into a full tunnel and Eli dropped into it with a heavy thud. He grunted as he brushed the dust off his shirt.

Monsun shuffled behind him—much harder for the burly Vindicator than for him. As the man's head appeared in the gap, he hauled him out by the shoulders, leaned him against the wall. Monsun nodded his thanks, too exhausted to say anything more.

Once the others had joined them, Eli held his Torch higher. He didn't need to, for the sunlight streamed through the gap in the rock and flared up through the tunnel.

"Whoever made this must have been a superb digger," Kyra said dryly. He grinned at her, despite the dread in his throat.

After a few minutes, they burst out into dawn light and a snowy cliff. Monsun staggered once and tripped, rolled down the face, tumbling in the snow. He hit the bottom with a squelch. Kyra rushed after him, slid down the slope, relying on her supernatural balance to keep her upright, sprinting over to her loyal Vindicator.

"Monsun? Monsun!" she yelled.

"He's pushed himself too hard. I don't know how we are going to get him out of here," Alsair said. Eli gritted his teeth and gazed down the valley in which they stood.

A thud sounded down at the end. They all stilled. Another *boom* rattled across the rock. The rear-guard had arrived, all one hundred soldiers, fully armed and battle ready. Panic set in Eli's chest. He couldn't get them all out in time.

He whipped his head to Alsair. "Any ideas?"

Alsair turned away from him for a what felt like an eternity. Eli's heart raced. It wouldn't be long before the soldiers saw them, and then it would all be over.

Alsair pointed at the other end of the valley. "We can get out that way." Something curled in his gut, but Eli stood his ground. They wouldn't be able to escape with Monsun in this condition. Those soldiers wouldn't stop for anything, even though Monsun had been their commander. They'd hack them all down.

The small gap in the rocks loomed. Merely a fissure extending through the cliff, widening at the base. Amongst the spindling cracks of rock, roots from an ancient tree clung fast to the stone. As Eli glanced at the tree, leaning precariously over the gap, small pinpricks of an idea congealed in his mind. Amora didn't hesitate before squeezing her way through it, Monsun grunting as he followed her.

A single raven cawed overhead as Alsair's eyes bored into Eli. The monk nodded once. Kyra started forward, turned sideways to allow Nix to go ahead. He waited until she was almost through before speaking. "I need you all to run as fast as you can. I'll hold them off."

Two female voices clashed at once. "You? Against a hundred soldiers?" Amora whispered at the same time as Kyra's loud curse. Eli steeled himself, but smiled at the girl. *No harm will come to you.* He'd made a promise. By the blood and magic in his veins, he'd honour it.

"It's time these soldiers learned what facing a Guardian means." With that, dug into his magic. Blue light flickered in the gap, and gold was already rising to meet it.

He leaped up, the strength coating him like a second skin, and he grabbed the rough bark and *heaved*, the tree groaning under the strain. It toppled and crashed into the gap.

But Kyra was already rolling underneath it, staff in hand. The tree thudded into the breach, splintering shards on either side. The trunk sealing their escape route. Colour drained from his face as Kyra faced him. "What have you done?"

252

Chapter 31

"We—we have to get you out of here," he breathed, every fibre of his being roaring at him to get her *out,* to get her somewhere safe. But she'd sealed herself in with him, the tree now blocking all passage through the breach.

"The *hells* I'm not staying," she hissed, every line in her body stiff with royal stubbornness. "We got ourselves into this situation. And now we're fixing it. I'm staying with you, Eli Serae."

Silver eyes glowing with anticipation met the blue depths of the sea as they locked gazes. His gaze flicked downward to her lips just once, and his heart quickened. Not because of the army. He moved forward, made to brush his lips against hers, heart hammering in anticipation. But as his eyes closed, a single callused finger pressed itself on his lips. He opened his eyes to see a cunning smile on her beautiful face, wicked and unafraid.

"Survive, and that's what you'll get," she whispered. He cursed under his breath but her smile only widened, even as her breathing was shallow. Kyra reached down to Nix, nuzzled the cub behind her neck, then murmured into her ear. The snow leopard blinked once and squeezed through the gap, the tiny leopard finding paths nobody else could.

"I'm so sorry, Kyra," he said. Because that was all he could offer.

Her gaze swung back to him and flames glimmered in her eyes. "Don't be. This is my choice. I'm done running."

He sucked in a breath. "We are going to survive this," he promised. A promise he wasn't sure he could keep. She nodded, and the fire that burned within him, within *her,* grew to an inferno.

Steel rasped on wool as he drew his sword, hefted the Torch higher in his left hand. Golden light spilled out around the valley, a beacon to show they still stood. He would defend it as long as he drew breath. More than just a boy, more than just a hunter, more than just a soldier.

More than a Guardian.

The only person to wield the Eternal Flame in battle. The Torchbearer for the continent.

His vambraces hummed, rife with Nestham-blessed power. Kyra merely flicked her staff to release the glittering blades glowing with gold, and stepped to his side, falling into a defensive stance. A *boom* shook the earth, travelling up through his spine and shaking his core. The soldiers appeared, a line of gleaming steel, filing like ants. The valley seemed to stretch out before his eyes as he took one step forward.

"For our friends," Kyra murmured.

"For *us*," Eli said. The fear, the dread had melted away. Now he would avenge two weeks of atrocities and release ten years of rage. "Your Highness," he smirked.

She bared her teeth in a fierce grin and ignited her Mark, prompting the staff's blades to shine with their golden hue. Two Marks blazed over the valley, twin blessings of Nestham. The soldiers halted, a ripple of tension ran through their ranks.

"That's not a Leranion legion," Kyra breathed.

They wore exclusively white, edged with gold. Nothing he'd ever seen before. The army halted just twenty paces away, shields and swords raised and bared. Eli planted the Torch in front of him. Marked a battle line with the golden Flame. He nudged Kyra, and she tensed, prepared to strike. His sword's hilt turned slimy in his hand.

Their leader, a swarthy man with a scarred mouth, touched the hawk feather bound to his sword and grinned fiercely. Eli snarled back and took one step forward. It was enough. The leader only shrugged, and the rest charged at the Marked, leaving him safe in the mass of his army.

Eli's heartbeat thudded in his throat.

Ten steps.

The soldiers thudded closer, their swords moving with controlled precision as they approached. His throat closed.

Five steps. The world fell silent. The valley narrowed, barely room for two to move at once. Eli's muscles tensed, and the roaring in his ears died away.

One step.

He dropped to his knees under a swinging blade. He stabbed forward with his sword, heard the squelch as it impaled a hand's length into the soldier's body. Hot blood coated his hand, spattered on his cheek. Shock coursed through his veins as the warrior toppled to the ground. His heart stopped. Just once.

Then the world roared back into existence and he parried, blocked and sidestepped on instinct. Every lesson, every hour of sweat and blood with Alsair in the mountain halls and the Sanctum, would keep him alive. Every single ounce of training, everything he'd endured—it came down to this.

He became a brutal force, an unbreakable wall. His heightened speed and strength gave him an edge over the soldiers who'd spent their lives killing. And yet, despite that, they seemed faster than usual. Beside him, Kyra was a whirling cloud of death, spinning and slicing with her staff, slashing until the warriors fell. The legion pulled back. A battle line reformed. Eli wiped blood off his face. The brutal clash had so far lasted only seconds, but five of the enemy already lay dead at their feet.

Eli stared into the harsh faces, now beginning to show a small amount of fear. The soldier facing him; he seemed ... off.

A shadow pulsed along the soldier's cheek, rippling, worming under his skin.

"Oh, mukk." *They're not human.* And he bared his teeth at them like an animal, a smile he had only given once before, to a Vindicator who had hunted him and now he would die for. The soldiers charged again, and Kyra and Eli slowly gave ground to the multitude of blows aimed at them. Despite his magic, the strength began to wane, forced out of him by these not-men. His arms turned to lead. But there was nothing to do.

Nothing to do but keep fighting. He couldn't Rift out of there. To do so would be to condemn Kyra to her death. They couldn't break position or they would both die. Her scream ripped out across the valley as a soldier sliced her arm and Eli, untested in combat, glanced at her on instinct.

The look cost him. His opponent slashed viciously downward and scraped his leg. He roared as the pain erupted through him, as his lifeblood spurted out of his body. His Mark dimmed, as his magic pulsed to the wound, fighting to contain the blood flow. The gash slowed to a trickle, but he slowed, his strength failing. His magic couldn't contain the flow of blood for long. And even if it did, there wouldn't be enough to fight off the remaining soldiers.

There were so many remaining. The warrior punched out with his shield and sent him stumbling backwards, his head already throbbing, white pushing in on his vision. He gathered his magic, his years of training and darted to the side, slashed up the man's torso. Blood bloomed on the purest white cloth and the warrior went down silently.

Eli roared his victory, feigning strength he didn't have, not anymore. It was part of the act Alsair had taught him. Pretend to be strong, pretend to be fearless and you would seem invincible.

His fingers twinged, then the feeling faded from his grip. *No.* No, he couldn't have burned through all of it so *fast.* Strong with and without magic, but once it faded, too weak to fight. This was it. Kyra's magic couldn't heal her and he sensed rather than saw her strikes slowing, as the gold light dimmed in the valley.

A *boom* rattled the ground, but he couldn't pay heed to it. Eli flicked his sword out, tried to gain a breath's respite. Two soldiers circled him. He tried to keep both in his view, but the one in front lashed out with his sword and kept him occupied. Eli parried frantically and stumbled to the side. The soldier behind him cursed as his blade whistled over Eli's head. The young Guardian launched into a barrage of strokes, desperately trying to keep both at bay. He went for a risky swing, and the soldier merely trapped his blade and smiled. The other soldier roared and swung at Eli's head.

In the instant he had, he wished he had got that kiss.

A roar split the air and red mist splashed onto Eli's face as his opponent's body fell apart, cleaved in two. Screams from the soldiers pierced his consciousness. A dark figure now stormed amongst the killers, wielding a massive battle-axe with the strength and speed of years of training. Someone who should have been on the ground in agony, but by some strength of will had followed the life debt's command. Monsun had come, somehow finding a way to get around the tree and help.

And behind him, a spotted shape slunk in and out of Eli's vision, even as he parried a soldier's stroke, the blood slowing out of his aching wound. A shape with violet eyes. Nix pounced on a soldier, her maw bared on his throat. He fell to the ground as the snow around his neck turned red.

A knife whizzed over his shoulder from behind before embedding itself in the shoulder of another soldier. Amora. Eli's heart broke at the sight. So young, yet fighting with the rest

257

of them. Kyra re-engaged with renewed vigour, even as her light, her strength, began to ebb.

On the last legs of her magic, as the blood ran down her arm, coating her left hand until her staff was sticky with it. She turned towards a new enemy, endlessly spinning her staff until the blades were humming. Eli never took his eyes off his opponent yet he found time to wonder who had sent her into his life. He locked blades with the man snarling at him from his scarred mouth, smiled serenely and shoved him backwards. The leader stumbled, his white cloak tangling in his legs. Eli wasted no time and his sword found purchase in his chest. He turned to the next soldier and glared.

Do you want this too?

And that was it. The other soldiers turned and ran, leaving reddened snow and white-armoured bodies littering the landscape. Eli's chest heaved, and he hopped on his good leg, staggered to Kyra's embrace, barely finding the strength to cling to her. Tears pricked in his eyes.

"We did it," he whispered. Somehow, they had survived. Her answering smile told him she couldn't believe it either. But his grin became edged, purposeful. "And I believe you owe me something," he smirked, relishing the blush that stole over her cheeks.

"I thought I told you to stay back at the tree," Monsun said to Amora. The girl shrugged and pointed at the soldiers on the ground.

"Why white? Surely the bloodstains don't come out of that." Everyone gaped at her. "What?" She shrugged.

Eli sighed. He was tiring of these constant interruptions. "Where's Alsair?" The old monk was nowhere to be found. Monsun's face tightened, blood coating his tattoo.

"He's up there," Kyra pointed. Eli spun awkwardly, cursing his injured leg, and glimpsed Alsair barrelling down the slope at them.

"We have to go," the monk panted.

"How many?" Monsun asked, his brow crinkling. "How many refused to fight?"

"It's not the army that's the problem." Eli tensed, braced himself for the blow. "There are two people approaching us from the cliff, and they aren't waiting for the army. One walks with a darkness within him. I can feel it." He paled. "It's like nothing I've ever seen."

"Then let's go," Kyra pushed. Eli nodded and made to turn to the breach, to leave this place of death. It was only then he could gasp. Monsun hadn't climbed around the tree.

He'd obliterated it, leaving shattered wood littered on snow. When Eli glanced at the warrior, a sheepish grin was the only explanation he received.

"I'm sorry Eli, but you can't leave," Alsair said.

* * *

They all stared at him, except for Monsun, who bit his lip and nodded, his silver tattoo contorting in grief.

"The darkness will kill anything it touches, except Nestham's Marked. You and Kyra must stay and face it." The ground swayed beneath Eli as his meagre breakfast threatened to return.

"Alsair! Look at them, they're drained," Amora insisted, the young girl finding a new strength from somewhere.

"Eli, Kyra. Trust me on this." Alsair's gaze softened until there was nothing but a bitter, broken love in his eyes. "There are many things you don't understand. Things I wish I could tell you, but I can't. Not yet." His piercing eyes fixed on Eli.

"You've always trusted me, Eli. I just need you to do it one more time."

Eli swallowed once and glanced at Kyra. Her eyes were as cold as the mountains beyond the Sanctum, and a single vein pulsed in her graceful neck. Her mouth twitched as she stared the monk down. She'd questioned his motives once before. Was she right to do so? At last, she sighed and nodded, her fingers intertwining with Eli's. He found them cold, clammy.

His mentor looked away and coughed once, wretchedly, as if releasing a long-held breath. "We need to leave right now." Alsair couldn't meet his eyes as he turned and shuffled away, like he'd just watched a friend die. Amora enveloped Kyra and Eli in a bone-crushing hug. Kyra held onto the little girl tighter than ever, pressing a kiss to the top of her head, until Amora too left them. Monsun turned to Eli, his expression gone, though tracts of silver mingled down his stone face.

"You paid the debt," Eli said. "The bond's dissolved." The crackling energy that had once bound them together melted away, leaving a strange void in its wake.

Monsun nodded. "Then thank you, friend." Eli reached out, and Monsun clasped his hand, their calluses grating together. The hulking Vindicator turned to Kyra and took a deep breath. His bow was as effortless as it was deferential. "It was my pleasure to serve, Majesty." Kyra threw royal protocol to the wind and hurled herself on the Vindicator, who caught her easily. They murmured something and Monsun set her back down on the ground. He bit his lip again and strode off. Eli wiped away the moisture threatening to spill from his eyes.

"Go, Nix," Kyra whispered. The leopard twitched her bloodied maw once and darted through the gap. Monsun followed, squeezing his large bulk into the breach again, between the pieces of shattered tree.

Eli turned to the far entrance of the valley. Beyond the remnants of fallen soldiers, two figures loomed, swaggering and stretching. Kyra's hand found his as they neared, then she tugged on his arm, spinning him into her until they were centimetres apart.

He met her gaze, as blue as the depths of the ocean. Though he'd never seen it, he knew whatever beauty he could find in the Sea would be nothing compared to what stood in front of him. There were no words they needed to exchange. Not as her lips crashed on his and he opened his fiery heart to her, letting the emotion, the pain, the heartbreak, the forgiveness and the strength flow over him. Not just duty, not anymore. What bound them was something far more powerful. Yes, to be a Guardian was duty, but there was so much more.

And there was nothing keeping them apart. Even Jaser had given his reluctant blessing. The rest of the world faded to the two of them, locked in an embrace an army couldn't break. When they at last pulled back, her breath ran in ragged pants, misting in his face. Eli swallowed once, not even bothering to fight the smile matching her own. His gaze swung back to the warriors and his mouth tightened. But he knew the light in his silver eyes was soft as he kissed her again, and again, and again. His magic flared and his wound knitted together, but the numbness in his hands remained. Her golden light flashed and her breathing steadied. The Eternal Torch still flickered ahead of them. A phantom hand touched Eli's shoulder, and he knew what he had to do.

One of the fallen soldiers carried a scabbard mounted on his back. With a few tugs, Eli freed it, and after wiping it down, strapped it on. Slid the Torch into the sheath. It didn't rattle at all, and golden light now glimmered over his shoulder. Kyra smiled at him with all the fire she could muster. Bloodied and exhausted, they turned to face their new enemy.

Chapter 32

The one on the left, a handsome man, smiled winningly. A white-clad warrior, his tunic immaculate and expensive—yet he seemed fit for battle. The tattoo stretching across his face, however, was darker than the night. Yet another Vindicator. If only he was as amenable as Monsun. What Eli wouldn't give to have the towering soldier with him now.

The masked man next to him did nothing, but Eli observed the way he stood, frozen in place, as if he was a puppet dangling on a string. A black cloak concealed his figure, and though he bore no weapon in his hand, twin vicious sabres poked out over his shoulder, and under that cloak, Eli guessed he carried enough smaller weapons to outfit a personal armoury.

Eli sensed Kyra tense at his side. They didn't need to speak, not as they moved as one.

"The Guardian himself," the Vindicator said. "If only I'd known what you were, back in Imbra. And"—the man turned to Kyra, his gaze taking in every detail of her heritage she couldn't hide—"they said that you were dead."

"They," Kyra quipped, "have been greatly mistaken."

The Vindicator grinned. "So it appears," he rasped. The blood roared in Eli's ears as the voice of his enemy reached him. That hiss, that smile of base cruelty. This was the man who had branded him.

Eli concentrated on his breathing, even as he observed every detail of his opponent. He couldn't let the warrior know how exhausted he and Kyra were. Every minute they spent waiting to fight, their magic was recovering, the twin blessings of Nestham reshaping themselves. The Vindicator idly swung his twin swords, as if warming up for a spar, not a deadly battle.

The snow stirred under unseen breath, and the ghost of a hand grazed his shoulder. *Go now, boy.* Kyra shivered next to him and they exchanged a glance. Just one was all they needed to convey the depth of emotion and pain and fear. But those would need to wait. Because that truly was Jaser's voice calling to him from across the abyss and expanse of death.

He marched forward, Kyra's steps echoing his, crunching on damp snow littered with bodies. His Mark flared as he shifted his grip on his sword, joined by the flicker of the Torch over his shoulder. He rushed the Vindicator and let out the roar of a conqueror.

The Vindicator merely held up a hand and a wave of pure night blasted them back. Searing pain coated Eli's arm as he landed on the snow, agony roaring up and back. Kyra let out a fragile moan by his side. And as he lay on the ground, he wondered if he had been wrong in trusting Alsair. He wondered if his mentor had just condemned them to death.

Cruelty edged the Vindicator's smile, honed in some hellhole Eli didn't want to picture. Darkness pulsed at his fingertips. This was no human. Either one of Temero's fell beasts, or the demon king himself, encased in a Vindicator's body. Eli raised himself up onto his knees, grimacing as he did so. As he met the man's gaze, the Vindicator's eyes grew black, pitiless. The soul that gazed out was not from this world.

Eli's Mark pulsed and he leaped to his feet—but the dark figure was already moving, a sword in one hand, the other reaching to his wrist. Eli ducked as a spike whistled overhead. Only his preternatural reflexes had saved him. His opponents were good. Lethal.

He risked a glance at Kyra and gasped. The girl was not standing beside him as she should have been. Instead, she was kneeling on the ground, gazing with unseeing eyes. A horrible keening noise slipped from her throat, and something lodged in

263

his own. He had lost her in some dark corner of her mind. Perhaps fighting the nightmares she still lived with. This battle would kill her.

He leaped forward, gathered her in his arms, and crashed his vambraces together, landing on the top of the cliff. Far beneath him, the Vindicator merely smiled, as if he knew Eli's plan, knew the power contained within the Guardian and his armour. Knew Eli wouldn't be able to keep his distance, not with his magic fading and his Rifting limited.

Good. Because he wasn't going to. "Stay here," he whispered to Kyra. She had no response. His heart shook. How long could she survive what looked like unimaginable torment?

* * *

Eli fell back into the world, into the valley, but when he returned, only one warrior faced him. The other—the other was already running to the cliff face, the cloak streaming behind him. Eli let out a silent scream and dug into his magic, but the Vindicator gracefully cut in his way, blocking the path to cut him off. Eli's eyes blazed with silver fire, and the man grinned at him.

"Now that's a sight I haven't seen in an age."

Oh. You're Temero. "Oh, mukk," he muttered.

"Don't worry. You're not even half the man Jaser was. This won't take long."

"When I skin you alive?"

"Someday, perhaps. But now," the Vindicator said as he gestured, "first you'll tell me exactly who you are."

And somehow, Eli thought he could trust the man, could share his name, his purpose. After all, what could he do anyway? They were nothing but insects compared to the vast might of Temero. In reality, it was all Nestham's fault, a vindictive Creator punishing those who would not follow him. There was only Temero, the one true saviour of Ekra—

Eli swore at his opponent. "Get out of my head!"

The man blinked once, barely showing surprise. "Fascinating. We'll do this the hard way, then." He sprinted forwards and met Eli's blade in a clash.

* * *

The Antarun heir, the young princess, died a year ago in the Kinar River.

Clouds of shadow parted before her and she stood once again facing a squadron of Eternal Guardsmen, her Musadim escort all lying slaughtered around her. She stepped back, her riding boot catching on the edge of the cliff, above the torrential river.

"You can jump, or we can kill you now," the burly man said, a sword pointed at her chest. All of seventeen, Kyra had trembled once. But when she saw her fear boosted her would-be killer's ego, she instead forced a smile and jumped into the raging river.

The ice had just melted after winter, and the water was seething, not only freezing her, but throwing her down into the murky depths. It poured into her lungs and she choked on the water, clawing for the surface, fighting to breathe. That stupid ceremonial dress—it dragged her down. It had been a battle to survive, but she'd made it. She'd sworn never to wear a dress again.

Yes. Whoever ordered the soldiers to kill her had succeeded—the Antarun heir, the Nameless Heir, was no more.

Jayne Farer died at Trayse's hands in a little valley a day from Mount Sancti. She died with the team she'd gathered over a year. They'd helped people in need, rescued hundreds from the Order's persecution. Too bad they couldn't rescue themselves.

And once again she was helpless and hopeless, kneeling in pouring rain, as lightning crackled over the scene of slaughter. She couldn't do anything but watch as an arrow lodged in Luca's chest, as the young man she had trained and come to love like a brother was struck down.

A sob caught in her throat as she stood in the field once again, her team surrounding her.

You failed us.

I did, she coughed. *I failed all of you.* That slaughter in the valley was her second death. Jayne Farer, the Ghost, died that day. Her friends, or the monsters they had become, lunged for her, but she rose and looked them all in the eye, raised a hand in their path. They halted, fangs dripping with ichor, and madness in their eyes. *But I will never stop trying to make it right.*

Her scene shifted. Now she stood arrayed in shimmering armour. A circlet glittered upon her brow, adorned with the sapphire of her household. The staff of Nesthamir rested in her hands, and Nix paced at her side, fully grown and completely attuned to her. And beside her, the young man with silver eyes. Eyes smiling at her with hope and pride and warmth. She'd gone to him under a false name, a false life, and they'd saved each other. She'd make sure they'd keep saving each other. Kyra turned and gazed out at her friends, once again fully human. Her family.

I love you all. Luca grinned, and the scene broke.

Kyra screamed as scalding heat ran across her face, as if it was being melted off—

This isn't real. And it was Eshe's voice that echoed in Kyra's head as her Mark flared, gold flickering over crystalline white. The pain faded away and Kyra blinked as her senses

266

absorbed light, sound, touch. Her sight adjusted, and she swore as a figure stepped in front of her, garbed in black and clutching two wicked sabres.

She bent a knee and pushed herself off the ground, the blades of Nesthamir whirring as she met her assailant in battle. She twisted and spun, her staff moving into that familiar blur, that deadly dance. But the figure could keep up with her in any move, fighting impossibly fast. As fast as one of the Marked.

Kyra thanked her father for the years of practice with the staff, thanked Lillin for perfecting her. She feinted and swung, rebounded off a glittering metal bracelet, slicing the man across the arm.

The man screamed, high and loud. Not a man's scream. Blood spurted out of the wound. But the bracelet shifted to black and she inhaled a bitter stench. A faint white glow flickered under the dark glove and the wound re-sealed, the figure heaving a breath. Kyra blanched, clutching her staff, leaning heavily on it. They clashed again.

* * *

Eli's magic was fading, his light dimming as the Vindicator swung strike after strike at him. Shadow pulsed at the man's fingertips, yet every time he came closer, the Eternal Torch glowed brighter. Eli had no time to contemplate, however, as the man lashed out with a brutal overhand. He dodged backwards and clashed his vambraces together, fell into the darkness, Rifted through to his chosen target. The Vindicator's back.

He thrust his sword straight into the white cloth.

The Vindicator let out an unearthly scream, and he toppled to the ground, blades falling from his hands. Instead of blood, green ooze poured out from around Eli's sword embedded in his torso.

Eli's chest heaved, and he swayed on his feet as he gazed down at his fallen foe.

Shadow leashed him and he was vaguely aware of toppling backwards onto the snow before his sight vanished. He stood in liquid night, eyes peering into nothing. Not even his flaring Mark pierced the twisting blackness. The ice blue barely highlighted his feet. The Eternal Flame, the other mighty gift of Nestham, barely made a dent.

This was no ordinary realm.

The weaving shadows scattered before him and a towering mountain stood proud over the plains, swarmed by a mass of vermilion. He knew what was coming, even as every bone in his body begged him to close his eyes. But doing so would honour nobody, for this was the past. The mass of red was a legion of Eternal Guardsmen. And the fire blooming from the mountain was the event that had set him into action. The destruction of his home.

For it had been his home, as much as it could have been. Though he had paced and fretted and made scenes, the monks had been patient and kind. They had shown him a different love he had never imagined, and taught him so much over those many years.

The scene shifted and another image lay before him. Dim corridors. Flickering torches. Screams and strikes of steel. Red pooling on the floor, the stench of blood in the air. Armoured soldiers rushing at men and women garbed in simple robes, with no weapons.

Except one. One monk refused to die as he sprinted through the corridors, grasping an ancient sword in his right hand, a package wrapped in weathered cloth under the stump of his left arm. A soldier leaped out in front of him, but the monk had seen him coming through piercing green eyes, and was already ducking and bringing his sword to his unprotected side.

Eli fell to his knees. If he had known what had happened that day he was hunting, he wouldn't have found the strength to push on. The screams of a woman made him look, even though he tried his hardest to glance away. Tears fell as he watched her, bound in chains and kneeling before the commander—who smiled and stabbed her in the heart.

Eli's hoarse cries faded into nothing in the shadows.

Another set of memories flashed before him, too fast to comprehend. The monk stumbling, dropping the sword and leaping into a waterfall. An emblem of a dove, crushed under a heel. A sapphire shattering from its casing in an elegant ring.

He could barely watch anymore, but the images kept coming.

Monsun, fighting, surrounded by enemies, roaring a battle cry as his axe swung vicious circles around his head. His opponents swarming him like ants over a carcass. His screams as they finally threw him to the ground, and the cries of fell beasts ringing through the air at their foe's fall.

Alsair, condemned to the butcher's block, his head rolling away, the crowd cheering at the fall of the last Jinnam monk, as his lifeblood drained onto the stones.

Amora, sunken eyes and gaunt cheeks, pleading eyes and leaden limbs, begging for food, and receiving a blade in the heart.

A silver-eyed girl, not even eight, reaching for gleaming metal, screaming, falling into violent waters.

And Kyra. Kyra was everywhere. Dying alone with a knife in her gut, suffering at the hands of the young man from Rankil, helpless before the feet of Trayse. Mourning over a dark-haired boy clad in black battle armour, a single arrow sticking from his heart. His smile mischievous, even in death.

Eli bared his teeth, leaped to his feet, and *roared*. Roared a battle cry, driven to madness by this darkness. He swung his sword and flailed at shadow, but to no avail. The shadow fought back, tendrils of darkness reaching for him.

He was powerless as they wrapped around his arms, his legs, his throat, and *squeezed.* His vision blurred. Outside this realm there was nothing. Did he have a body? He no longer remembered. And then the images started again. An explosion, rubble and debris floating through the air, until—nothing.

Morning.

A sweet voice, one he would listen to all day if he had the choice. Eli blearily opened his eyes at the soft light flickering through the open window, as gauzy cloth stirred in the morning breeze. Golden light flared throughout the room as he rolled over on the soft mattress to see Kyra's deep blue eyes, half-closed in bliss. Her skin shone in dawn's light, despite it being a few shades lighter than he remembered.

"Morning," he murmured. He brushed a hand down her silken hair, aching to reassure himself that this was real, that he had made it.

"It's real," she whispered. He sighed in relief and lay back on the mattress, staring at the ceiling. On a whim, he glanced at his hand. No Mark adorned it, just as no brand marred his bare chest. They were as smooth as the day he was born. The same for Kyra.

"What happened?"

She quirked her lips. "I don't know. You tell me."

"I dreamed we were out in the cold. In a blizzard. Our friends pulled us out."

Confusion showed on her face. "Friends? You mean the court?"

"What?" He shook his head. "No. I mean Alsair, Amora, Monsun."

"Eli ... I don't know who they are. You must have imagined them."

270

Desperation washed over him. "But they're our friends," he whispered. "They have to be real."

Her eyebrows drew together in concern, and she brushed a hand over his face. "It was just a bad dream. But you're awake now," she whispered. A happy ending. After all, he'd fought and bled. "Isn't this what you wanted?" she asked. "A quiet life?" He caught himself nodding. "You could have it," she pressed. "Just stop."

"Stop what?"

"Stop fighting," she murmured. Could he do that? He wanted to. Nestham above, he *wanted to.*

No. He thought he'd wanted that life. A life of peace, the one he'd lost in Laif. But she'd given him the life he truly needed. A life of adventure, surprise, and passion. The real danger was in forgetting who he was. "I'm sorry," he whispered to Kyra. "But I can't."

She bit her lip and pulled away from him. "Too bad," she hissed, and creamy skin was suddenly nothing but wispy smoke.

The luxurious room lit with golden light disappeared into mist. He stood alone in the shifting shadows, again helpless. A man appeared ahead of him, with a warrior's posture and a curling tattoo.

"You? I killed you," Eli whispered, even as his heart fell into darkness.

The man's mocking grin told him otherwise. "You'll never be a Guardian. And your lover will die, just as you will." He vanished. Eli sank to his knees. But the tendrils came back, squeezing, choking the very air from his lungs. The fog swallowed Eli's screams.

* * *

The man was good, Kyra conceded. But she was tiring, the golden light from her hand dimming and ebbing, her own breathing growing laboured. Blood dribbled down her chin, courtesy of a vicious punch earned by getting too close. The staff afforded her reach, but she'd learned the hard way just how quick her opponent was with those nasty little spikes on his arm.

"Who are you?" she hissed at the figure. He stopped, frozen in place as if shaken by the question. As if he couldn't remember his own name.

Finally, he breathed a word. "Alondra."

"Why are you doing this?" she asked, trying to buy time, to let her magic recover—Eli's screams shattered the valley, carrying rolling agony and rending her heart. The *fool* hadn't run. He'd gone back to face their enemy *by himself.* He'd be slaughtered.

Kyra roared as she leaped back at the man, and darted close enough to land a slash at his neck. It sliced through black cloth and rang on steel. The hood tumbled from the man's head and a tightly wound braid fell out.

Glowing silver eyes stared back at her. The woman went rigid, then turned and sprinted away. Kyra froze in shock, not even daring to move. For that was a face she recognised, despite never seeing it before.

Eli screamed again. *Hurry,* that voice nagged, ancient and wise beyond all time. *You must save him.* But she was on a cliff, with no way down to the valley floor. Meanwhile, Eli was somewhere, begging for her help.

Where is the path, where is it where is it—the woman had gotten here somehow. Likely was returning the same way. Kyra spun with a curse and her eye fell on red blotches on snow. She tracked the blood trail through icy trees.

The ground gave away suddenly, and she halted with one foot in thin air. The land slid away into a snowy slope. With no choice, she sucked in a breath and leaped, skidding down the cliff face, her boots barely keeping purchase on the wintry carpet. She hit the bottom and launched into a full sprint, rushing towards where she'd left Eli.

The ground swayed around her as she looked down. Blood everywhere, leaking from a gash on her ribs. The pain, once dulled by the fury of battle, now hit her full force and she sank to her knees, pressing a hand to her ribs, finding it immediately coated in sticky red.

She would have collapsed right there if not for one image in her mind. A face alight with joy and laughter, smiling at the stars. That same face narrowed in tension at a standoff. The way his brow twitched, and the way he danced through war.

The screams were much closer now. But as Kyra collapsed onto the snow, the one thing she was holding onto was regret at not being able to see him one more time.

Get up. That voice again.

Why now? she cried in her mind, a desperate plea. *I can't go on anymore.*

A phantom hand gripped her shoulder. You have walked through fire, fallen through water, and fought through shadow. Do not let him die after everything you've endured. Your story does not end here. She glanced up. And saw the ancient Queen holding out a hand.

Family was more than blood. She gripped that hand and arose.

* * *

The darkness was madness and joy and agony, destroying him even as it remade him. His Mark pulsed, blue light warring with shadow. And yet, the blood-red glow under his shirt was just as bright. A Guardian claimed by a God and by a Demon. He walked a line flirting with darkness, and one day he would pay

273

the price for it. But not today. Fighting the blackness that kept him under, he opened his eyes.

The Vindicator stood above him, green oozing from his chest. "I wish you could have seen it," he grinned. "The face she made when she threw herself at me."

"Who?" Eli breathed.

Nesthamir screamed through the air and the Vindicator's head toppled from his shoulders. Head and body fell to the ground. The world burst into light—beautiful, angelic light. When Eli reopened his eyes, it had vanished. The Vindicator's body was already rotting, as if it had been dead for weeks. But beyond, screaming north on a frenzied wind, was a drop of liquid shadow.

"I hope there's a special place for you in the Hells," Kyra snarled. She dropped to her knees next to him. "Are you okay?" she breathed, almost like a prayer.

"I'm fine," he trembled. How the Vindicator had spoken rocked him to his core. But something steadied him. A tether now connecting him to Kyra, crackling energy linking them together. Her swift intake of breath told him she felt it too. "The life debt." He didn't know if she'd keep it intact. But whatever she chose, he would support her.

"Eli," she said, as her voice cracked. "Will you return to Imbra with me? Serve me?"

"Always," he said, lacing bloodstained fingers with her own. "To Imbra and whatever comes after, if that's your wish."

"It is," she smiled. His heart soared and a great weight seemed to fall away. "Then Eli Serae, I absolve you of this debt."

The bond splintered and shattered. Eli gasped as the energy crackled away into nothing. "What did you do?" he hissed. His breathing turned into a ragged pant.

Kyra smiled softly. A princess didn't look at him. A queen did. "I always wanted it to be your choice."

His own choice, as every shackle he had ever felt slipped free. Jaser's burden, the dual Marks on him, the weight of Mount Sancti's fate—they all shattered into darkness. How could he deserve her? He kissed her tenderly, feeling her smile into it, then deepening the kiss. His heart stirred despite his awful condition, as they intertwined for an eternity, until Kyra broke the kiss with a groan. It was only then he noticed the blood coating her ribs.

He swore, his heart shooting into his throat, but she only smiled as her eyes fluttered once and she collapsed on the snow.

Chapter 33

No. *No,* she couldn't die now. This couldn't be it. Kyra lay on the snow, the white rapidly turning red. Her breathing became shallower. Her golden light faded, then died.

A single tear fell from his cheeks. What could he do? To lose her now, after she'd saved him ...

He reached deep inside his magic, felt the pulsing core of the gift that Nestham had given him. His Mark flickered, then melted away, spent, exhausted from his battle. Rifting wouldn't be an option. And Kyra had severed the life debt that would have given him the strength to repay it.

What if she had known?

He hefted her into his arms, gritted his teeth against the dead weight. Took one step. Kyra screamed, a horrible, blood-curdling scream, and spots blurred in the corners of his eyes. Her blood leaked onto his arms, gluing them together. So he set her back down, screeched for help, but Alsair and the others were likely too far away to help them now.

And in his grief, he cursed his mentor for sacrificing Kyra to fight his battles. Alsair had played them like a game-master on the hellin's board, and they were all his pawns.

He touched his Mark, then the brand under his jerkin. It glowed faintly, a deep red. Fiery wrath stirred inside him, something that had been there all along, yet awakened the moment the burning iron imprinted itself on his chest.

Nestham had claimed him.

But so had Temero.

A loving hand brushed along his cheek. He could use its power and save Kyra. Where Nestham's gift had faltered, Temero's would provide his strength, cost be damned. So he let his brand grow, focused on the raw power imprisoned in his chest. The red expanded until it coated his body, a shimmering shield of malevolence. He placed his hand on Kyra's wound.

Only to have it knocked away by a weak slap. "Don't you dare use that to save me," Kyra said weakly. "You can't sacrifice your soul."

"I can and I will," he hissed.

"Eli," she whispered, "don't lose what makes you worth that blizzard." She took a shuddering breath and that light he had admired in her eyes died, even as they fluttered shut.

No.

"Stop," Jaser growled from behind him.

* * *

The shield shattered into shards of light and Eli froze. Kyra's breathing hitched, and he glanced down at her, the terror threatening to overwhelm him.

"What did you do?" Jaser hissed.

"I—"

"It doesn't matter."

"I can't do anything," Eli screamed through a tightened throat.

The man's eyes glowed with a comprehension that had been centuries coming. "Your power isn't half of mine," Jaser breathed. "It's different. I don't know how, but you're not the Warrior I thought you were."

"Jaser, you're really not helping ..." Besides, he was a warrior. Wasn't he?

"That's why your healing magic is so strong, somehow you got more of that," the old Guardian began muttering, shaggy black hair falling into his creased eyes as he paced back and forth. "You don't have full power, somehow. Unless ..." His eyes widened.

"Jaser!" Eli yelled.

"You're the Healer. *So heal her.*"

Eli's world went still. "What?"

"Focus your magic, Eli."

He tried, but his strength was already so drained. That second pit, the part of him he had sensed but never activated—it now lingered out of reach, tantalisingly so, a maelstrom of power he couldn't touch.

"I-I can't," he sobbed. "It's locked."

"Try again."

"It's not working! My healing is just automatic. I can't control it!"

"Kyra dies if you don't!" Jaser snapped. That single, brutal statement blasted through him with all the subtlety of a war axe. The old Guardian knelt next to him, but anger blazed in every part of his being.

Morning, Kyra whispered in his mind. A future promised in an effort to deceive. He didn't care where it came from, he'd fight for that, regardless. His Mark blazed a brilliant icy blue, and he screamed. Deep within his mind, he descended to that churning furnace of power. Of pure, radiant *light.* He screamed as the lock clicked open and he threw open the door to the roiling storm of magic. He was light; he was power; he was—a Guardian. The Guardian Healer.

Tears fell down his cheeks, glittering in his light. And just like that, it was over. His incandescence died, and he collapsed to the ground, barely able to move. He had burned out the last dregs of his magic, leaving only ash inside a fiery heart. Had it worked? He gazed upon Kyra's face, so drawn and pale. Nothing.

He couldn't draw breath in his lungs as the seconds stretched out. Five. Ten. *Why, Nestham?* A pulse of golden light skittered over the valley. A second later, it became a living flame as Kyra stirred, her wound knitting together.

278

"What happened?" she breathed.

He swallowed once, dried his tears. "You came back."
She closed her eyes and took a deep breath. Her face, already pale and drawn from the blood loss, whitened even further.

He looked up from Kyra to Jaser's shimmering form. The silver eyes, mirroring his own, now smiled sadly.

"Thank you," Eli croaked.

Jaser smiled. "It was a debt long owed." The eyes faded into nothing, but the phantom hand's touch remained.

He slumped next to Kyra's still form. "I don't feel like moving for a week," he grumbled. She laughed weakly and, damn it, the sound was a delight to hear. After a minute, the first dregs of his magic began to refill. Strength returned to his body, but he could feel the difference. It was no longer two chambers.

No. Two parts of him now ebbed and flowed, as if fire intertwined with living light. However, he realised what he had been working with, the fire, the warrior's strength, was dwarfed by the healing power that now dwelt inside him.

The Guardian *Healer.*

He'd never believed that was his destiny. Since arriving at Mount Sancti, he'd known where he stood. A warrior, trained by the best. A living weapon. But no longer. No life debt bound them together, and he sensed that there never would be, almost as if the magic knew something far stronger bound them now.

His magic began to refill, and he stood, taking Kyra's hand and raising her up. She leaned into his strength and they began to hobble through the snow. The breach loomed, and they looked for traces of their companions.

They didn't have to wait long, as soon Monsun hobbled to them from the other side of the breach. Alsair's grave expression didn't change as he took in the situation in front of him. Amora let out a small cry and rushed to Kyra's side, followed by Nix, who twitched her tail anxiously despite the order Kyra had given her hours earlier to stand down.

Alsair glanced at Eli and Kyra, at the battered and bloodied faces, at the hand Eli wrapped around her waist to keep her upright, at the way her head rested on his shoulder.

"We have good news," Monsun said with a faint smile. "Temero's lackeys are on the run and my legion remains loyal. I've sent them back to Imbra to ready our arrival." Their first allies in the capital. Monsun's eyes glistened. "Who was that you fought?"

"A Vindicator, but it was something else. One of Temero's minions, no doubt."

Monsun hiccupped, tears streaking down his face. "Cedwin," he choked out. He dropped to his knees, beside the corpse.

"I'll help," Eli murmured. Kyra straightened beside him, nodded slowly. She staggered to Alsair as the monk stretched out his hand. Eli knelt beside Monsun and placed a hand on his shoulder.

"For what you have given, we thank you," he murmured, forcing himself to stare at Cedwin's body.

"May we always remember your sacrifice," Monsun said.

Monsun hummed the funeral dirge, and Eli picked up the tune, trying his best with a mouth parched from terror. They removed their cloaks, and as best they could, wrapped Cedwin in them. The numbness remained, but Eli held it. For the sake of his friend, the Vindicator.

* * *

Later that night, they huddled in a cave as Alsair coaxed a meagre fire. Monsun sat by the wall with reddened eyes, Amora asleep by his side. He had barely spoken a word since the battle with the Vindicator. Kyra dropped down next to Eli.

280

"Did you know Cedwin?" he murmured.

"No, he must have been appointed after I left."

They lapsed into silence, their backs to the rough stone, studying the flickering flames. Eli almost expected Jaser to materialise out of the fire, but he could feel the old Guardian's presence retreating, even as his thoughts churned with Jaser's commands.

Not just to fight, but to heal, with two eternal beings warring over his soul. He'd already told Alsair about it. Not for long, but then he hadn't needed to. Alsair's jade eyes had pierced him, unmoving, as Eli explained what had transpired.

Kyra elbowed him in the side and it instantly brought him back to the present. He grinned at her, the weight of the battle slowly releasing him from its grasp.

"What happened when you left me?" she whispered, as if she had been building up the courage to ask that for hours.

Eli sighed. "I thought I had killed the bastard, but then he put me into some trance."

"What did you see?"

"Mostly Mount Sancti," Eli replied, his gaze lost in the shifting fire. No need to mention the other vision. Not yet. But he would keep fighting until it was a reality, one day. One glorious day. "Thank you for freeing me," he breathed. Kyra's smile was brighter than the firelight spilling through the cave, and she kissed him hard. Eli ignored Alsair's elderly chuckle.

Hours later, he slipped from her grasp, headed out to the mouth of the cave. His eyes trained on the glimmer of Nestham's Shield, the brilliant set of stars in a liquid black sky, and smiled.

Imbra. Where new battles and challenges would face them. But for the first time, he felt as if he wasn't running away from something, but running toward it.

Towards home.

Epilogue

The wind howled outside the King's study at Imbra. The servant, her blue uniform edged with royal silver, knocked delicately on the oak door. No call, no grunt answered her question. Perhaps His Majesty was asleep at his desk. It wasn't uncommon for that to happen. It was a bad idea to interrupt the King when he hadn't answered. Still, she had a duty to perform. She knocked again, harder. Listened harder.

A guttural cry rang out from within the chamber. Her heart shot into her mouth and she crashed through the door, gasping at the sight before her.

Blood and vomit mingled on the desk and rich carpet. King Hadrian gagged once, and his body crashed to the floor.

Acknowledgements

This book wouldn't have lasted the first month without so many people here today. And while I only have a couple of pages to thank everyone, here we go!

To my wonderful editor, Belinda Pollard, for patiently correcting my (grammatical) flaws and explaining the tangled web of publishing. Also, thank you for the amazing mentoring in these many months. Through wildfires and pandemics, your optimism and cheer has bolstered me so many times.

To Mum and Dad, thanks for teaching me never to give up, but also to know when sometimes things are more important than this book—family, and the seventeen assignments I have due! Also cheers Dad for calling this a hobby back in 2018—finally, I have fulfilled my quest to prove you wrong. Love you guys.

To We are Huan's, I couldn't have done this without you. Ben, Superior Steven, Matt (Whitney) and Matt (Sticks), you guys have been my rock from the beginning. Starting to work on Legend so many years ago got me back into writing, and I'm not sure *Torchbearer* would have been here without it. Special thanks to Ben for helping me with marketing and bullying/encouraging me to lift my game with content creation, and to White-Smith for all your wonderful art and design. Whitney, your claim on this book due to getting me hooked on Ranger's Apprentice has been noted.

To Ryan, with whom I have had the mis/fortune of sharing literally every role at uni together, thanks mate for everything. Thanks for the banter at uni, thanks for the competition on Monday nights, and thanks for being a huge support when I needed it.

And to Ellie, who's never turned me away when I've had a problem. I'm looking forward to next year guys, when we can go through this madness again!

To Marieke, my accountability partner, thank you for all the discussions we've had on the joys and horrors of writing. Venting to you keeps me sane, and I'm so grateful for it.

To my beta readers, you have been amazing, your patience and encouragement was amazing. You made my days better whenever I read the comments left on my half-finished manuscript.

To my support networks: the Plex, Salt, and Uni: each and every one of you, and frankly, anyone who ever smiled when I said I was writing a book. Thanks for allowing me to bore you with my rants and fanatical discussions about people who don't exist.

To Anakin: I'm pretty sure I was going to write some joke about how most authors' pets give them cuddles and support, but you hated my study. Forget all that. Thank you for everything. I miss you, little buddy.

Above all, I thank God for the ability he's given me, and I am grateful to share it with all of you.

Finally, thanks to you, dear reader, for sticking through with *Torchbearer* to the end. I hope you enjoyed reading it as much as I have enjoyed writing it. If you have, please consider leaving a review. It would be much appreciated!

About the Author

Steven is a resident of the most isolated capital city in the world: Perth, Australia. He is currently working on the sequel to *Torchbearer*. To find out more, visit **riftsingerpress.com** and follow **@srthiele** on Instagram.